An Endless Memory

CROCUS VALLEY, BOOK 5

MARIE JOHNSTON

LE PUBLISHING

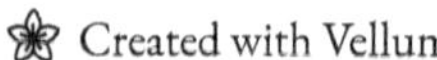 Created with Vellum

Get married or move out. Those are my options, thanks to the trust my grandma left and my aunt is determined to enforce.

From Marie Johnston comes a single-mom, marriage-of-convenience romance.

If I don't get married, I'll have to find somewhere to live that I can afford with two kids and a lot of debt—and do it without losing my brand-new job. When my aunt confronts me on the move-out deadline, I try to buy time. I blurt out a name. I tell her I'm engaged to Eliot Knight.

Eliot's my boss's brother and he's been around the vet clinic where I work. He's hot. He's charming. He's who I'd pick if I had to marry someone at a moment's notice. But he wasn't supposed to hear me. He wasn't supposed to get dragged into my mess. And he wasn't supposed to agree to help me. Now, we're Mr. and Mrs. Knight.

We only need to be married for a year, and he runs his family's ranch in another town. Three hours away. Yet circumstances keep throwing us together, and I get a lot of time with my new husband. I fall hard the first time I hear him say, "My wife."

But our lives are still separate. At the end of the year, I'm afraid I'll get to keep my house, but I'll lose my heart and be left with nothing but endless memories.

One

ELIOT

"Push it hard, Wilder. Just get down in there."

My brother was on his hands and knees. He aimed his glare up at me. "Not helping, Eliot."

I grinned. "It's a dryer vent. Don't let it beat you. Mind over matter."

"I like it better when you're cranky," he muttered and continued working on the dryer we promised his wife, Sutton, we'd install in the clinic. The expansion of her clinic hadn't stopped. Instead of the two-room, one-veterinarian clinic she'd opened, she now had four exam rooms and three veterinarians under her.

It was Saturday, but the newest vet tech Sutton hired arrived earlier. I heard her cooing to the two cats and one dog being held for monitoring over the weekend.

"Fucking finally," Wilder grumbled and groaned as he backed out from behind the dryer, still on all fours.

"You gonna be okay crawling around on the ground with those babies?"

That earned me another glare. "I'll be fine. I can tell them what a jackass their uncle is."

"You'll have to be more specific." We had two other brothers and a brother-in-law.

He gave me a dubious look. "No. I won't."

I chuckled. "What else do you have on your honey-do list?"

He rose, cutting his groan off and giving me a warning glare. I did my best to appear innocent.

"I need to change a couple of light fixtures and then she wanted the garage rearranged so Doc Julio can load his equipment and pull the trailer out easier."

Doc Julio was the large-animal vet. From what Wilder said, the guy preferred to be outside and working all day. If he had to work on anything furry without cloven hoofs, he got cranky.

"Is the new girl working with him?"

Wilder adjusted his grungy ball cap and shook his head. "No. The plan was the new hire would work with him, but Lily just had a baby. Sutton asked the other techs if one of them wanted to work outside the clinic more, so they made a rotation schedule."

"All that to hire the new girl?" Sutton was known to go out of her way for her employees, but she was already rearranging work schedules for someone brand new?

"Lily was going to vet school and dropped out. So Sutton's getting a highly knowledgeable tech."

"A vet school dropout?" A knowledgeable tech was one thing. A high-maintenance hire right before having twins was another.

He shrugged. "I don't know the reasons. Sutton clicked with her."

Whatever. It was my business to keep the ranch going so Wilder got his inheritance payouts. He'd been in house-husband bliss since he'd quit his job, moved to Crocus Valley, North Dakota, and dove into helping Sutton expand her veterinary clinic.

I was here to lend a hand or moral support. And because weekends in a big empty house were starting to wear on me.

"How's Sutton? For real this time." I'd asked before, and he'd given me the standard "fine" answer, but there was an edge to him I hadn't seen since he'd gone through the divorce with Sutton.

They were remarried, and she was expecting. He should be elated, and it wasn't this dryer stressing him out.

A muscle jumped in his jaw. "The doctor mentioned bed rest at the last appointment. Her blood pressure is starting to creep up."

"What's that mean?"

"To keep herself and the babies healthy, she'll have to park it in bed until she delivers. No work."

"Shit."

He nodded, his Adam's apple working. "I'm just worried, you know?"

I didn't. "I can believe it."

"It's not just her physical health and the twins. She'd be stuck in bed watching TV and..." He drew his brows together. "Well, if you knew how she grew up, that's going to be hard for her. She had very little parental attention and was left home alone a lot."

"Damn." Now that he mentioned it, I only met

Sutton's parents at their first wedding and now Sutton was due with twins in four months. I didn't recall another visit from them. As if I'd know. I lived three hours west, across the border in Montana.

Frustration at being so far removed from my family welled up. When our father died, he'd tied me and my three brothers to that damn place. Only my sister had been free, but he'd shit all over her in the will and trust.

Everything worked out for her, and my brothers had found loopholes to get out of their inheritance stipulations without losing out on the money. They all settled in Crocus Valley too. But I was the ranch manager. I had to be there full-time—morning, noon, and night. My vacations were visiting my siblings, nieces, and nephews. They would come out to the ranch and help a few times a year to meet the demands of the inheritance, but those visits were decreasing as their families grew larger. My sister and all three of my sisters-in-law were pregnant too.

I was starting to feel left out.

Who was I kidding? I'd felt that way for a long time.

"I gotta run out to the truck," Wilder said, giving me a break from the path my thoughts took. It wasn't like I could change things.

"I'm gonna grab a drink while you do that."

Sutton had added a nice break room with the expansion, and all the employees kept it stocked with snacks.

"Just keep the door shut. They have a repeat-offender Dalmatian in the back. He's a wily fucker and he'll go straight for the break room and get the fridge open before you know it."

"Repeat offender?"

"The owners swear he's not acting right, he's been puking, insists the clinic keep him overnight for observation. There's never anything wrong. Now, they've been dropping him off on Fridays. Sutton thinks he's too much dog for them, but they won't admit it. She's afraid they're going to euthanize him."

I winced. I could get weary of the cattle and horse-breeding operations, really fucking tired of the daily grind, but I didn't envy Sutton for a lot of aspects of her job. "That sucks."

"Yeah. He is a handful. The techs have been working on training him, but he's only a year old."

"Still a puppy." A puppy that needed a job, not to be cooped up all weekend. All our ranch dogs over the years had been the same.

Wilder and I left the new laundry room. He broke away to go out the back door where he was parked outside the garage. I continued down the hall to the break room.

There was a plastic container of thick frosted cookies on the table. Since it was the weekend, could I assume those were open season?

I went to the water jug that kept water at the perfect cold temperature and got a small cup. The jug glugged as water poured out. I should get one of these for the shop.

A skittering of claws on tile sounded down the hall. The new tech must've taken the Dalmatian out for a bathroom break—

"Bug! Dang it!" a woman called from the hallway.

Somewhere in the building, a squeal pierced the air. A blur of white and black charged into the break room. A leash trailed behind him on the floor. "Hey, boy."

The dog charged the table, bodysurfed the top with his upper body and knocked the cookies to the floor. I started for the dog when a blur in blue jeans and a gray scrub top rushed in. This must be Lily.

"Bug! No." She dove for the leash, but the dog spun around and hunkered the front of his body down. His mouth lolled open like he thought it was a great game they were playing.

Lily straightened, her back to me. The top of her head wouldn't reach my chin, but the jeans she wore molded around a nice, round ass.

She stuffed her hand into her scrub pocket and then held it out. "Sit," she commanded, a treat sitting on her palm.

Bug ignored her and spun around instead, his claws skating across the floor.

"Bug, *sit.*"

He tried to race around me, but I scooped up the leash and held tight. Bug darted away and damn near yanked my arm off when I stopped him. He was a strong dog.

When Lily turned, I was faced with wide indigo eyes surrounded by dark lashes. She had equally dark circles under her eyes, but they didn't detract from her loveliness. Her hair was cut short, and it puffed into a halo around her head. She looked like a coked-out pixie.

"Thanks." She was out of breath.

When she pushed her hair off her face, my gaze was drawn to her chest and—*shit*. "Um..."

"I'll take him from here." She held her hand out, her expression no-nonsense with flushed cheeks and wild hair.

"You have, uh..." I kept my gaze firmly on her face. Should I tell her? Pretend I didn't see anything? Would she want to know? Wilder had said she'd just had a baby.

A squall sounded again from somewhere in the building. Was that baby *here*?

"I can take him," she said firmly.

"Sure. Yeah." I handed the leash over. I'd keep my mouth shut.

The dog nosed at the cookies on the floor. The lid had popped open when they hit the floor.

"Bug." She sighed.

"Don't worry," I said. "I'll clean them up."

She barely spared me a glance. "Thanks. Can you make sure to keep the door closed after I leave?"

"Mommy." A little blond girl was in the doorway. "Kellan's crying." When her eyes landed on the dog, she gasped and grinned. "A Dalmatian!"

Bug lifted his head, his tail wagging. Cookie crumbs fell off his chin.

"Not now, Cali. Can you go sit with Kellan until I get in there?"

The girl's wide brown eyes pinned her mom, and she pointed at Lily's chest. "You're leaking."

"What?" Lily looked down. She stiffened. She folded an arm across the wet spots. "Cali, please go wait with Kellan."

Bug lunged against the leash. His tail was going wild. He was so interested in Cali he'd run her over if he had a chance.

Lily needed help. A lot of it.

"I can put Bug back in his kennel," I offered.

Lily didn't look at me. Her neck was as red as her face had been when she'd chased Bug. "No, it's fine. I got it under control."

Bug barked, and we all jumped. The crying grew louder.

"How about I help with the baby? I've got plenty of nieces and nephews. Cali can boss me around and tattle to Wilder if I do something wrong."

Cali grinned, showing off two missing front teeth.

Lily peered at me from the corner of her eye. She was half turned, keeping the wet spots over each breast as hidden as possible. "No, really. That's fine. I've got it." Bug strained against his leash and coughed. He was going to choke himself out.

"Follow me," Cali said, beaming. She marched out of the room.

Lily side-eyed me. "Cali, come back, please. Bug will trash the office."

"I can get the baby or the dog."

Alarm lit her eyes, too close to panic for my liking. She must be worried for her kids and her job.

"How 'bout I get the baby and comfort him until you kennel Bug? Honestly—I'll keep the door open—except the break room one—and Cali can watch me like a hawk. We can come find you."

"Are you coming?" Cali called from partway down the hall.

I looked at Lily.

She danced sideways when Bug lunged for the cookies again. "Yes. Okay. I'll only be a minute."

I dipped my head. This had to be nerve-racking for her. I was a strange guy with her kids, but she might be afraid of losing her job if she lost the dog again and Wilder witnessed it. I was fairly sure she wouldn't, but I wasn't the new employee.

I stepped into the hallway. "Lead the way, boss lady," I said to Cali.

I left Lily to handle Bug, though she could've used

help with that too. Something about the undercurrent of defensiveness made me think she wouldn't ask for it.

Cali skipped to the offices. Her pigtails bounced. Her hair was a lot lighter than her mom's. The crying got louder the closer we got to the office door.

Inside, I found a baby strapped in his carrier in a stroller with a red, angry face and wild hair that was as dark as his mom's. His little hands were balled into tight fists. "Goddam—dang, he's a fresh one, ain't he?" Little Kellan couldn't even be two months old.

Cali giggled. "He cries a lot."

I unbuckled the baby from his straps and lifted him. His bottom was soggy, and judging from the state of Lily's shirt, he was probably hungry. I cradled him in my left arm. "Where's his diaper bag?"

Cali dug out a backpack from behind a desk.

"Wanna dig out a diaper and wipes to have ready for your mom? Maybe a new outfit?"

She nodded and retrieved them for me. She also tugged out a plastic pad and proudly brandished it.

I took them from her and set them on the desk so they'd be ready for Lily. Kellan cried and squirmed. The dampness from his butt seeped through my sleeve. "I'm Eliot Knight, by the way."

I was awarded with her toothless grin. "Cali Wilson—wait. Mommy changed it to Duke."

Kellan kept crying, so I gently swayed from side to side. Cali hadn't produced fresh clothing. "Is there another outfit in that magic backpack?"

Cali yanked out a tan onesie. It flopped open to reveal what I'd guess was a milk crust. She wrinkled her nose. "Ew."

"Maybe there's another?"

"Nopers," she sang.

There was a fresh diaper waiting for him. That would be enough. They couldn't live far away.

Kellan quieted to steady whimpers, warning me he'd blow again. "Okay, champ. Let's clean up the break room until your mom can feed you. Coming along, boss lady?"

She followed me down the hall. "Mommy feeds him with her boobs."

The last thing I needed to be thinking about was Lily's boobs when I was holding her new baby.

We approached the door to the holding area, where we could hear movement and the occasional command from Lily.

"Mo-om," Cali called through the door. "We have Kellan."

"Uh, just wait a minute, please," came Lily's harried reply.

We went into the break room, and I shut the door.

"Think we can find a broom?" I squatted and picked the empty cookie container up. Kellan started crying again, a start-and-stop wail that was different from his five-alarm beller earlier.

Wilder opened the door and poked his head in. "What the—" His gaze landed on Cali, then the baby in my arms. He swung his attention back to Cali. "Hi. Cali, right? Your mom told me about you."

She scooted closer to me. Suddenly, she was shy as could be.

"This is indeed Cali," I explained. "She's in charge, and this is Lily's son, Kellan."

"We have different moms," Cali informed us.

Both Wilder and I blinked at her, unsure how to respond.

I was the first to recover. "Cool." Was the dad different or the same? None of my business, but I was curious. Wilder said Lily was a single mom. "Wilder and I have the same mom and dad, but I'm the better brother."

Wilder narrowed his eyes at me. "Better at lying maybe. I'm gonna go check on Lily."

Lily came to a stop behind Wilder, her gaze wide, taking us all in, finally landing on me, then dropping to her son. "I can take him."

She scooted around Wilder. She wore a different gray scrub top, but there were faint disks of moisture soaking through.

I handed Kellan over. His volume decreased, and he turned his face into her chest.

"We have everything to change his diaper ready to go in the office. His clothes are damp," I said.

"The extra was dirty," Cali announced. Loudly.

Lily's shoulders drooped. "Oh, right. I have to wash that. Come on, Cali." She led her daughter out and stopped right outside the door. "I'll be in the office for a little while."

Cali peeked around her. "Feeding Kellan with her boobs."

Lily briefly shut her eyes and sucked in a breath. When she opened them again, she looked at my chest. "Thanks." Then she was gone, closing the door behind her.

Wilder and I stared at the door for a moment.

"Be right back." Wilder disappeared. When he returned, he had a broom and dustpan. He scanned the mess. "I take it you didn't shut the door?"

"No, but I met Bug the Dalmatian."

He grunted. "He's a lot of dog."

"I didn't get a chance to introduce myself to Lily."

"Yeah, she's...got her hands full."

She was a cute disaster but a woman who had to juggle a lot of responsibilities. Just the type I stayed far away from.

Lily

It'd been two days since my milk letdown in front of the hottest man I'd ever set eyes on and the mortification was only starting to wane. I'd started wearing two breast pads in my bra to keep from having another accident. Not only had I looked incompetent at my job—again—I presented like a walking calamity.

I hadn't even been walking. I'd been running after Bug, and I hadn't even been able to catch him. Mr. Melt My Granny Panties Off had to do it.

I was cleaning out the holding cages when my boss appeared at my side. Her long blonde braid was wrapped around her head. She always appeared so calm and serene. I'd hear cats screaming from her exam room, and she'd walk out nonplussed. As for the cat, it'd have gotten its shots, its ears swabbed, mite treatment rubbed in those ears, and a rectal temp taken. Sutton didn't need people catching dogs for her.

Someday, I'd have my shit together.

"Can I talk to you for a minute, Lily?"

Her voice might be sweet, but tears pricked the backs of my eyes. I was going to get fired. All weekend, I'd cared for Bug and the other furry guests that were stuck until

Monday, but the one time I'd messed up, there'd been witnesses. Her husband and, judging from the resemblance, one of his brothers.

The better-looking brother, if I had to say so. I wouldn't ever speak my thoughts out loud. Wilder was handsome enough. Ruggedly hot, if I were into that kind of thing. But I wasn't. Carter, my ex-husband, had ruined good-looking men for me.

Wilder's brother could get a girl out of her man-hating era. He could help a girl forget she was about to lose the job she'd moved to another state for in order to have a fresh start. Back to the beginning, so to speak.

The beginning of another end.

I inhaled until the pressure of the tears ebbed. "Sure, I have a minute. I just finished."

I checked the time. The daycare was militant about picking up the kids before they closed, which, of course, I understood. If only their closing time wasn't right when my shift ended. Finding another daycare was on my to-do list, but that list was massive, and my evenings were dominated by tiny beings. And the daycare was wonderful.

Damn.

"Will I make you late?" Sutton asked.

"No. No, not at all." I wasn't telling my boss I had to leave. I was the new girl.

Her shrewd gaze didn't ease. "Is there anything I can help with? Wilder told me about the issue with Bug over the weekend."

"I had it under control." I would've. Eventually. "He got away when I was locking the door to the fenced-off area, but the cookies were the only casualty." They'd been stale by Saturday anyway. I'd tried one. So had Cali. We both ate the cookies anyway.

"Bug is a special case." She sounded resigned.

He would continue to be a special case. He was a good dog, energetic, but he wasn't aggressive or fearful and he tolerated kids and other animals really well. He needed space and something to do, and if he wasn't busy, he needed the piss run out of him three times a day. His family wasn't able to provide any of that.

She folded her hands over her belly. "Wilder said you had your kids here."

Panic pressed against my chest walls. "Is that a problem? I'm so sorry, I should've asked. At my last job, we were allowed to and I didn't think—"

She waved her hands and shook her head. "No, it's absolutely fine, and I know you know what animals they should and shouldn't be around. But you can let me know if the weekends are too much right now."

The tears were threatening to return. They were almost a constant these days. Everything was too much, but that wasn't Sutton's problem. She'd been nothing but generous and she was continuing to blow me away. How long before she got sick of making adjustments for me? "No, it's fine."

She lifted her brows. "You barely got a maternity leave. If you need more time off—"

"No." I almost shouted. "No. It's fine." Nothing was fine. I needed the paycheck. I had most of the vet school education but not the job. My student loans were staggering and all mine. If I hadn't been able to move into my grandma's old house, I'd still be living with my parents. They'd done so much for me. I'd needed their help, but if I couldn't survive a month at a new job while living on my own, what did that mean about me? "I'm good. It gets us out of the house for the weekend."

Her expression was dubious. "Okay," she said slowly, like she didn't believe a word I said. Probably because I was lying. "Please know I understand. You can come to me if there are any issues. I know you just lost your grandma."

I didn't win the battle against the tears. I swiped at my eyes. My grandma hadn't been aware of much during her last months, or it would've killed her to know I had gotten divorced before Kellan was born. She loved Cali and that I'd had a family when the rest of my siblings were single with no kids. "I miss her."

Sympathy filled her eyes. "I'm sorry."

"Thank you. Being in her house with all her things helps." Having a fully furnished house also kept my parents and brothers and sisters from worrying about me. "I really appreciate you taking a chance on me. I'm sorry about Bug."

"You did well with him. He's...a lot." She glanced at the clock on the wall. "You have to go, right? Doesn't your daycare close soon?"

It closed five minutes ago. I'd get charged ten dollars for every five minutes I was late. "Yes. Soon."

"Gosh, I'm sorry. Go. I'll get the wash going."

Normally, I'd be horrified she had to clean up after me, but I had to get to the daycare. "Thank you."

"And don't forget Friday is the party. It's for family and coworkers in case I get bed-rested during one of my OB visits and miss all the summer festivities. No need to bring anything but the kids."

"Is that the party you're throwing here?"

"No, Friday is at my place. The open house for our clients will be here." She shrugged. "We like an excuse to grill and visit."

What was that like? My family sometimes gathered for a major holiday. Not often enough.

Relieved I hadn't upset my boss, I filed the party details away for later. I didn't run out of the room, but once I was free from her sight, I scurried as fast as possible. The daycare was a quick drive, but another ten dollars was tacked on before I arrived. I hurried to the door and knocked, waiting for Wanda to answer.

Wanda ran an in-home daycare, and she'd been recommended by my coworkers. It was a miracle I even found a spot for a baby. Sutton had hired me two weeks before I gave birth. I had taken a scant six weeks off, but part of that had included Grandma's funeral, relocating, and finding childcare and getting Cali enrolled in school.

I was exhausted.

Cali opened the door and beamed at me. Wanda was behind her. She already had Kellan loaded in his carrier and his diaper bag packed.

"I don't close at the clinic the rest of the week," I said by way of apology and explanation. I'd been late three times last week.

Wanda smiled. "How about we give you a month to adjust before late fees set in?"

"I can't let you do that." Yet it'd be awesome. Everyone was doing so much for me. I had to take care of myself. I'd relied on my ex-husband and had been left with little more than debt. "I know about the time issue, and I'm late."

"It's only a month." Wanda handed over the car seat. "If this is going to be a regular thing, you'll be paying enough after that. Give yourself some time to adjust."

Wasn't that what Sutton had basically talked to me about? I didn't have the luxury to adjust. Two kids depended on me to keep it together, and since their father had chosen not to, I was stuck.

Wanda's kindness burrowed into my stress, easing a small part of it. "Thank you," I said, my words thick. She shouldn't have to waive her fees because my life was a mess.

"No worries. I know how it is."

I didn't say anything, but Wanda had three grown kids and a husband who seemed to adore her and supported the daycare from what I'd seen. I hadn't known a supportive husband or one who thought the moon and earth revolved around me. "See you tomorrow."

She might regret the month of no extra fees. The rest of the week, I'd be at her door the minute she opened in the morning. I would dump the kids on her and run to work. I might not be paying ten dollars for every five minutes I was late to daycare, but I'd be showing up to work five to ten minutes late instead. If there were limits to how understanding my boss could be, I might, unfortunately, find them.

I hated to lose Wanda, but I'd have to find a new daycare. I couldn't risk my job, and I couldn't hemorrhage money because of my hours.

I hefted the diaper bag over my shoulder and gripped the car seat.

Cali slipped her hand into my free one. "What's for dinner?"

"Uh...sandwiches?"

She groaned. "Always samwiches."

"I know."

Grandma's house was five miles out of town. Technically, her address was Coal Haven and all her land was in

Coal Haven, which was nine miles from Crocus Valley. She'd be dismayed I worked in Crocus Valley instead of in the town she loved, but there weren't many other vet clinics in the area. The only other vet clinic was run by a notorious womanizer, and I'd already been there and done that with someone like him and had the newborn and divorce papers to show for it.

It didn't matter if I worked in Coal Haven or Crocus Valley. The cost of living in either one was cheaper than in a bigger town.

I coasted down the long drive that had grass poking between the wheel divots. It needed more gravel, but that went way down my growing list of shit to get done. Cats darted in the door I kept cracked in the barn. The barn cats were half-feral. Later this summer, I'd trap them and take advantage of the employee discount for neutering and spaying.

The proud farmhouse sat in an *L* of trees that were three rows of pine, ash, and bushy lilacs. I barely registered them blooming. It was early June and they were my favorite blossoms. Grandma's too. She couldn't enjoy them this year; I should be.

A month had passed, but my dad said it was no issue if I moved into her house. Grandma had told me she was leaving me the house and the forty acres it sat on. The rest of the land and property would be split among my siblings. My dad's sole sibling hadn't had any kids. We assumed Aunt Linda would get the money from the estate. My parents were doing well enough since my dad was the CEO of King Oil in Billings.

Go home and be dependent on your parents like you were with me. My ex's words were poison.

I got closer and noticed a silver car parked by the

garage. It was vaguely familiar. I pulled into the detached garage. By the time I got out, my aunt Linda was hovering by the silver car, her face pinched. Her husband, Darren, got out from the driver's seat. I didn't expect them to visit this soon after I'd moved in. Or ever.

"Hi." Aunt Linda and I had never been close, but there was no animosity between us. She hadn't seemed to know what to do in a house bustling with six kids, and Darren just ignored us.

She smiled, but the tension around her eyes remained. The fine material of her skirt wrapped around her legs in the wind. All my life, she'd worn floral dresses and put her hair back in a twist. "We need to talk."

Another person tracked me down to talk? Was she worried like my boss was? Did she feel bad that she lived in town and hadn't stopped in yet?

"Sure." I got Kellan's baby carrier out. Cali crawled out the same door and hid behind my legs. "Come inside."

I led them to the side door that faced the garage. Inside, the smell of Grandma's lavender perfume still lingered, bringing comfort. The main difference was there were no longer the savory scents of a delicious meal cooking or the sweet smell of a fresh pie or cookies. If life slowed down, I'd make some cookies with Cali.

I'd have to get a little more sleep before I could tackle a real meal.

Just being home caused the fatigue to settle heavily on my shoulders as if my body sensed a bed nearby. I didn't sleep in Grandma's bed. Her mattress was older than me, and the guest bedrooms were less worn. I had moved into one and squashed the bassinet in the corner. Cali often slept with me, too, until she got used to her own room.

As if my sleep wasn't terrible already. To top it off, I often ended up in the second guest room to keep Kellan from waking up Cali.

"Have a seat." I carried Kellan through the laundry area and the small dining room to the living room and sat on the couch to unbuckle him. Pressure was building in my boobs. I hoped whatever my aunt and uncle needed to talk about was over by the time he needed to eat.

Cali sat next to me, scooting right into my side.

Aunt Linda hovered under the plaster archway that separated the living room from the dining room. If I could ever afford to remodel the house, I'd open up the wall between the dining room and equally small kitchen so everything wasn't so compartmentalized.

My grandma's cat, Pebbles, sauntered by Linda. My aunt's face softened when she looked at the cat. She loved the old kitty, but Darren hadn't wanted to take Pebbles. So the cat had stayed. She was mine.

Honestly, Pebbles had made the move easier. My ex had gotten our dog and cat in the divorce since they'd been his before we married. He'd thrown a fit about my corn snake, Flakes, when I'd moved in and had gladly given him up—along with the kids. He'd made it clear he'd ship Flakes on my dime to my parents. My dad took Flakes on another trip, and the snake was in Grandma's old room.

Pebbles jumped on the arm of the couch and curled up.

"Come on," Darren said, guiding his wife with a hand on her back. He held an old-fashioned leather brief-case in his hand. "Let's get this over with." He let her sit on the threadbare recliner that was probably older than Grandma's mattress.

"What's going on?" I propped Kellan against my shoulder and patted his back.

Everything was fine. It had to be. I'd gone through enough, right?

"I'm just going to come out and say it," Linda said, fanning her hand over her dyed-brunette hair. She swallowed hard and my anxiety grew until I wanted to squirm off the couch.

Whatever it is, make it go away!

"I'm the executor of my mother's estate." She licked her lips. "And it's come to my attention that while yes, you get the house..." She closed her eyes. "She made a trust. With stipulations."

"A trust?" Grandma hadn't mentioned one.

Darren huffed. "Yes. It stipulates that you have to be married for at least a year between when she passes and when you can fully inherit the house. Otherwise, we—Linda—controls the estate."

A nervous giggle left me. "Right. Married."

They both stared at me, no humor in their expression. I barely registered Cali tickling Kellan. My world was narrowing on my aunt and uncle's serious expressions.

"No," Darren said. "I'm afraid Annie had it in her head that including marriage parameters in her will was a good thing."

Annie Duke had been a fierce romantic, but this sounded ridiculous. And highly inconvenient.

It couldn't be legal. "She wasn't in her right mind—"

"She did this years ago," Aunt Linda said hoarsely. "She was healthy, and well, she probably thought it wouldn't be an issue, especially with you and Carter."

My laughter came out like a hyena. Pebbles' expression turned alarmed. Carter would've crapped himself in public and rolled in it before he entertained the notion of moving to the town where I'd been born. But he would've gladly sold the house and funneled the money into his mismanaged vet clinic.

"Why would she even think it was a good idea in the first place?" My voice was pitching up. My ex's voice filtered through my head. *Come on, don't overreact.* The hit of anger was swift.

Kellan let out a cry as if he sensed my stress. Darren flinched. Pebbles scurried off.

Linda folded her hands. "She, uh, apparently liked the story West told her about his old boss."

West was my dad. Weston Duke. He'd taken over King Oil in Billings for the previous CEO and owner, Gentry King. I'd met the man, but what story would he have that inspired my grandma to screw me and my siblings over? They were all single and now I was too.

"Gentry King's late wife left a trust for each kid, but they couldn't access the money until they'd been married for a year and it had to happen before they turned thirty. In their case, it was a trust fund. In this case, the land and all her properties are included in the trust."

"But I'm thirty, and I'm the youngest."

Darren's scowl deepened. "Annie gave a time period of six years before the trust lifts and we can sell."

"It's actually seven," Linda clarified. "Whoever marries last will need to do it before the six-year mark so they can have a year. Then we sell. And donate all the money."

Everything my grandparents had worked their entire lives for would be gone? If I didn't marry? The good news was that I had six years.

But I needed the house *now*.

My steady breathing quickened. Any faster and I'd hyperventilate. I didn't have the spare income for rent. I'd have to quit a job I adored and move to Billings to live with my parents—*again*. That wasn't the end of the world, but it'd be the end of me as Lily Duke, trying to prove she wasn't incompetent. A large part of my pride died. Carter claimed I couldn't do anything without my family.

"Is this necessary?" I croaked.

"We are going to enforce the trust," Darren stressed. "It's what Annie wanted."

Linda glanced at Darren. She looked almost as hopeless as I felt. Darren had been Mr. Ambivalent my entire life but now he was dedicated to carrying out my grandma's wishes?

"We'll give you until the end of the month," Linda said gently.

Shock made me sit forward. I switched Kellan to my other shoulder. He was already rooting around, accidentally headbutting me. He'd start crying to get fed soon. "The end of the month? For what?"

"To find a new place." She pursed her lips. Whatever bad news she was telling me, at least it wasn't easy for her. "You need to move out...unless you're married by then." She exchanged a look with Darren. He gave her an encouraging nod. "It's in the papers that couples need to reside on the land or property for that first year. So if you're dating and you want to fast-track the nuptials..." She spread her hands before dropping them limply to her lap.

I'd have to move out within a month? My parents would be faced with moving me for the third time in less than a year. Instead of moving forward as an adult and single mom, I was sliding back. "C-can I have some time before you talk to Mom and Dad?" I groaned. "You have to tell everyone else, don't you?"

Linda hesitated and exchanged a glance with Darren. "I have some time yet before I'm required to inform everyone. I'll give you that time before we both have to deal with the stipulations of the trust getting out. I'm not exactly looking forward to ruining everyone's day. Thanks to my mother, I'll be the bad guy until this is over."

Their expressions weren't wavering. There was sympathy but no leeway. I'd have to find a husband in a few weeks, or I was losing this house.

Two

LILY

I shoveled chips and dip into my mouth. The end of the month was in a couple of weeks. I'd done nothing but comb rental properties. Either nothing was open soon enough, the space was too small, or they didn't take pets. I would not abandon my animals. My deadline loomed. Twice, I'd picked up the phone to call my parents, but Carter's voice ran through my head. *You can't change your underwear without asking them what pair you should put on next.*

I wanted to call my oldest sister. She was the most even-keeled. Violet was logical to the point of being irritating sometimes. But then I'd have to tell her about the trust. She'd feel obligated to tell the others, and the Duke Hotline would light up. The last time that had happened was when I left Carter. I didn't need to start another text frenzy because of me.

I held out hope I'd find a place to live or meet a nice

guy who wanted a quick commitment. The thought of dating made me nauseous. The idea of marrying because I had to? I turned livid. I had a lot of regrets about marrying Carter. The kids weren't one of them and that was about it.

Time to return to ignoring the issue. Sutton's house was smaller than my grandma's place, but she had her garage doors open to house the food. We were outside and surrounded by several quiet acres out of town.

Sutton's brother-in-law, the one I'd embarrassed myself in front of, was at one of the grills. I'd purposely trekked as far away from the grill as possible. Was it possible he wouldn't recognize me? The rest of her family was here, along with all of my coworkers.

I sat in a chair next to Sutton on the edge of the concrete pad. I didn't know my coworkers well enough to intrude on their little groups. Cali had no such reservations. She was running around the yard with Sutton and Wilder's dog, Oreo, and several other kids. I'd been told their names, but there was no way I could recall them. I didn't even know the name of the sister-in-law who was holding Kellan so I could eat. She was bouncing with him at the edge of the concrete slab and chatting with a few coworkers.

I had nothing to discuss. I was single and soon to be homeless.

"What do you think so far?" Sutton asked. She had her hands resting on her rounded belly. She frowned. "I suppose that might be hard to answer since I'm your boss."

"I love it." That part was easy. I did love my job. Yes, I'd been scatterbrained, but so far, everyone was writing it off as new-person slips. I'd forget to start the washing machine or clean an exam room between patients. When I was in the room with the client and the veterinarian, I was on. Outside of that, I might leave my coffee cup on the bathroom sink. Doc Julio found it in the microwave one weekend from the Friday before.

I was also a little in love with this party. My coworkers made up less than half the people. Sutton's family was large, just like mine. They had fun together. Kids frolicked. People laughed and talked. My siblings and I had been close growing up, but once we'd finished school, we'd dispersed all over the country. They rarely called to chat, and even though we got together for holidays, it wasn't often all of us.

I had wanted to invite them out, but Carter had hated their interference. He was used to parents who only cared about how people perceived them.

I loved working for Sutton, and I would be envious of her private life if I had the time to dwell on it.

"I really appreciate the opportunity to work at your clinic." I pushed some dip around with my chip. "I'll get better, you know, when I get more sleep."

She chuckled. "Don't worry about it. We've all forgotten to get weights."

Maybe once. Last Tuesday, I'd gotten one weight on a kitten and had to rush to do every other patient midexam. My mind had been somewhere else since Aunt Linda's visit. Stupid marriage stipulation. Should I ask to talk to Sutton privately and tell her? Maybe she knew a single guy who was willing to marry a stranger to save her house.

Ugh. No. I wouldn't ask someone to give up a year of their life for me. I was not irresponsible. I was not impulsive. Marrying a stranger would be both.

A shadow fell over us. I looked up, and my heart

skated right into my throat. It was *him*. The brim of his ball cap was pulled down low, his T-shirt hugged his impressive pecs, and the blue jeans were just porn for women. The way he stood in boots and how his pants draped around his legs—he was all strength and good looks. Add in that I couldn't forget how he'd looked holding a baby tucked into his arm, and the hot flash was unavoidable and not at all from my postpartum hormones.

His brown gaze was speculative. "How do you ladies want your burgers?"

Sutton screwed her face up. "I guess I have to pick well done for the babies."

The corner of his mouth ticked up, and he aimed his gaze in my direction. "Lily, right?"

He remembered? My heart skittered sideways like a startled crab. I dug in the depths of my brain. "Yes. Eliot?" Cali had given me the play-by-play of every second with him. He might as well wear a cape in her eyes. I had tucked all the knowledge away. If I dwelled on it, I'd wish for something silly, like an impromptu marriage with a stranger.

"At your service." God, his voice was pleasingly deep. "How do you like your burger?"

I studied the remaining chips on my plate. He was too painful to look at. "Well done, please."

"Cheese?" he asked.

I waited for Sutton to answer, and when she didn't, I peeked over. Her face was tilted to the sun and her eyes were closed.

He gestured his metal spatula toward her. "I already know she wants two slices, fully melted."

"It makes you the favorite brother," Sutton murmured.

His eyes crinkled with his smile. "I'm going to tell Cody and Austen."

Her eyelids fluttered open. "No, Cody's my favorite when he checks the books for the clinic and Austen's my favorite when he gets Vienne to make her bacon ranch salad for my cravings. Ansen is my favorite when he gives me his training expertise free of charge."

"Someday, I'll get everyone's names down," I said, ignoring the way my pulse wanted to kick up around Eliot.

Sutton smiled. "The Knights are all named after classic female authors. And Aggie is a Barron now since she married Ansen. You'll start meeting his relatives." She thought for a moment. "Actually, you probably have. The goats from a week ago were Ansen's sister-in-law's. Anyway, Agatha Christie Barron is her full name."

The rest started clicking in place. "Austen is Jane Austen?"

"Cody cheats," Eliot added. "His real name is Alcott."

"Louisa May Alcott." I summoned more names. "Laura Ingalls Wilder. And Mary Anne Evans, writing as George Eliot."

Surprise brightened his eyes. "No one's ever gotten that."

For once, I didn't feel like a failure. "My mom's shelves are filled with women authors. She writes kids' books. Cali's her number one fan."

"Eliot," Wilder called from the grill. "I'm going to touch your meat if you don't get back here."

"You'd better not," Eliot growled. Shivers erupted

over my skin from his voice. Pleasing and deep, with no hint of a whine like my ex. "Cheese?"

"No, thanks. Dairy gives Kellan gas." Mortification swept through me like a pasture fire. I worked with a lot of women and moms. My verbal filter was off. Wasn't leaking in front of him enough?

"No cheese it is." He spun on his heel and was gone.

"I'll never quit embarrassing myself around that man," I muttered.

"Don't worry. The dog incident didn't faze him. I'm sure he doesn't know what you meant."

She didn't know about the milk stains on my top. "Hope not."

"It's fine. Eliot's a good one. I'm so glad he could come down again for this. It's so weird having him in Buffalo Gully while the rest of us have moved here. You've lived in Montana too, right?"

"Billings." When I interviewed, I told her my family used to live in Coal Haven. I didn't remember much of the area. I was pretty young when we moved, but I'd shamelessly used the connection to help land the job.

"Eliot's a good one. A little grumpy sometimes. You ever need anything, just holler. All of us will help out, and when Eliot's around, he will too. I'm sure you'll be seeing more of all my family."

Unless Eliot had a friend who needed to marry someone immediately and wasn't a creep, I wasn't so sure. Her family might be around more, but I wasn't sure where I'd be at the end of next week.

Eliot

. . .

Cody stopped next to me by the grill. He and his second wife, Tova, hadn't been married for that long, but it was nice to see him looking like the brother I'd grown up with. His jeans were a little nicer than mine and he wore a polo instead of a T-shirt, but it fit him better than a suit and tie.

"You're staying away from Sutton's new hire, aren't you?" he asked in a quiet tone.

I glared at him. I wasn't a horned-up teen anymore, and sometimes he forgot that. "I'm not hitting on Lily."

She was cute. The way she flushed when she saw me and then avoided me hadn't gone unnoticed. The dark circles were still there, but there was a heaviness in her eyes that hadn't been there when I'd first seen her.

"Just making sure," Cody said easily. "I saw you talking to her, and she looked like she was going to light on fire from her blush. I wasn't sure if you knew that she's got a lot going on."

"Like what?" I made it sound challenging, but I really wanted to know. I could tell immediately her life wasn't easy. She had to bring her kids to work, and she clearly hadn't asked Sutton to forgo being on call. Sutton would've done it.

"Weston's talked about her a little."

I shoved burgers around on the grill. Everyone had their first serving and I was cooking seconds. I searched my brain for Weston. Cody had mentioned the guy. Weston Duke did business with Cody for Knight's Oil Wells. Weston was her dad? "Wilder never said she's a Duke."

Cody shrugged like this small of a world was no big

deal. "One time, Weston grumbled about his youngest's pathetic husband, said it seemed like he was keeping her away from her family, but that she was also hardheaded and did her own thing."

Good thing she was away from that pathetic husband, but I steered clear of stubborn women.

"Ruiz hasn't talked to you about downsizing?" Cody asked.

My mind rerouted at the subject change from Lily's family to our family lawyer. Lorenzo Ruiz had been our father's lawyer, but thanks to the way he'd kept the trust from being ironclad, he was ours.

I shook my head. "I told him I was selling another five mares this year and only breeding five."

Cody's brows lifted. "Five?"

My brothers and I couldn't sell the land, and we had to keep the three portions of the Knights' businesses going—the oil wells, breeding purebred Arabians, and the cattle ranch. But our father, Barnaby Knight, had never said we couldn't downsize the numbers we ranched or sold.

I nodded. "I can't keep good help for long enough to care for the horses. The cattle make more money and require less travel and marketing."

"You don't have to train cattle to be ridden," Cody agreed.

I couldn't work with the horses like they needed while overseeing the cattle. I was in the middle of nowhere in eastern Montana. The location didn't have the draw the western side of the state did. The guys I hired to work for the ranch were transitory at best. If they wanted to work long term, there was usually a reason they preferred to stay off the grid, and they weren't always the people you wanted around. Sometimes, I found a real one, but the physical demand of the work often limited their career.

My phone started vibrating. I groaned. My family was with me. If I was getting a call, then something was wrong.

Cody waved his hand. I gave him the spatula and went farther into the garage to take the call.

"Knight," I answered.

"Eliot." My bookkeeper Chambers's voice cracked on my name. Adrenaline pulsed into my veins. I paced the garage. "Silas nailed the corner of the barn with the Kubota."

"What?" I turned my back to the open doors and lowered my voice. "He's fine, right?"

"He's, uh...drunk."

"Fuck." I pinched the bridge of my nose. Chambers wasn't in charge. He'd never ranched on his own, just grew up in the life, but he was the honorary second-in-command while I was gone. He worked from the house and liked to be in everyone's business. I trusted his wisdom, probably because he'd been my history teacher and football coach. He shouldn't have to deal with this. "He's fired."

"I gathered as much. I think he did, too, because he quit. I told Alexander to watch him pack and drive his truck to the motel where he can sleep it off. I'm heading out to follow him and pick Alexander up. Are you going to press charges?"

Silas was a guy whose wife left him, his kids didn't want to speak to him because he fucked around on their mom, and he didn't know how to handle a life without a wife doing everything for him. He probably tried calling his ex, hit the bottle, then decided to be useful...by fucking up my barn and tractor and making the other guys work extra.

I would probably be more pissed if I was there. Silas was a sad sack on his best days, but involving the police would only give us all headaches. "Nah. We'll file with the insurance company. Make sure to charge me for the extra time and mileage."

Chambers only grunted. "I'll start the insurance paperwork when I get back, but...I'm not sure about the barn."

Goddammit. "That bad?"

"It's not good. We've moved the bottle calves to the pasture between the older barn and the stables, and we moved those foals to the stables."

Thank fuck it was summer. We could play musical pastures. Chambers didn't need the headache. He wasn't supposed to be full-time, and this weekend would be double time for him. I looked around at everyone. Over half the guests were my family. I'd been gone too much and this was my consequence. A drunk employee. "Fine. I'll be there in a few hours."

"You don't have to cut your weekend short."

And he didn't have to do my job on his days off during what should be his retirement. The bookkeeping job was to keep him out of his wife Roxie's hair. "Talk to you soon."

I tucked my phone away. When I turned, all the burgers were off the grill and Cody had shut it off. My appetite was shit after that news, but I'd grab some food to go.

"Trouble in paradise?" he asked.

"Chambers is handling it, but he shouldn't have to."

"He's a good guy. What happened?"

"A little tractor meets barn after a few beers."

He whistled low under his breath. "Need help with anything?"

"I'm just gonna tell everyone bye and head out."

"This looks serious." Tova sauntered toward her husband. Her dark hair was gathered in a bouncy pony-tail, and she wore a loose yellow sundress. She walked right under Cody's arm. A perfect pair. No one could tell by looking at them that she had been a burlesque dancer when he'd been an uptight widower. "Cody's running the grill. What's wrong?"

"I've gotta get going," I answered.

She patted her husband's stomach. "Let's send some food with him. Are you coming back next week to help finish the clinic before Sutton's office party at the end of the month?"

Another night away? I'd never been gone from home this often unless it included transporting horses.

"Remember, we're doing the Fourth of July picnic early since it's on a weekday," Cody added.

I loved spending the Fourth with them. Sutton had hosted a big family picnic, but this one would be at Cody's and would be within the window to shoot off fireworks.

But this was my second time in Crocus Valley in a month. I was the boss. The ranch needed my presence. "I don't know."

"You're cutting this weekend short," Cody said. "Come on down. The ranch will still be there and then you can stay for our Fourth of July party."

"We'll see." I tabled the decision for later, once I knew how much damage was done to the barn.

I found the rest of my siblings, told them a quick version of what was going on, eased their concerns, then walked toward Sutton. Cali ran up to Lily, gave her a batch of wildflowers she'd picked from the property, then ran away.

Lily was grinning when she glanced up at me. Need punched me in the dead center of my chest. What would it be like to be at one of these family gatherings and have a woman smile at me that way? What would it be like if that was one of my kids who ran up to my wife? To not have to watch the clock for when I should leave, or worse, worry that I shouldn't have been gone in the first place?

She dropped her gaze, a flush darkening her cheeks. The smile wasn't for me. She wasn't mine. And neither were her kids. I had to leave, and I couldn't see my situation changing anytime soon.

Three

LILY

It was Friday and the end of the month. The clinic was having its open house. Everyone was standing around and laughing. The garage doors of the clinic were open, and the floor had been hosed off. A few tables were set up and filled with food.

Meanwhile, I wanted to cry. Every blink pushed back tears. I was supposed to be moving to another house, apartment, condo, or townhouse. I was not. I didn't even have a toiletry bag packed.

Instead, I had picked up Cali and Kellan from daycare and came straight here. Kellan had fallen asleep in his car seat. Cali was so excited. She'd talked nonstop after the party last week, jabbering about how fun the Knight and Barron kids were. She'd been understandably disappointed when she learned the open house wouldn't have all of Sutton's family.

Fatigue swamped me. Kellan continued to snooze in his car seat stroller. Would he sleep tonight? God, I hoped so. My vision was crossing. He'd been extra fussy the last week, like he'd fed off my stress.

I pinched the bridge of my nose. What was I going to do?

I was so tired.

Where in the world would I take the kids? I'd avoided my aunt and uncle's calls and texts. They'd show up soon. They'd see I wasn't moved out. I'd have to call my parents. I should've done that right away, or at least as soon as it was apparent there'd be no house to rent within my budget. Now, they'd have to rush to Crocus Valley to save me. Just like before. My brothers and sisters would hear about the trust in a frantic way and that'd stress them. Ugh. I should've put more thought into all this.

Part of me hoped Aunt Linda wouldn't be so stern. She and Uncle Darren wouldn't kick me out with a kid and a baby? Maybe?

Shit.

I glanced around the clinic and blinked. *Pull it together.*

Could I sleep here? How long before someone noticed?

Sutton approached me. I blinked and straightened. Did it make me look more awake?

"Are you doing okay?" She rested an arm over her belly. She had an ob-gyn appointment on Monday, and she suspected she'd be put on bed rest for good instead of reduced work hours. We'd all been doing what we could to make things easier around the clinic for her, and she'd backed off to less than a quarter of the clients she used to see. What was she doing standing and talking to me?

"I'm fine. How are you?"

She lifted a shoulder and munched on a celery stick. "Nervous. As long as everything's okay, I don't mind being stuck in bed." Doubt flickered through her expression.

"I'm sure it's scary. You're worried about the babies but also about the business you built."

She smiled. "Yes, it is scary. I have a really good crew, but it's not that. I used to sit around and watch a lot of TV when I was younger, and I'm afraid it'll feel like I'm regressing. But I have a light at the end of the tunnel with the babies." Her grin turned dreamy. "And I won't be alone this time either."

"Wilder seems very supportive." He was a doting spouse. The way he watched Sutton with an eagle eye, his gaze full of adoration, should be sickening. Instead, it was just another Knight showing me how low I had settled with Carter.

"He worked hard on being the spouse I need." Before I could figure out what she meant by that, she looked over my shoulder and a wide smile spread across her face. "There's my favorite guy."

"And your second favorite, right?" Eliot's voice washed over me like warm caramel sauce.

I didn't know he was coming to the open house. He'd rushed away from the party a couple of weeks ago, and I thought that'd be the last time I saw him. I was sure I would be quitting my job and leaving town at some point in the next twenty-four hours.

Wilder went right to his wife's side. He snatched a cookie off the plate, and she adopted a fake scowl until he hand-fed her. She gave him a secretive smile, and he returned it with a smoldering look.

Gah. My bar had been on the damn floor.

Cali ran up to Eliot. Her toothy grin was filling in. "Remember me?"

Eliot dropped to a squat. "Let's see...Cooper?"

She giggled. "No."

"Gumball?"

She shook her head, her smile firmly in place.

"You must be the really smart and strong Cali, then."

She nodded. "Yup."

"Having fun, boss lady?"

Cali nodded. *My* day certainly brightened. The only time my tired gaze uncrossed was to admire his wide shoulders. I discretely looked down at my chest. No leakage. Good.

He gave her a fist bump, and she ran off. He straightened and looked right at me with soulful brown eyes I could swim in all day. "Lily. How's it going?"

"Oh, you know. Living the dream."

His smile was warm, and I basked in it until he turned his attention to Kellan. "There's the sleeping champ."

I could draw a full breath now that his attention was off me. Was this guy for real? He greeted my baby and seemed genuinely delighted to see him. Why couldn't I have married a guy like him?

I shoved a carrot stick in my mouth.

"Hey, Lily," Wilder said. "I was out with my brother-in-law the other day to go look at a horse, and I saw your house. That's a nice place. Well kept up."

He was making idle conversation. I appreciated it, but also, I'd rather not talk about the house right now. "It's like a time capsule. Grandma kept the original woodwork."

Sutton brightened. "You remember Vienne and Austen?"

I nodded. Another devastating brother-in-law of hers with a woman who had all her ducks in a row and not floating off in different directions to get lost in the reeds.

"They redid their house..." Sutton frowned and looked at Wilder. "Was it two years ago?"

"Pretty much," he answered.

"Now they flip houses—ethically, of course. I'm sure if you need a hand with anything, you only have to ask. They'd be happy to help."

Wilder nodded. Everyone said they were happy to help. I was like a billboard that screamed, "I'm a mess."

I stuck with "Thanks" for a reply.

Eliot turned back to Wilder. I gave myself two seconds to ogle the way his butt flexed under the denim. He was the best-looking Knight brother, and it wasn't just because he was the only single Knight. He seemed the most mellow, but there was a hint of sadness in his eyes that called to me.

I was romanticizing him, but I could use a little fantasy. My reality sucked.

"Did you get food yet?" Eliot asked Wilder.

Wilder didn't look like he wanted to leave his wife's side.

Eliot pivoted toward me again. "Lily, can I grab anything for you while I'm getting a plate?"

He was so damn polite. His mama had raised him right.

I was trying to think of something just to continue the interaction with him when Sutton's gaze drifted over my shoulder.

"I'm not sure I know her," she murmured. "Is she a client here?"

I turned and my stomach slammed to the ground. My aunt was here. Stress lined her face and her frown was sandblasted into her skin.

Linda was outside of the garage, at the edge of the parking lot, talking to River, one of the other techs. River was pointing at me and my aunt nodded.

"I—I do."

Sutton pinned me with her gray eyes. "You don't sound thrilled."

I was not. "She just isn't the happiest person in the world." Why did she have to track me down at the open house? "I didn't realize she was visiting. She's probably worried about why I'm not at home." I forced a bright smile, but inside my ribs, my heart hammered until I worried it'd quit and I'd just collapse. The kids would go to my parents. *Lily should've known better. Lily should've told someone. Lily should've planned like a grown-up.*

Someday, I'd wipe Carter's voice, and his mother's, out of my head, but today was not that day.

My aunt spotted me, and her gaze sharpened. Her frown grew impossibly deeper, and she marched in my direction.

"Lily." Her voice was a whiplash. "A word."

I smiled at Sutton, panic clawing at my chest. *Please spare my dirty laundry from getting aired.* "Excuse me, please."

I put my hand on the stroller to take off the brakes. My throat grew thick, and I wasn't sure I'd win the battle against my tears.

Eliot waved me off. "I'll watch over the little guy. If he starts crying, I'll find you."

I would brush Eliot off, but the conversation with Aunt Linda would be too serious for interruption if Kellan woke up. "Sure. Thanks."

I walked into the clinic, not waiting to see if Linda would follow me. She did. Her footsteps even sounded stern.

I turned into the offices. The building was blissfully empty, but the sounds of laughter and talking were strong enough to drift in. Perfect. I could hear exactly what I was missing as I begged for more time.

My aunt entered and walked straight to a desk. It wasn't mine, I didn't have one, but she sat primly, regret and disappointment scrawled over her expression.

I faced her, my back to the entrance. The silver lining was that she didn't bring Uncle Darren. "I'm sorry I haven't gotten back to you. It's been busy—"

"Are you moved out yet?"

It took everything in me not to hang my head. "No," I whispered.

"Are you married?"

"Aunt Linda, I need more time."

"Lily." She sighed and looked every day of her sixty-two years. "I could've kicked you out right away. We did give you time."

"Not enough. I have two small kids."

Sympathy burned in her eyes. I was almost surprised to see it. "It's not my choice, but I am the executor." She clenched her jaw. She glanced away and determination filled her gaze.

No, no, no. She was going to kick me out. I had enough money for one night at a motel, and then I'd have to go back to Billings. There was no place big enough to move the kids and animals too, and I couldn't stay in a hotel for a couple of months with all that. My parents would take me in. I'd have to quit my new job only six weeks after I started. I'd get a shitty reference if I quit over a weekend. That'd make two vet clinics I'd left under less-than-ideal circumstances. Add in my withdrawal from vet school and I was a less-than-ideal prospect to hire. My career might be over.

"Aunt Linda…"

She shook her head and closed her eyes. "I'm sorry, Lily. The rules are in black and white. I've already bent them enough." She opened her eyes and gave me a direct stare. "I have to continue fulfilling my duties. I gave you time and your siblings need time."

"I appreciate it," I said, my throat tight. "I really do."

Linda rolled her lips in, considering me. "Darren will help you pack tonight until West and Magnolia get here."

My aunt knew me well enough to know I couldn't get out of this mess without them. To be fair, I was in a unique situation. But I thought that at thirty, I'd have a good job, money in savings, and a big degree to show for my college debt.

I didn't want my uncle to help me pack. I'd get the kids settled, and Dad and I could come back for the rest. Unless he and Mom needed to be close to home when the others learned about their absurd inheritance stipulations. At some point, I'd have to call Sutton and tell her I could no longer stay in Crocus Valley.

I could weep.

There had to be something. Panic made me claw at the edges of my brain. There had to be some way.

Grandma laid out exactly how. The only thing that'd save me was a man.

"What if…" The only thing that would buy me time

was Linda thinking I'd be getting married real soon. I never told her I didn't have a boyfriend. I could buy myself some time. Tomorrow, I'd call the same rental properties I'd talked to earlier and accept the first opening. Maybe Mom would let Pebbles and Flakes stay at her place. Maybe my parents would help with hotel expenses.

I needed help with so much. Humiliation dug into my ribs.

"What if what, Lily?" Linda peered at me, a spark of hope in her eyes. She didn't want to be the bad guy. Yet she would be. I could save us both with a little fib.

"What if I have someone?"

She lifted her chin, interest in her eyes. My hopes rose. Would this work, if only for a weekend? I didn't know what the time would buy me, but I had to try.

"You have someone?" she asked, dubious.

"Yes." I drew out the word. "I didn't want to rush him. I mean, I never thought I'd fall in love again." I spoke slowly, like I was reading about mammal reproduction for the first time.

"And you're getting married?"

I nodded and forced myself to hold her gaze. I just needed the weekend. I could secure the animals, get myself and the kids settled in a motel, and put money down for a rental deposit. After I borrowed it from my parents.

Her eyes narrowed. The stench of my lie was rising up. Either that or my deodorant couldn't stand up to new-mom stress. "What's his name?"

All she needed was a name. What should I say?

The only name that popped into my head spilled out of my mouth. "Eliot."

"Eliot who?"

"Eliot...Knight." Shit. I should've made up a last name.

"At your service," Eliot said from the doorway.

I gasped and spun around. Kellan was throwing his head around on Eliot's shoulder. He let out a cry. Three seconds ago, he'd been as silent as the man holding him.

"Eliot." All my dismay poured into that one word. My heart clawed into my throat. I could vomit everything I'd eaten for the last month. If I thought I was humiliated before, this was nothing.

"Oh." Linda's voice perked up. "This is him?"

Why didn't I make up a name? Why did I name him? It was not wishful thinking. It *wasn't*. I just didn't know any other single men.

"Eliot Knight?" Linda prompted again.

"Yes," I squeaked.

Linda's brows lifted. Kellan slammed his mouth against Eliot's stubbled cheek. "Slow down, champ. I don't have what you want."

"When's the wedding?" Linda asked.

Eliot glanced at me like he was waiting for me to answer too, like this was polite conversation that didn't involve him. It shouldn't have involved him.

Linda lifted her brows, giving him a pointed look. "Do you have a date? I assume it must be soon."

Incredulity filled Eliot's gaze. A chuckle came out nervously. "Did I miss something?"

Was I really going through with this? If I didn't, I'd be quitting for sure and moving. I'd never see Eliot again, and my humiliation would be just for me, for during the middle of the night when I was alone in bed and reliving all my mistakes.

"The wedding," I said woodenly. I couldn't meet his

gaze. I kept mine on the teardrop bottom of my baby, whom he was holding. "Remember how I told you"—I squeezed my eyes shut—"shortly after we started dating that I would lose the house if I wasn't married for a year? And how Aunt Linda was being lenient and letting me stay in it until then?" I peeled my eyes open. If my heart rate climbed higher, I'd pass out.

His disbelieving gaze was on mine. Kellan was getting noisier, but he had nowhere to go in Eliot's strong hold.

My hope wavered, rose a little, but it was still at the bottom of the world. Eliot wasn't calling me a liar in front of my aunt, so I forged ahead. "Well, I didn't want to rush you, but she gave me until today to move. I thought we could have some more time, you know...since our love is so new?"

His eyes narrowed but in that *This can't be real* way. "Today?"

"Yep." I popped the *P*. Shame was branding itself into my skin. "I had to be moved out by today."

"Unless you're married."

"Mm-hmm." My cheeks were on fire. I could melt into a puddle and sink into the foundation.

"How long have you been dating?" Linda asked as she scrutinized Eliot.

Might as well dig the hole deeper. "Since I first moved, actually. I met him right after I started here. Eliot is Sutton's brother-in-law."

"That's not long at all," Aunt Linda said. She exhaled, the sound somehow full of skepticism.

No, it sure wasn't long at all. "We're willing to rush to get you the documents you need."

"And you're okay with that?" Her gaze was sharp enough to stake Eliot in place.

The heat of Eliot's gaze lifted off me. "Like she said, we're willing to rush."

Oh god. Was he... Was he playing along? Relief almost knocked my knees out from under me, but I forced it back. The fallout was waiting for Linda to leave. Then I'd have to tell Eliot the whole story. He deserved as much. Would he recount this whole situation to Sutton? They'd have a good laugh. I'd be the butt of a ridiculous joke, but I would likely keep my job and a roof over my family's head. Who needed pride when I had that?

"Well." She clapped her hands together, then rose. "That is good news."

Oh my god. It worked. I caught a giggle before I cleared my throat. I bit the inside of my cheek to keep my giddiness from showing. I could figure my life out.

Eliot tilted his head, studying me, his expression tightly neutral.

"Perfect." Linda clasped her hands together again, like she was unsure of what to do. "I'll need the marriage certificate next week."

"That soon?" I ignored the scrape of Eliot's gaze. He'd started bouncing the more Kellan moved. I'd been so nervous through the conversation I'd left him holding the baby. And he'd done it.

Linda squeezed my elbow as she passed. "I already gave you weeks of extra time. Please understand."

She'd have to tell the others soon. I wanted my situation solid before my family found out. Would Linda go for one more favor? "Can you wait to tell Mom and Dad until after we're"—I swallowed hard—"married?"

"Yes," she said quietly. "I imagine they would have a lot to say."

After my shit show of a marriage, they would not love

hearing that I'm running into another one with a stranger. I needed time to call them first and explain. Before that, Eliot needed answers.

"I also need to let you know that both Weston and I have to sign off on the marriage after a year. My mother wanted to make sure there weren't shenanigans to get the inheritance."

"Shenanigans?" My voice went high, and a nervous laugh came out. What had Grandma been thinking?

"Sounds like you don't have to worry even if the nuptials are rushed." Linda's smile was relieved. She crossed to Eliot and stuck her hand out. "Nice to meet you."

He slowly clasped hers and gave her hand a perfunctory pump.

"Welcome to the family," she said right before sidling around him and out the door.

She took all the air with her.

"What the hell was that about, Lily?" Eliot asked incredulously.

My emotions welled over and tears poured out. I gave in to the relief, sank to the floor, and cried.

Eliot

Goddammit, I broke Lily. Guilt wound its way across my throat. I didn't mean to swear, but it wasn't every day a guy tried to help a woman and then was told he was marrying her.

What the hell had I walked in on? I'd heard my name,

and suddenly, I was engaged. Not only that, but the lady who was just here wanted to see a marriage certificate, or she'd kick Lily out of her house.

Didn't she know Lily had two small kids?

Kellan's cries were growing more powerful. I squatted by his sobbing mom. She'd covered her face with her hands.

"Hey," I said softly. Her shoulders shook harder. "Hey."

She continued to cry.

"Lily, I'm sorry."

For some reason, that made her cry harder, and Kellan's volume increased.

"Look, the champ's hungry. I need an explanation, but he's got to eat first."

She nodded, sniffling and finally lifted her face out of her hands. "I'm so sorry."

Holy shit, she looked haggard. The dark circles under her eyes that had been there before were more prominent against her pale skin. Now, the whites of her eyes were bloodshot. Her short curls were a haphazard mess around her head, but it was a style a lot of people probably paid good money for. What did I know? This was the first time I'd made a woman cry. I'd never given them a reason to get emotional about me. The way I'd snapped at her reminded me too much of my father for comfort.

She wiped off her face. "Uh, that was a mess. Such a mess. I should've been ready." A fat tear rolled down her cheek.

"Hey." I swiped the teardrop off her cheek. "Look, I have no clue what just happened, but it's clearly distressing you, and I can barely hear you over the champ. Feed him, and I'll check on Cali."

"I'm not distressed." When she caught my look, she shook her head. "Yes, I'm *very* stressed. But I'm also relieved." She pressed her fingertips to her temples. "Embarrassed. I need to go."

No matter what she said, she was distraught and I didn't want her driving off. "Tell me where your keys are and where you're parked. I'll get that stroller monstrosity loaded up. I'm sure Cali can help. Then I'll drive you home. Come out when you're ready. Sneak out the side door so no one sees you. Sutton will understand and won't make a scene."

"Why are you being so nice?"

"Listen, if my family hears you claim I'm nice, they're going to have questions, and I can't have that."

Her mouth twitched and the panic in her eyes ebbed. She let out a gusty sigh. Kellan only partially calmed down.

I held out my hand and helped her up. Her fingers felt tiny in my grip, but she was strong. I handed the baby over and left the office. I stepped to the side a few feet before I took off my ball cap and ran a hand through my hair. What the hell had I gotten myself into?

Something about marriage and moving and... *marriage*?

In the garage, there was laughter and lightness. Wilder hovered over Sutton. I'd been late today thanks to calls with the insurance company and breaking my damn back to make the barn structurally sound again, but I'd decided to come to Crocus Valley anyway. I thought the getaway would be good. Now I had a crying woman and I wasn't sure what else on my hands.

...you know...since our love is so new?

How about nonexistent? I barely knew the girl. She

was a cute single mom who lived three hours away from me. She worked for my sister-in-law. I hadn't planned to do more than admire the way her ass filled out her jeans at the last company picnic. There was nothing between me and Lily and her cute button nose, but apparently, we were getting married? Next week?

Why had she said my name to her aunt?

I didn't know the story, but I couldn't believe an aunt would kick a young family out of a house. I also had no idea why a marriage was pertinent to keeping the place. Wasn't Lily divorced?

Lily couldn't have a high opinion of men since she was stuck in a new town with a new job and two small children by herself because of a divorce. I didn't know why she and her ex split, but he was a fucknut. I didn't need details.

I'd have to get all the information before I breathed a word to my family. Would they warn me about Lily, or would they warn Lily off me? I was about to turn forty, and I'd never been married. I hadn't even been in any long-term relationships.

Wilder spotted me. "Everything okay?"

No. Not at all. "Lily's not feeling well. I'm gonna load up the stroller and Cali and pull around to the side door. She doesn't want extra attention."

Worry darkened Sutton's gaze. "Right. She doesn't seem like that kind of person. Thank you, and tell her to call me if she needs anything."

How did I tell Sutton that it sounded like Lily needed to get married? To me?

I couldn't comprehend being a husband by this time next week. One, I didn't know the bride. Two, I had more than a job. I managed Knight's Arabians and Cattle

Company. I had employees who counted on me to make their living, and I had siblings who needed the place to thrive enough to pay them the inheritance we'd worked our entire lives for.

No matter how married I was, I couldn't pull up my roots and leave. If I could, I would've done it years ago.

Four

LILY

To add to my humiliation, I had fallen asleep on the short trip to the house right after I'd given Eliot directions. With Cali in the car, we couldn't talk about much, and Eliot seemed to understand. He hadn't pushed for an explanation.

I blinked my eyes open just as Eliot pulled to a stop in front of the house. Good thing he'd driven. For a few blissful minutes, I didn't have the weight of the world on my shoulders.

Cali unbuckled and leaned forward. "Mom? Can I watch shows on the tablet?"

Grandma hadn't believed in TV, but she'd had Wi-Fi to stream radio stations. Cali needed to be distracted while I talked to Eliot. "Can you watch them in your room? I have to talk to Eliot."

Cali jumped up and down as much as she could in the SUV. "You're staying?"

Eliot's shuttered gaze slid from her to face out the window. "For a bit."

He was probably ready to run. I'd dragged an innocent man into chaos. Carter would laugh and claim I'd done the same to him. *Some days, you're like living with a tornado.*

Eliot hauled the car seat with Kellan in it, and I carried the diaper bag. Cali disappeared in a heartbeat. At least she'd had time to eat. I'd gotten a few bites in before Linda had shown up.

I sank onto the couch. Eliot looked around the house, curiosity more apparent than trepidation or impatience. Did he see a place that had a little bit of each decade from the last seventy years in it? Oak kitchen cabinets from the nineties. Furniture from the eighties and early aughts. Wallpaper from the sixties and a touch of the seventies. I had a lot of work to do.

I would've had a lot of work to do.

He finally took a seat, perched on the edge of the chair Aunt Linda had sat in when she'd delivered her bad news.

"It's just what I said." I started unbuckling Kellan. The long end table of Grandma's was pushed against the wall to protect my shins and so I could lay out Kellan's various playthings.

I set him on a play mat. He loved the faux grass next to the bright-blue fake river.

"You have to get married or lose your house?" Eliot asked. "How can that be?"

"Once you understand this isn't my house, maybe it'll make more sense." I fought back a yawn. Exhaustion was deep in my bones, but I had to tell him everything. I owed him. "I mean, I thought it was. Grandma always said she'd leave it to me. She passed away shortly before I moved here. So when I got the job with Sutton, I thought it was fate." Everything was finally working out for me, or so I had thought. "Dad gave me his keys and said I should just move right in."

"And your aunt will really kick you out?"

My heavy eyelids made blinking hard. The ten-minute snooze barely dented the hours of sleep I was missing. "I believe so. If she wavers, her fence post of a husband will do it."

"Fence post of a husband?"

I lifted a shoulder. "That's what his personality reminds me of. He's just kind of there."

The corner of his mouth ticked up. "Why'd your grandma— Never mind. I'm sorry for your loss."

"Thank you." I missed Grandma, but right now, I was upset with her. She screwed me over. "As for your other question, I'd like to think that Grandma thought I'd still be married and wouldn't be in this predicament."

"And what predicament is that, Lily?" he asked quietly.

I blinked, but the tears had already sprung into my eyes. "My parents would take me in, but can you imagine moving back in with your parents?"

"They're dead."

I recoiled at the frankness of his tone. "God, I'm sorry."

He rubbed his temples. "Shit, no, I'm sorry. My mama ran out on us when we were all still kids, and she did it because my father was a massive bastard. To give you an idea, he left my sister Aggie's inheritance to her now husband, who was the guy she left at the altar. He did that when he thought they had separate lives."

"That's awful." I had issues with my parents, but they'd never hurt me like that. If anything, they were too loving. Carter had claimed they were enablers, and while I'd learned how much of a dick my ex really was, he hadn't been entirely wrong. What had it been like for Eliot to grow up under the opposite?

"It all worked out because Ansen fell hard for my sister again and donated everything to her animal rescue. But to get back on topic—what else? It's not just moving back in with your parents."

I didn't want to tell him my baggage, but at the same time, he'd already witnessed my worst. "This job. My ex is a veterinarian. Guess how we met?" I tried to make the question light, but my shame broke through.

"You worked for him."

"Stereotypical, right? I was in vet school and working a few hours here and there. You know what's even more predictable?"

"He continued to fuck the staff?"

My cheeks heated, and I dropped my gaze to Kellan. "I found out I was pregnant right after I asked for a divorce. He got a lawyer, and I got nothing." I chewed my bottom lip. "Not nothing. I got the kids. I didn't care about anything else, and I knew I couldn't fight him and his parents, who wanted a more impressive daughter-in-law."

"He wants nothing to do with the kids?" Eliot held up his hands. "If it's none of my business, just say so."

"I think I made it your business. Cali's mom signed away custody and left her with Carter shortly after we met. Cali was six months old, and I adopted her after we got married." I'd always been honest with her, and with the name change, she'd been asking questions before school started in the fall. Hence her two-moms announcement in front of Eliot when we first met. "Carter isn't interested in being a dad. He's interested in doing what he wants when he wants."

The rumors I'd heard after the divorce were like soaking my wounds in salt water.

"So, to answer your question," I continued, "I won't get a good recommendation from him. If I up and quit on Sutton to move to Billings, then how hard will it be for me to get a job? I'm just going to look like a vet school dropout who can't hold a job." Which was exactly what I was.

"Did leaving vet school have to do with your ex?"

I nodded. I dropped my gaze again. Kellan wiggled against the mat, kicking his legs out. Drool dripped out of his mouth. I grabbed one of the many cloths I stored around the place and swiped his face clean. "I quit school to work and took care of Cali because Carter was the main breadwinner. He made a good argument about how raising Cali would be better if we were married and I was around more. That I'd have a more flexible schedule as a tech."

"What a bastard." His tone was heated, and pleasure rolled through me. Yes. My ex was a bastard. I knew it, but I'd never turn away extra validation.

"That's the general consensus with my family too, but I was second-guessing vet school. I just wanted more time to be with Cali and be involved in her life. Carter wasn't home a lot, and I hated having her in daycare. Once I got done with school, that wouldn't change. I'd just have more stress." I lifted a shoulder. "My family thinks I made an excuse, but it's true. I was doubting my career."

He propped his arms on his knees and pressed his fingertips together. He was all cowboy CEO right now. My mortification didn't detract from his hotness. The muscles in his forearms bunched and flexed, and I had no right to notice as acutely as I did. "If you don't marry someone next week, you'll have to move everything out—"

"It's not mine. I could only bring what fit in my car and my parents' pickup from Kansas to Billings, so I didn't have much to move in here."

"Jesus, Lily."

"I know. I'm a mess."

Pebbles prowled into the room, making a mewing noise like she was agreeing with me.

Eliot's gaze softened when it landed on the tabby. The cat swiped her body against his shins, and he scratched her head.

Pebbles moved on, and Eliot's expression turned introspective. The corners of his jaw flexed. "I wasn't thinking you're a mess. I think you've got dealt a shit hand. And now you have to marry to keep a roof over your head and your job." He shook his head, anger brewing in his brown irises.

"I have to be married a year before the house will be put in my name. I'm really sorry to drag you into this. You don't have to marry me, of course, I just had to buy some time with Aunt Linda. I couldn't find an adequate place to move into, and I thought, I don't know, that maybe she would go easy on me. But she's not. In order to stay, I've got to live with my husband for a year on the property—or at least make my aunt and uncle think he lives here. Know any single guys who want to settle down now?" My thready laugh fell flat.

His gaze was on me, burning right through me until I was uncomfortably warm.

"Trust me," I said, struggling to make my voice stronger. "I got this. I've landed on my feet for the last year; I can keep doing it. You can go, but I'm sincerely sorry for what you walked in on."

He didn't answer, but his gaze intensified.

"I've disrupted your day enough, but if you could keep this between us until I figure everything out? I really love working at the clinic. Sutton keeps surprising me with her generosity, and I don't want her to doubt hiring me. This story is...crazy."

He didn't respond right away. My anxiety tried to increase, but my adrenaline had run out. I was depleted.

My yawn couldn't be stopped. I smothered my mouth with my hand. I just had to hold it all together a little longer. When he was gone and when Cali and Kellan were asleep, I could have a little panic session and start gathering numbers to call in the morning.

"How tired are you?" he asked.

"Excuse me?"

"When's the last time you've gotten some decent sleep?"

"Um..." I bit the inside of my cheek as I thought back. "I got that nap in the car."

He exhaled a "fuck" and rose. "Go to bed, Lily. Tell me what to do, and I'll take care of it. You need to sleep."

I could laugh, that maniacal cackling of someone too overwhelmed to think straight. "I can't go to bed. There's too much to do. Lying to Linda bought me a few days. That's all."

"Go to bed," he said firmly and propped his hands on his hips. "Because over the weekend, we're going to have to figure out how this marriage of ours is going to work."

Eliot

Everything Lily told me rebounded inside my head as I rocked Kellan and read a book to Cali in one of the guest rooms. The little girl was tucked under a comforter that had more flowers than any flower beds I'd ever seen.

I'd been on uncle duty before, but there hadn't been many times I'd flown solo like tonight. And to do it with two kids I barely knew served only to make me wonder how much I'd missed out on with my nieces and nephews.

Cody and his first wife had lived in Buffalo Gully when his oldest two were born. Before she died, his wife had preferred Wilder and Sutton for babysitting. Which had been fine. I'd been younger and not used to kids.

Then Aggie and Ansen had Ro. Cody met Tova and they had Charlie. Aggie and Ansen had Tripp next. Now Sutton and Wilder were having twins, Aggie was expecting again, so was Vienne, and Tova had just announced she was pregnant.

Ten nieces and nephews. How much would I miss in their lives?

I shook it off and turned the page. Cali's blinks were getting long. Lily had made her change and clean up before she laid herself down. She'd pumped when I promised her I wouldn't gag when handling a bottle of breast milk. My insistence that I'd handled milk from several animals in my career didn't comfort her like I had hoped it would. An embarrassed blush had flamed across her cheeks.

I finished the last page of the book. The author was listed as just Magnolia. Cali said it was her grandma. "Time for bed."

"I sleep with Mommy."

New house. New town. Was she scared in this strange room? Lily needed sleep. Kellan would be in her room. How much quality rest would Lily get with two kids? Not much, judging by how she'd been out within seconds of driving. "If I check all over your room and make sure it's safe, can you *try* falling asleep in your bed first?" It was an old negotiating trick I'd heard Cody use a few times.

Her lips puffed out. "Monsters like to hide under the bed."

"Whoever told you that don't know monsters. I heard they're afraid of kids." She gave me a dubious look, but I nodded. "Haven't you watched *Monsters, Inc*?"

"Watch a movie 'bout monsters?" Her doubtful expression didn't waver.

"Tell you what, I'll look anyway. Monsters don't like me, that's for darn sure."

She wearily pulled her blankets up. "Night, Eliot."

"Night, Cali."

I glanced down at Kellan. His little lips were smushed against each other. He was snoozing solidly, having fallen asleep during the first book we read, somewhere between when the mouse got a cookie and made a damn mess.

I got up, nestled Kellan in the crook of my elbow, and checked the closet and under the bed. Kellan snoozed through the whole process.

"All clear and I'll be right outside." I was about to walk out of the bedroom.

"Eliot?"

I bit back a smile. She mostly said the *L* sound, but there was a hint of a *W* in there. She'd probably outgrow it as soon as tomorrow, but that, along with her enthusiasm at seeing me, melted my heart a little more each time I saw her. If kids liked me, then I wasn't too far gone from civilization, surrounded by isolated men on my big ranch in the middle of nowhere. "Yeah?"

"Can you keep the door open?"

"You got it." I turned the light off and kept the door halfway open.

The hallway light stayed on, giving Cali some light to go to sleep with and so I could lay Kellan down.

I glanced down at him tucked against my chest, his fingers lax under his chin. I didn't hold sleeping babies often. I played with them or held them so my siblings and their spouses could eat or visit without a human barnacle.

His little mouth moved like he was suckling an invisible bottle.

Cute little bugger.

Lily's door was open too. Was she afraid to shut herself completely away from her kids? Duh, of course. We were practically strangers.

Yet, I was marrying her. Within days.

I'd checked the courthouse hours. We could go there Monday, say our vows and this nightmare would be over for her.

Or I could leave. Tell her I couldn't marry a stranger. She'd understand. She'd been terribly sympathetic and had given me several outs. Yet I had stayed and told her to go to bed. I was a single guy. I never wanted to try and fail at a relationship and prove my mother right, but I could use my bachelorhood for good. I could give it up and help a mom and two kids. And a cat. Add in more barn cats she'd probably care for.

I was getting married.

I stepped into Lily's room and let my eyes adjust to the darkness. The smell of old perfume faded, and the scent of baby powder and sunshine filled the air. Lily's soft breaths were barely audible. A bassinet was by her side of the bed.

I laid Kellan down. He made a little squeak and I froze. Did I wake him?

I played statue until his breathing returned to being even. Lily didn't move. She was exhausted. I'd seen it when I first met her.

No wonder she was so worn out. She was worried about her job, her home, and her kids. Life was stressful enough with just one of those issues. She'd have all three if I didn't help her.

Before I left, I looked at her small form in the bed. The comforter was almost exactly the same as the one in Cali's room. A shitload of flowers. I took one last inhale before I left her room. The rest of the house had a scent that reminded me of my house when Barns was alive. A little stale.

I shook my head, grabbed the baby monitor, and left the bedroom before she woke and caught me watching her. The last thing that woman needed was some dude leering at her while she slept.

My stomach rumbled as I went to the kitchen. I hadn't had time to eat at the party.

In the fridge, I found milk, eggs, and Lunchables. I closed the door and checked the counter. Bread and apples. The sink held the clean bottles Cali had told me were for daycare. I looked in the freezer. Bags of frozen milk lined one side and TV dinners for kids and adults filled the rest.

Was that all the woman ate?

My stomach was fussing up a storm, but I didn't want to dig into her ready-to-eat staples, none of which were appetizing anyway, so I went in search of a deep freeze. I doubted there was one on the upper level, so I found the door to the basement. A musty scent got stronger the lower I went. The basement was furnished, and it was like stepping down into a time capsule. Upstairs had a mixture of styles. Downstairs? Welcome to the '70s.

The orange shag carpet crunched under my feet. I found a laundry room. I checked the washer. There was a load inside that was damp. I switched that to the dryer.

Next, I checked the freezer. All I needed was a steak or a pound of hamburger. Anything but the boxes of disappointment she had in her fridge freezer upstairs. I opened the lid and groaned.

White packages were piled on each other enough to cover the bottom, but the amount of frost lining the outside wasn't promising. Even the freezer burn would have freezer burn.

I picked up one that looked newer. When I made out what was inside, I jolted and dropped the baggie. "Jesus."

Why would Lily have dead mice in her freezer?

I closed the lid. Dead, frozen mice. What the hell had I gotten myself into?

A shadow moved next to me and I jolted. The cat blinked at me as she marched by.

I took my hat off and stuffed it back on. Goddammit,

I wasn't usually this jumpy. Scared by a cat that looked as old as this house.

I shook my head and gave up on my foraging efforts. I wasn't eating mice. Pausing, I glanced at the cat. She didn't look like she had the energy to eat mice. I doubted Lily and the kids were munching on them. What was in the house that ate mice?

Whatever it was had food.

Was Lily always this short on decent eats? The freezers weren't full. She had no crib set up. She said she had left with what could fit into her car and her parents' pickup. All of the furnishings were her grandma's.

Rage boiled inside of me. Good thing her shitty ex was in Kansas.

The anger made me hungrier. I couldn't run to the gas station or the grocery store if it was open this late.

I went upstairs and paced around. I could go one night without food. Or I could call in a favor from a brother. One who'd keep his mouth shut when I explained why I was at the house of one of Sutton's employees. Would he believe I wasn't here to take advantage of the tired but sexy mom?

I called Austen.

He answered with a muffled, "Yeah?"

"Can you get off your wife and run a couple errands for me?"

"One, jackass, we're done. For now. Two, what the hell do you need me to do for you that you can't do yourself?"

"It's a long story that I can't tell you right now. I'm helping out Lily from Sutton's clinic, and her kids are asleep and she's asleep and there's no food in the house."

The silence stretched on. "You're at *Lily's*. She just had a baby."

"It's not like that." I pinched my eyes shut. All my brothers were too damn nosy—and too suspicious of my intentions. I'd have to give him some info. "Not exactly. We're getting married."

"What the fuck?" he sputtered.

"You can't tell anyone. Not yet." I'd have to make time for an explanation. "She can't keep the house if she's not married and then she'd have to uproot the kids and quit her job. It's her grandma's stipulations."

"Grandma's stipulations? What kind of crazy bull—"

"Of all people, we should be familiar with relatives fucking us over after death." He went quiet, which was exactly what I expected. Barns had been selfish in the trust he'd formed before he died. I was as stuck as Lily. "I'll explain more later. Right now, I'm really damn hungry, and I need my overnight bag. Can you grab it from my pickup?"

"Sure. Whaddaya want to eat?"

"Anything that won't give me gut rot."

"You realize only the gas stations are open right now." His heavy exhale gusted over the line. "Just so you know, I'm telling V so we can be shocked and appalled together."

"I'm with you, man. I'll tell the others at the picnic." A worry for another day. A day real soon.

He grunted and got off the phone.

I sat on the couch and stared at the wall, working over everything Lily had told me until headlights swung down the drive. I hooked the baby monitor to my belt and crept out the door. I didn't care to wake Lily, but I certainly didn't want her to run into Austen. I already felt like I was invading her place.

Vienne hopped out first with two plastic bags in her hand. "You're getting married?" she whisper-shouted.

Her sandals slapped the ground. She was in shorts and a T-shirt like my brother. I'd make a joke about them being married so long they were dressing alike, but humor wasn't my priority.

I nodded, my throat working. Saying the words to her made it more real. *Married*.

Her gaze dropped down. "Oh my god, is that a baby monitor?"

"You'll have to get familiar with one in, like, six months."

She gave me a saccharine-sweet smile. "Don't wiggle out of telling us what's going on, Daddy Eliot."

"She needs sleep." I told Lily if Kellan woke up tonight, she only had to feed him, and I'd rock him until he went to sleep. She'd warned me he was fussy. She'd made a lot of excuses as I had herded her to bed. She'd been ready to drop, or she might've kicked me out.

Vienne's eyes went liquid. "Aw, you're so sweet." Concern infused her gaze. "Marriage?"

"For a year. Then the house will be hers."

Austen approached and handed over my duffel bag. "Are you moving here?"

Did he sound hopeful? I shook my head. "You know I can't do that. This house isn't hers as much as the house on the ranch isn't mine." I had to be married to my job to stay in that place. *Thanks, Barns.* "I can't risk it. We just have to make her aunt think I'm residing here."

I took the bags from Vienne. She stared at me. Same with Austen.

"You're supposed to marry her and live here?"

I shrugged. "We have to provide a marriage certificate. Otherwise, we could fake that too."

"Shit," Austen said softly. He held his hand out. "Gimme your keys. We'll drop your pickup off."

Relieved I wouldn't have to herd everyone out of the house to get my pickup in the morning, I did as he asked. "Thanks."

He inspected me. Most of the time, I didn't see much effect of the military on him. He was the same laid-back Austen. Then moments like now, when I itched under the collar from his open scrutiny? Yeah. I could see it.

"You're welcome," he finally said. "See you Sunday?"

"Yeah. I'll see if..." I waved toward the house. "I'll see if she wants to be there when I tell everyone."

"Tell her we'd love her and the kids to come no matter what," Vienne said. "You know Cody and Tova won't have an issue with it."

Cody would have *thoughts* about the marriage. Most of them critical.

"Will do." Humbled that my family might be aghast that I was marrying a single mom whom I'd just met but that they understood and would support her, I went inside.

As I dug out fruit and nut packs, containers of meat and cheese, and a few candy bars because Austen knew I had a sweet tooth, I appreciated their efforts more. I wouldn't be a present husband, but my family was here to watch over Lily. Something I couldn't do.

Five

LILY

The night was a blur of feedings. Just as I'd wake to Kellan's cries, I'd find Eliot handing him to me. I'd nurse, and as soon as Kellan fussed after he ate, Eliot was quietly knocking on the partially open door. He'd take Kellan, and I'd drop into the deepest slumber I could remember. Repeat. I hadn't been this exhausted in vet school.

I was dimly aware of the sun rising outside for the last two feedings, but when I blinked my eyes open, panic rose. It was well into the morning. The angle of light streaming through the windows wasn't normal. Neither was the silence.

I scrambled for my phone. Eleven. Oh no.

Alarm pumped through my veins as I catapulted out of bed. Where were my kids? I bumped out the door and careened down the hall to Cali's room. I'd left her alone with a strange man.

A hot, considerate, basically a miracle guy. But I didn't know him.

What had I been thinking? My boss vetted him, but what did that mean? I should've—

I came to a halt when I took in Cali's bedroom. The longing was almost as strong as the relief. Cali was on her stomach on the bed, kicking her feet behind her. She had on headphones while watching her tablet.

She grinned at me. Only partially mollified, my gaze darted to the rocking chair. Eliot was snoozing with Kellan curled on his chest. Kellan's face was turned to the side. He puffed air out of his mouth a moment before Eliot did the same.

Eliot's ball cap was on the floor, and his rich, chestnut hair was ruffled. Dark lashes swept over his cheeks. His face might be lax while sleeping, but he still had a jaw carved from stone, only this late in the morning, it was dusted with dark stubble.

For the first time in months, a kindling of desire curled through my belly.

Nope. I could not go there. The guy had given me almost fourteen hours of sleep. No orgasms could compare, and I was wrong to be so attracted to a man I was cornering into a marriage.

I turned my attention to Cali and tapped at my ear before putting my finger to my lips.

She took her headphones off.

"Did you eat yet?" I whispered.

"Eliot made eggs."

I nodded, and she put her headphones back on. He let me sleep, and he cooked. This guy might just be perfect. Maybe the trick to picking a man to marry was to get one who wasn't interested in me.

How long had Kellan kept Eliot up?

I backed out of the room.

In the kitchen, embarrassment filled me. I usually got groceries on the weekends, but I had purposely let supplies dwindle. Less to move or trash that way.

I checked the fridge as if food would miraculously appear. There was a plate with Saran Wrap on it. Behind it was a bottle of lemonade.

Where did that come from?

"It's yours."

I yelped and jumped away from the fridge. Eliot was standing behind me. Slumbering Eliot didn't destroy my nerves as much as sleepy, tousled Eliot. He blinked, and the corner of his mouth lifted. He held Kellan facing out. I got a drooly smile from my son.

"Morning, baby." I held my arms out. I couldn't look at Eliot. It would sear my retinas as thoroughly as staring at the sun. "Thank you. I haven't had that much sleep in years."

"I can see why you needed it. Little man likes to party at all hours." He lifted his chin to the fridge. "I hope you don't mind. I called in a favor from Vienne and Austen. They brought us some food."

"I'm sorry. I was going to get groceries tomorrow if I was still in the house." I grimaced. Not only did I fail to impress his siblings with my scant pantry options, but they had to ask why he'd been here that late. "Did you tell them?"

He nodded. "They'll keep it quiet until we can explain. Which brings me to this weekend."

"What about it?" Kellan was wiggling around and self-consciousness was digging in. I had woken up after being nearly comatose for fourteen hours. All night, I'd risen like a zombie to nurse and then went back to my grave. I hadn't showered or brushed my teeth since I'd woken up. How bad did I look? Was my shirt crooked? It didn't feel askew.

"Cody's having a Fourth of July picnic on Sunday. We can tell everyone then."

"Everyone? All at once?" Another Knight family gathering? He had a big family. I was used to the same, but my siblings were all currently single. They could be a force among themselves. If they had spouses, did the scrutiny and questions double, or was it different for Eliot? He wasn't the youngest like me.

Could I plant myself in the center of a giant unit of supportive siblings and tell them I entrapped their brother for the next year? My heart rate crept up.

"It'll be fine," he said.

Did I look ready to bolt? I had nowhere to go, and the diaper bag needed to be reloaded with fresh diapers anyway. "There are a lot of you."

"Yeah." He huffed out a laugh. "I told you about Aggie and the inheritance money?"

I nodded. Kellan squirmed. The last time I nursed must've been around nine. He'd be rooting at my shirt. I swayed side to side with him.

"She got away free and clear. Barns—that's my dad, Barnaby Knight—wrapped up our ranching and oil well operation into a trust. In order to get any inheritance, my brothers and I have to work for the family company."

I didn't understand. His family lived in Crocus Valley.

He nodded like he wanted me to know he was getting there. "Cody runs Knight's Oil Wells. He used to be the accountant for the ranch, but with his growing family, we were able to justify hiring a bookkeeper that he oversees. And that's the loophole Wilder used. We hired another guy, but technically, Wilder is still a ranch employee. He comes out to help with moving cattle and working them and the horses."

"Right, you breed Arabians."

"Then there's Austen. Barns was actually a little considerate with him. He let Austen choose between a bigger inheritance if he got out of the army and worked the ranch, or he'd give him a smaller cut if he went on to get his full military retirement. Austen picked retirement."

"That leaves you." Was it all dumped on him?

"Yep. Mine's a little more complex. I was ranch manager when Barns died, and if I want to keep my job and have a place to live, I have to stay ranch manager. My inheritance is my paycheck, like my siblings."

"But it's your only job. The others had different careers." Sutton said Wilder had been a deputy in Buffalo Gully.

"Yep." A dark shadow crossed his face. He was as tied to his place as I was mine.

"That sucks." I wanted to live in this house, but he didn't sound fond of his home. Dedicated, yes. Nostalgic? Nope.

"Sure does. But I'm telling you that to point out that my family will understand and help us out as much as possible. We're going through it with our own trust."

The idea crawled along the back of my neck. I wasn't dragging his family into my problems any more than I had. "I'm fine. I mean, as long as we have the marriage certificate... How are we going to do that?"

"We can ask Sutton and Wilder what they did for their second round of vows."

"They got married twice?"

"They were divorced for a year, separated for longer."

"No kidding?" Sutton seemed to have her life pieced together perfectly, but she had made comments that alluded to how it hadn't always been like that.

Cali wandered in, her headphones still on.

Talk of marriage would have to be tabled. Eliot and I had a lot to cover, and I needed time to figure out what to say to Cali. The divorce had been a lot to talk through, and occasionally, she still needed reassurance that it hadn't been her fault. "Hey, kiddo. Hungry?"

"Yep."

"I have to get groceries." I looked down at my shorts and T-shirt. I'd have to nurse, then shower, or vice versa, and then get Cali dressed in something other than pajamas. Kellan was in his sleeper too.

"Go feed him and get ready." Eliot went to the fridge. "I'll figure out lunch."

"You've already done enough. I'm sure you have family waiting to hear from you after you left the picnic last night."

"They've gotten along without me for years."

Why was it so easy to trust him?

Because, for once, I couldn't see what was in this arrangement for him. I wasn't a ready-made mom for his neglected daughter. I wasn't a wife who would work at his clinic for cheap. And I wasn't running his errands.

A girl could get used to this.

A girl should know better than to think anyone else can clean up her disrupted life.

"I've gotta ask one thing," he said.

There it was. The ask. He'd tell me what he expected out of me. Should I tell Cali to give us a minute?

"I looked for food downstairs. What's with the mice in the freezer?"

Lily

Flakes had been fed a thawed mouse before we left. His tank was in the main bedroom, a juxtaposition compared to the old-fashioned style of the space.

Cali had talked Eliot through the whole process. He'd been patient, but judging from the wary look on his face, he would've rather released the snake into the wild and flushed all the mice.

After I had showered and dressed, I fed Kellan and dressed Cali. Eliot had already heated up a frozen dinner for her. The retching sound she'd made over the gooey brownie made it as far as the bathroom, and I'd known exactly which kind he'd tried to serve.

Now we were at the grocery store. Eliot attracted attention from everyone we passed. Sometimes, he ran into someone who thought he was one of his brothers. With the Knights in town, it was like tall, dark, and handsome grew on trees.

"Ooh, Mommy. Granola bars." Cali pointed at the shelves.

Eliot grabbed the box she was most excited about. He'd cleaned up, but his scruff was still in place. I couldn't quit letting my gaze stroke over it. Instead of concealing his jawline, the dark stubble enhanced it. He had his ball cap pulled down low, and he was studying a box of granola bars Cali was asking for as he held Kellan in his other arm. The bars were name brand.

"You can put that back. We usually get a different kind." A cheaper kind.

Cali let her shoulders hang. "Mo-om. These are better."

Yes. They were. Those granola bars were definitely a case of generic not being the same. "You know we don't eat those."

Eliot was studying me. "How about I get them for me? I might share one."

A large grin spread across my daughter's face. "Yeah!"

He quirked a brow at me, and I shrugged. I knew what he was doing, and it made Cali happy. One box of granola bars wouldn't hurt. He put the box at the end of the cart.

I shook my head, but my smile broke through. I circled around the aisle and went for the beef display.

"Nope." He tugged the front of the cart, and I was helpless to push it after him.

"I need to get some hamburger."

"I've got a place you can get hamburger. Let me make a call."

Sutton had mentioned their freezer was always stocked with Knight beef, but Eliot wasn't likely to haul a cooler of it in his pickup at all times. "You can't raid from your siblings."

"No, but Aggie's husband has a lot of ranching cousins who'll stock you up with good beef."

My alarm was rising again. I'd love to buy from the source. I used to do it when I was married, but without a veterinarian's salary, that wasn't happening. "I can't afford bulk fresh meat like that."

"My treat."

"Eliot—"

He turned, and I was pinned by his intense stare and Kellan's dark-blue one. "If I'm staying with you through Monday, I'm going to need more than that freezer-dried food in the basement. You don't want me diving into Flakes's stash, do you?"

Cali giggled.

"I don't have a small appetite," he added. "My treat." He turned back around. Since I was sick of discount beef, I followed him.

He loaded up the cart with more eggs, milk, yogurt, cereal, fruits, and frozen veggies than one man could eat in a weekend. My suspicions were growing before we reached the cashier. When it was time to pay, he handed Kellan to me and dug out his wallet.

"Eliot, you can't—"

Another dark, quelling stare. It should upset me, not make molten lava flow through my belly and circle down. I was not attracted to his high-handedness.

"He's going to share his fruit snacks," Cali whisper-squealed.

Didn't all rugged ranchers want princess fruit snacks after a hard day's work?

I waited until we got the kids and the groceries loaded into the car. He'd never given the keys back to me after he'd driven here. He put the cart away, but I stayed outside the vehicle.

As much as I wanted to indulge in being a passenger princess, I had to address his intrusiveness in the store. "I'm going to pay you back."

"Don't worry about it."

"I do worry about it."

He stopped next to me by the passenger door. I had to tilt my head back to look at him.

He waited until he had my full attention. "It's okay to get a little help."

"Not always."

He held my stare, then his gaze traveled down my face, down my neck, to my collar. "It'll bother me if I don't, and it'll sure as hell bother me if you try to pay me back. I don't cook for more than one unless I'm running the grill at family events." He skated his gaze away. "And those don't happen in Buffalo Gully as much as they used to."

That sense of loss in his voice matched the heavy air I'd first noticed about him. "Isn't your family all up in your business?"

"Not anymore. When we were younger, my brothers did their thing and ignored me unless I wasn't pulling my share around the place."

Oh. Well... "What about Aggie?"

"She was usually upset she wasn't included enough."

My points were falling way short of their goal, but this had hit home. "I've had to pay for the help I get in the past."

His gaze sharpened. "How so?"

"Carter's parents were hypercritical. If I asked them to watch Cali, they'd ask him if I was doing my share around the house. Was I contributing? Could I handle the duties? Why was I always calling my parents or my oldest sister, Violet? So I didn't."

"And your family? Didn't they check on you?"

"I think they got discouraged, but I do have to learn

to live on my own." Having a guy pay for all my groceries wasn't the best example of fending for myself.

He arched a brow. "Most people have a support system. Your ex-in-laws sound like jackasses."

A laugh sputtered out of me. They were jackasses, but were they wrong? "I agree, but I can do it. This is just a hard season in my life."

"Lily Duke, you burn your candle at both ends. Sometimes you gotta let a guy blow on you." He frowned, then his eyes widened. "Shit, not what I meant."

A giggle left me, morphing into a genuine laugh that rang through the air. It'd been forever since I'd laughed. "That's how I ended up in this situation."

He grinned, and thankfully, I was laughing so hard I was already out of breath, or the view of him with a full smile would've stolen every particle of air I didn't have to give.

ELIOT

On Sunday, Lily, the kids, and I were loaded and heading to Cody's. He'd have his shop open for the picnic and then he'd have a cordoned-off spot to shoot fireworks. I didn't know if the kids or Lily would make it the whole night.

I drove through Crocus Valley and aimed for the other side of town. Lily's knuckles were white on the bowls she held. She had insisted on making a pasta salad and a dessert for the family picnic. The corners of her eyes were pinched. She was stressed.

My nerves were on high alert. I'd spent the morning messaging my employees, telling them I might need another day away for family business. Hopefully, there'd be no more tractor DUIs while I was away.

Chambers told me to tell everyone hi. If I mentioned I was getting married, he'd be delighted. If I told him I was leaving my wife in Crocus Valley alone with her two kids, he'd kick my ass like a proper dad.

I had messaged Austen and told him to let the others know I was bringing Lily and we had to talk to everyone. That way, my siblings were prepared to see me show up with her.

Last night, she hadn't let me do bedtime duty alone. She hadn't let me do much. She'd made a delicious cheeseburger pasta dish for dinner, then she had rocked Kellan while I read a book to Cali.

We didn't talk about the wedding or discuss how the residence would work. Between the groceries, feedings, naps, playtime, meals, cleanup—there hadn't been time. Or so I told myself. Once we started discussing details, then it'd become real. From her story, she'd been manipulated into marrying once. This time wasn't much different. But I'd treat her better than that dick ex of hers.

By the time I was done with the story and Cali was tucked in, Lily had been yawning. I'd sent her to bed, then remained vigilant on baby duty all night. Kellan and I partied for a few quiet hours when he fussed every time he wasn't held, then he'd passed out.

Instead of the couch, I got her grandma's old room. I dozed in the lingering scent of old perfume, with a corn snake in a large enclosure pushed between two dressers.

"Is Ivy going to be there?" Cali asked. Ivy, my niece, was a few years older than her, but Cali idolized her already.

"Absolutely," I said. "I bet she'll show you her goats."

"Goats, Mom!" Lily had decided to tell Cali about us later. Otherwise, she might blurt it out before we even reached the shop.

Lily smiled at me, and I grinned back. The moment

stabbed right through my psyche. How easily could I fool myself that this was real? My bachelor days were done. But that would be fake. We were pretending.

I parked. Cali shouted, "Ivy!" and ran out.

Lily let out a slow exhale. I grabbed her hand. "We got this."

She gazed at my big hand over her small one. Her skin was warm and soft like I imagined the rest of her body was. I'd caught a glimpse of her white bra when she'd been sleeping last night. I'd felt like a damn creeper, but also—I had no regrets.

She swallowed hard. "Is it going to be okay?"

"Promise."

She lifted her gaze to mine. Denim-blue eyes that should be full of humor were too serious.

"You have beautiful eyes," I murmured.

A faint blush stained her cheeks. "Thanks. They're the only thing that survived the pregnancy unscathed."

"Trust me, Lily. I don't know what you looked like when you were pregnant or before, but nothing got ruined."

The flush deepened.

Fuck, I was flirting with her when she was worried about being driven off by my siblings. "Come on. Let's get this over with."

She dropped her gaze. "Right." She tugged her hand out of mine and got out of the car.

I had a second before she opened the back door to curse at myself. Get this over with? *Good one, Knight.*

I carried the diaper bag. The kids were playing in the yard by the shop. Cody had a volleyball net set up, horseshoes, and a few more lawn games were scattered around. The goats eyed us from their enclosure on the other side of the shop. He also had a few head of cattle for his kids' 4-H projects. His dog was running with the kids.

Several pairs of eyes watched us approach. The curiosity prickled along my skin.

Tova came to take the food. Her dark hair was pulled back in a bun and she wore a loose pink sundress that matched what I saw little Charlie running around in. "Lily, so nice to see you again. We have a spot in the shade for you and Kellan."

Lily's smile was shy. She looked ready to bolt, but her spine was straight. While she might seem timid, the woman was lined with steel. And covered in that satiny skin.

Tova took the food to the long table. The rest of my family greeted us. Cody watched me with narrowed eyes. Austen and Vienne were like a pair of grinning teenagers, in on the secret everyone else would soon learn. Austen saluted me with his beer. He and Vienne always drank the same thing. Some sort of inside thing they had. Sutton was sitting with her feet on a cooler. She looked concerned. Wilder hovered over her, looking grim because his wife was worried. Ansen stood behind Aggie, his hands around her waist and his chin on the top of her head.

A beat of envy passed through me. My brothers were older than me and still having kids. They had true partners in life. I was entering a marriage arrangement with a woman who was a stranger.

That wasn't totally true. I knew more about her than most women I dated. Although *dated* was a strong word.

"Austen said you had to talk?" Cody wasn't one to wait on business.

Grateful he broke the ice, I nodded and exchanged a

glance with Lily. At her faint nod, I answered. "Yep. We're getting married."

Sutton's jaw dropped. Wilder and Cody wore matching poleaxed expressions. Austen and Vienne were avidly watching everyone's reaction. Aggie's eyes were wide, but her husband smirked, probably because he still remembered how my brothers and I had run him off when he and Aggie were supposed to get married the first time. We were brothers now, but he liked my discomfort. Tova gasped and grinned like she was delighted.

"Let me explain." I told them about the trust stipulations. Lily scooted closer to me the more I talked. A guy could get used to her physical proximity.

Cody shook his head, but understanding filled his gaze. Same with everyone else.

Sutton put her feet down. "Lily, you could've come to me."

"I didn't know what to do." Lily's voice was slightly stronger. "I'm really sorry about dragging him into this, but I gave my aunt a name to buy time and then he walked in."

She'd said my goddamn name. Not some guy from her past or even a fake name. She'd put a lot of trust in me since we met. I wouldn't take any of this lightly.

"How's this going to work?" Cody asked.

"I just need to be married for a year," she said. "Eliot can go about his life, and I'll live mine. We'll tell my aunt he has to commute for work."

Our arrangement wasn't ideal, but what choice did I have? "It'll have to look like I live at her place and work out of town." If my family had any tips, I'd love to know them. "Her dad and her aunt need to buy that this is real."

Cody frowned. "You'll need to change your address. And move some stuff in."

"And you'll need to come to Crocus Valley more regularly," Wilder said, his tone neutral. He knew how hard it was to commute. "Where does your aunt live?" he asked Lily.

"In Coal Haven," she answered. "I don't know how often she'll stop in. My parents probably won't make it here more than a few times a year."

"You can use work at the clinic as an excuse anytime," Sutton offered. "We'll all cover for you."

Lily smiled at her. I stroked my hand down Lily's arm. I wanted to tuck her into my side and keep her safe.

"Should work," Austen said. "Anyone asks, we'll say you met through Sutton, fell madly in love, but have yet to iron out the logistics."

"She darn near swept me off my feet," I joked to take the focus off the knot forming in my chest.

Lily snickered. "That was Bug."

Cody's frown deepened as he looked between us. "Will you be married but living the single life in Buffalo Gully? Are you going to go back and announce that you're married?"

Cody and his damn need to have everything lined up. I could control myself.

As if he saw the irritated expression on my face, he shrugged. "What if Weston decides to travel to Buffalo Gully for a surprise visit?"

Lily glanced at me and moved a few inches away. "I don't see why you have to give up your personal life. I mean, as long as you're discrete you're free to...uh, date."

She would raise two kids by herself while I could fuck

around? We both lived in small towns, and Buffalo Gully wasn't that far away from where her parents lived in Billings. The world could be a connected place. I wasn't letting her family get word that her husband was inside another woman while she was short of sleep or crying on the floor.

I was better than that. "There is no single life while I'm married." I shook my head. "No. It's fine. I've gotta be at the ranch as much as possible if I'm going to be gone more."

All my brothers raised their brows. Fucking Ansen smirked. He was enjoying the hell out of this.

"You need a prenup," Cody said. He smiled at Lily. "No offense, but you'd want to protect yourself too."

The idea of a prenup scratched under the surface of my skin. Lily wouldn't try to take me to the cleaners. I didn't have to know her long to know she wasn't like that.

Lily snorted. "All he'd get is debt."

"We don't need a prenup. Nothing is mine." I returned Cody's hard stare.

"Married for a year," Wilder echoed. "Shit. When's the big day?"

"Monday, if that's even an option." I checked with Lily. Her nod was shaky. Her aunt needed a document as soon as possible. "The courthouse is open."

"I can do it during lunch," Lily told Sutton.

Sutton shook her head. "You are getting the day off with pay for a wedding. No arguments."

Lily bit her plump lower lip like she'd been ready to do just that.

I clapped my hands together. They had the news. Lily hadn't relaxed, and she was still holding the baby carrier.

"I know you fools can't make a good burger. Let me start the grill and get this party started."

Lily

Cali danced in the yard with the other kids. She'd gotten a tour of the place and all the animals. I was surprisingly relaxed even while surrounded by Eliot's family. They'd been strangely accepting, but from what Eliot had described of their situation, it made sense. Their support reminded me of my family. So did their readiness to step in. I got lucky with in-laws for a fake marriage.

"I'm really happy Eliot's helping you," Sutton said to me. "He's a good guy. A little grumpy, but it's just a hard shell."

I hadn't seen the grumpiness. "He's been so helpful. I've caught up on so much sleep."

"Good to hear."

"How are you feeling?"

She pursed her lips. "My blood pressure is still creeping up. My doctor's appointment is tomorrow, so I might not see you at work on Tuesday. I'll work from home, and Wilder will be my legs."

"How's he doing with all this?"

"Fine, but also so worried." She shrugged. "We're so close, you know? But Wilder's keeping me distracted, and he's stocked up on puzzles." She grimaced. "I'll most likely be doing desk work remotely."

I hadn't worked at Sutton's Animal Clinic for long, but I only knew the job with her kind smile there.

"What does your family think about all this?" she asked.

I ran my lower lip through my teeth. "They don't know."

Her eyes went wide. "What? How don't they know?"

"My aunt gave me time." I let out a dry laugh. "And I think she's not looking forward to facing down everyone with the details."

"What do you mean?"

"Aunt Linda doesn't have kids, and it's just her and my dad, so Grandma divided the land up, and none of my siblings are married."

Sutton braced her hands on the armrests and leaned forward. "*All* of your siblings have to get married?"

"All five of them." And they didn't know it yet. "My dad's going to flip." Everyone would. Aunt Linda would have seven people facing her down between my five siblings and two parents. I wasn't close with her, but I could commiserate. I was also salty toward her.

Sutton gasped. Aggie and Tova approached. Vienne ditched a tame game of volleyball to come over. Austen had been barking out orders for everyone to take it easy and keep it safe for her.

"Mind if I join?" Tova asked, pulling a folding chair closer.

Aggie did the same and grabbed one for Vienne.

Sutton glanced at me, an apology in her eyes.

"Not at all." I didn't mind talking with them. Their demeanor was different than Carter's family. I sensed nothing but genuine concern and caring from the Knights. I should have been gun-shy after my marriage, but I was also exhausted from the last month of stress. I was trusting them with my biggest secret, one that involved more than me. I wouldn't keep Eliot from getting help where he could. He would be giving up a lot.

He should've run as soon as he heard me say his name.

I was surrounded by women who reminded me of my sisters. They would be in-laws for a year and already I was more comfortable around them than my former in-laws. "I was just telling Sutton about how my family's going to react when they learn what they have to do. They'll each have their own property to inherit."

Everyone was looking at me, waiting. That part was new. I got run over a lot in our big family gatherings.

"I have three sisters and two brothers," I explained, "and if they want the property my grandma's leaving them, they all have to get married and live there too. I have the house and forty acres." I ticked one finger up. "I'm not sure how the rest is broken up, but there's a cabin that Grandma kept up on the far edges of the land. My grandpa built it so he and his hunting buddies would have a place to stay. She rents it out now." I put another finger up. "Then there's a house with some acreage she and Grandpa bought on the edge of town. It bordered some of their land, and they wanted a rental property." A third finger. "Then they bought another section that had an old house on it. Grandpa liked to rescue homes. Um... I'm not sure if there's just land left or if they bought more that they didn't talk about."

Vienne danced her fingers up one of the long necklaces she wore. "They'll all be moving here?"

"I really don't know." I would love to have them live close. I barely remember the days when we lived in Crocus Valley, but I recalled being happy. Our house had been smaller but everyone had been around. After we moved to Billings, everyone grew up and went to college one by one until only I was left. I missed the chaos of a full house. I missed having family close.

Carter had tried to seclude me. I could see that now while I was surrounded by near strangers. I hadn't been able to form a support network like this when I'd been with him.

"When does this all have to happen?" Tova sounded as scandalized as Vienne had.

"Seven years." After a year of wondering where I'd live, where I'd work, and trying to answer people who asked the same, tonight was refreshing. I got the perk of being the first to hear everything. "Seven years from when Grandma passed, everything that isn't claimed will get sold, but it can't be sold to family."

"What happens if someone doesn't marry, or the marriage doesn't last?" Vienne asked.

"I dunno. I think Aunt Linda would sell it and donate the money."

Aggie tipped her head. The wind rustled her fluffy curls. Mine would puff out like that if I didn't use product after my shower. I'd look like an electrocuted dandelion, but on Aggie, it was pretty. "What's your aunt's incentive to see everyone succeed in marrying?"

I chewed my lower lip. "I don't know." Like me, my aunt probably didn't want to see what my grandparents had worked so hard for getting dissolved. Grandma had wanted us happy, and this was her wild way of forcing our hands, of molding us into her vision of happiness. But what did my aunt want? Certainly not the headache of telling everyone about the rules and then enforcing them.

Tova frowned. "There must be something she gets for the ideal resolution your grandma wanted."

I could ask my aunt, but ultimately, I wanted the house. I could commiserate with my siblings, but they'd have to figure it out for themselves.

"Does she want them all to return to Coal Haven?" Sutton asked. "They were all born there too, right?"

I nodded. "Yes, and my mom wished we could move back. She never liked Billings as much, and she missed helping my grandparents farm and ranch. Grandma loved my mom, so maybe this was a way to get us all to relocate?"

"Do you want them to?" Sutton asked.

Longing tugged at my heart. I wanted this with my own family—barbecues, parties, and laughter. "Sort of, but we're not close like you guys. We all scattered after high school."

"We weren't as close as we are now," Aggie said. She lifted her can of sparkling water toward a house across the road. "The guys would gather for working cattle and stuff in Buffalo Gully, but they weren't especially close. I moved first and then life kind of piled all of us here, and it changed. Except for Eliot. I wonder if sometimes he isn't worried we'll forget about him."

I'd never forget Eliot.

"Now we have an excuse to see him more." Sutton grinned at me. "Thanks to our future sister-in-law."

The longing pulled harder on my heart. Future sister-in-law for a year. There was an expiration date on this relationship.

Seven

LILY

"Bye, Mom." Cali gave me a kiss and ran into daycare. Her friends were already inside. I was on the stoop with the baby carrier.

My stomach was in my throat. Eliot had called the courthouse. Just our luck, we could get a marriage license and get married on the same day. The justice of the peace was in the office and could fit us in.

How romantic.

I passed off Kellan. Eliot said he'd shower and get ready while I did the daycare run. I'd been wanting to hurl all morning. I had put on my jeans and a scrub top like I was going to work in case Cali questioned my clothing. I hadn't talked to her yet. What would I say?

Hey, can you pretend Eliot and I are married but also know that he's not your dad? I couldn't get her hopes up. She adored Eliot and his entire family. If she thought she was a Knight like them? She'd be elated.

95

Oh god. I'd have to change my name. I'd just reclaimed Duke. But to be believable, I'd have to become Lily Knight. The kids' names wouldn't have to change. Dad and Linda would have to understand.

Wanda smiled at me like she was wondering why I was still standing in her doorway and not rushing off. I forced a smile I hoped looked normal. "Thanks, Wanda."

She stepped back to shut the door. "Have a good day at work."

Sure. Just another day.

I drove to the house. Eliot's pickup was parked outside the garage. Dusty and only slightly beat up, it looked natural. It looked like it belonged.

"Not that kind of deal," I muttered as I crossed to the side door of the house. I could not fantasize about my future husband.

I stepped in. Should I change clothes? I'd put on a different top, but—

A shirtless Eliot was positioned at an ironing board. A white-with-brown-stripes dress shirt was hanging off each side. He must've found Grandma's iron, and his muscles were in full flex as he used it.

My mouth went dry.

Carter did not have a body like that.

I wasn't a sheltered girl. I messed around in high school. In college, I'd dated a couple of guys, but no one serious. In vet school, I was swept off my feet by a smooth-talking veterinarian. But my experience did not include muscled pecs and veins running down biceps to sinewy forearms. And those shoulders? Perfect to hold onto.

I trailed my gaze across the dark dusting of hair on his chest and followed the trail down to his abs. He was wearing jeans, but the clasp was open and the black waistband of his underwear was visible. I jerked my gaze up, terrified but also hopeful that I'd see too much.

He glanced up. His hair was combed to the side like today was special.

I continued to stare.

A twinkle lightened his eyes. "Keep staring, Lily pad, and I'm gonna start to blush."

I snapped out of my trance. "Oh my god. I'm so sorry."

His chuckle was deep and vibrated right down to between my thighs. I had a baby. I was postpartum. I had loads of stress. I was not supposed to get turned on in a blink. Not by the guy I was going to marry.

"Don't be sorry," he said. "A man doesn't mind when a beautiful woman's checking him out."

I rolled my eyes. "Putting it on thick, Romeo."

"Nope." He set the iron down and shrugged into his shirt. More bunching and flexing. I was a hussy, eating him up the way I was. "Cody lent me one of his shirts. How's it look?"

A squeak left me. Hot? Sizzling? Like I could rip it right back off?

He grinned again, sending my insides into a tailspin, making long-forgotten nerve endings fire. A steady beat started between my thighs.

Alarm flooded my veins. Was I...horny?

The smile didn't leave his eyes. "Ready?"

That shocked me out of my stupor. No. I was not ready. "I have to change."

"You look fine."

I put the back of my hand against my forehead. "Swoon."

He stilled and considered me. "Lily, I'm starting to think no man has shown you how attractive you are."

My hair was pinned off my face, the curls weren't frizzed yet, and I'd even shaved my legs sometime in the last week. That was the extent of my beauty regimen. "Men have been an overall letdown, present company excluded, of course. I'm going to change, then I'll be ready."

I scooted around him, praying I didn't touch that hard body of his and find out how ready I was to have sex again. Bad idea.

When I peeked at him, his gaze had dropped to my chest. Heat wicked up my neck and stopped. He was probably checking to see if I leaked again. Would I ever get over the mortification of that?

In my bedroom, I stared at the meager amount of clothing I'd brought with me from Kansas. Did eloping call for slacks? My first wedding hadn't been much more than a small gathering in a church, but I'd at least worn a dress.

I changed into my only one, a light-purple dress with daisies scattered all over. Not the same dress from my first wedding.

Time to get married. Again.

All too soon, we were at the courthouse, filling out the paperwork for the marriage license. My stomach was going to toss up the pancakes and eggs Eliot had made for breakfast this morning. Kellan had slept through much of the night, and Eliot had been awake before all of us.

The clerk chattered away. "It's so nice North Dakota doesn't have a waiting period. I mean, people can fly to Vegas in less than three hours and get married, so why not do it in the comfort of your own hometown? At least in the same county. Sometimes, when you know, you know. You know?"

"Absolutely," Eliot answered easily, and she smiled. She was young, but she wasn't taken by Eliot. Her eyes had flared when she'd seen him, but she wore her own giant diamond, and from the way she gushed about the ease of getting wed, she had probably utilized the lack of a waiting period.

She tapped on her computer. "All right. Johanna is ready whenever you are. Are your witnesses here?"

"We are," Cody said from behind us.

Aggie was with him, beaming in a maternity dress that wasn't much different than mine and wearing cowboy boots. Cody looked like he was ready to go to a board meeting for the day. We looked like we were going to a nice place to eat.

A shiver ghosted over my skin. We were getting closer and closer to saying "I do."

"'Bout time you showed up," Eliot joked.

Cody checked his watch. "We're ten minutes early."

"Just so happens, you're right on time." When Eliot smiled, I caught the lines of strain around his eyes.

Guilt gnawed into my stomach lining. He had to be stressed. The guy had a lot on his shoulders. He didn't need my problems piling it all higher.

The girl grinned. "Come with me."

Eliot ushered Cody and Aggie to go ahead of us.

I tripped over my feet taking a step. The butterflies swelled in my stomach, pushing out and growing uncomfortable. If my nerves were this bad, what was it like for Eliot? I'd been through this before. He hadn't.

He put his hand on my back. His heat seeped

through my dress, dulling my anxiety but increasing the thrum he'd ignited when he'd ironed without a shirt.

The girl disappeared into an office.

"How are you doing?" I murmured to him.

He only thought a moment. Then he ran one of my stray curls that had escaped through his fingers. "I'm doing just fine, Lily pad."

He'd used that name twice now. No one had ever given me a nickname.

The girl popped her head out. "I thought I lost you." She smiled, taking us in.

We looked like a couple in love, getting one last lovely whisper in. Suddenly, the desire to be just that was strong, causing an urge to run to whisper through my brain. I swallowed hard.

This was a deal. He was helping me because he was a nice guy.

He gave me a reassuring smile and took my hand in his. His skin was warm, and I soaked up the comfort. He nodded at his brother and sister and led me in.

My mind blanked in and out the whole time. Introductions. Johanna was short with dark hair. She gave an explanation of how the little service would go, the paperwork afterward, and then the vows.

"Do you have the rings?" Johanna asked.

"Sh— No." Eliot patted his shirt pocket like he might've forgotten rings we never bought there. "I'm sorry. We were too excited to think about the details."

Carter had wanted my ring back, but I wouldn't have worn it anyway. "Neither of us have jobs that are good for rings."

Relief crossed his face. Johanna nodded, only mild surprise in her expression.

I faced Eliot. He held both of my clammy hands. My knees were shaking. Oh god. I'd done this once before, and it was a disaster. This time, I knew the relationship was ending in divorce. There was comfort in that as I recited my vows. I wouldn't be taken by surprise again.

"I now pronounce you man and wife," Johanna said warmly. "You may kiss the bride."

I sucked in a breath. A kiss? How did I forget that part?

A kiss.

Heat filled his expression, and his focus was on my mouth. Nothing else existed in my world at the moment but him.

He dipped his head down, his hands tightening around my fingers. Slowly, we got closer. Then his lips touched mine, ever so softly at first, then increasing in pressure. The heat that had flooded me when I saw him shirtless made a return, swirling through my belly and settling lower.

He released my hands to wrap his arms around my waist. I gripped those wide shoulders I had appreciated earlier. Now I knew what they looked like underneath his carefully ironed shirt.

The man *ironed*.

He held me, deepening the kiss but keeping it chaste. I'd never felt so secure, so safe. I definitely hadn't buzzed with this much anticipation on my real wedding day.

Real. Wedding. Day.

This day was no different than that one. Only the man had changed. The empty pit in my stomach yawned open.

He pulled back, releasing me like he wasn't ready. His

gaze searched mine, questioning if I was okay, if he went too far.

My smile was probably shaky, but the sweeping relief was intense. I could keep the house. I could keep my job. "Thank you."

His eyes warmed. "You're welcome."

There. It was done.

And that kiss…

My knees were wobbly for a completely different reason.

Cody slapped Eliot on the back. "Good to go."

The justice beamed at us, not at all thrown by our nonjubilant reaction. "I'm honored to be part of your big day."

Today was the beginning of the end of the marriage. How odd to know that up front.

After we signed and submitted everything required and I got a copy for Aunt Linda, we walked outside to the small parking lot and stood between the two pickups.

Aggie gave me a quick hug. "I know this is temporary, but welcome to the family."

Cody shook Eliot's hand. "You need anything, holler. Keep the shirt. Wedding gift."

Eliot tugged at the collar. "You know I don't dress up."

"It's good for you." Cody turned to me. He didn't seem like a hugger. Instead, he shook my hand. "Remember, we're not far away if you need anything. Call any one of us."

I nodded, numb.

Good thing "young Lily" hadn't known she wouldn't grow up to be a happily married veterinarian who saved kittens and puppies. All my illusions had been shattered.

At least I knew where I stood with my career and with relationships.

"Lily." Eliot's voice was soft, searching.

My husband.

I could blame the sun for why it was hard to look at him, but my nerves had returned. The man was indeed different with his hard jaw, keen eyes, and that sweep of dark hair. He'd shaved, but I'd like to trace his jaw. I bet stubble was already there.

"You have to get back?" I asked.

"Eventually," he said. "My guys can function without me a little longer." He didn't sound confident. "Want to go eat and celebrate?"

"I feel like there isn't much for you to celebrate."

"Don't think like that. Have you been to Hummingbird's yet?"

"No, but I've wanted to." I loaded into the pickup, knowing full well he hadn't disagreed with me.

Eliot

It took inhuman effort to keep from watching Lily's mouth as she took a bite and chewed. I knew how those puffy lips felt. Even worse, I'd held her briefly, had my arms around her soft, curvy body, and soaked in her warm sunshine smell.

Thelma swung by to pour more coffee for me. She was Tova's surrogate grandma and had worked at the diner for years. Cody and Tova said she didn't have to work, they had made sure of it, but Thelma had asked what else she'd do all day. She claimed she was too old to hike or skydive or run the Mafia, so she might as well serve greasy food.

"Thanks, Thelma."

She grunted and peered at Lily's cup before walking away. Lily hadn't touched hers. She said she wasn't giving Kellan more reasons not to sleep all night, but it wouldn't have mattered. Thelma would've poured her a cup anyway, and she had.

Lily cut into her caramel roll. Our conversation had been awkward and stilted. Figuring out living arrangements now that we were married shouldn't be so uncomfortable, but then it was usually the other way around.

I downed a sip of the scalding, bitter-as-tar coffee. Just how I preferred it. "The next time I come out, I'll bring clothing and stuff."

She got that timid look in her eye that I hated. "When are you returning?"

As soon as possible. But that wasn't feasible. I could only spare time when needed to keep my absence from being a burden. "When do you need me?"

Her lips parted. The way her mouth captured my attention... The coffee wasn't hot enough to burn this inappropriate lust out of my brain. That pouty lower lip needed a good nibbling and not from her. I bet it'd taste sweet from the roll. Her flavor would be sugar and sunshine.

Goddamn.

"Why don't you see what works for your schedule?" She poked her fork into the roll.

I wanted to leave her with an answer, but I didn't have anything. I was down an employee, and I'd been gone for almost four days. She was right. I had to see what work was like before I could plan to get away again. "We'll do that, and you'll call Wilder if you need anything." She opened her mouth, but I leaned forward and put my hand on hers. "You're going to argue that Wilder's taking care of Sutton. So I'm going to tell you to call Austen. Or Cody. Or Ansen. I have four brothers—and don't tell Ansen I included him, or he'll be even more of a dick."

Her lips curved into a smile. That mouth. I could spend all day exploring that lush body of hers. But I wouldn't be. I was celibate for the next year.

Why'd that feel like a relief? Like she'd just saved me from having a beer in town on a Friday night and trying to keep things light with some girl. We'd mess around. Too often, she caught feelings, and I'd have to tell her that the ranch wasn't mine. That the house wasn't mine. That I wasn't good for more than a good time. No way would I prove my mama right and be nothing but a disappointment to a woman.

Lily didn't need me for any of that. She only needed me for me, even if she didn't want me. Though the way she'd looked at me this morning...

She chewed her bottom lip and stared at my hand on hers. She couldn't eat with me holding it down.

I pulled away. "What about the winter?"

She cocked her head. "What about it?"

"Do you have snow removal figured out?"

"I think Grandma hired a service. I'll find their contact information."

"There's a snowblower attachment for the lawn mower. Maybe when I'm back, I can take a look."

"You don't have to," she said and shoved her food in her mouth. I was focused on how her lips wrapped around the fork. "My dad made sure I can change oil and run yard equipment."

"Three of the tires are flat."

She lifted a shoulder and sawed another hunk off her roll. "He taught me how to change those too."

Another strand of patience frayed. "Lily, I know I'm supposed to be nothing but a name on the marriage license and a few shirts in your closet, but I can't just ignore you for a year."

She blinked at me with those big eyes. "You can, though. My dad, of all people, should understand commuting for work. He has hundreds of oil well employees who do the same. I have no idea how much Aunt Linda will visit."

"But she lives in Coal Haven?"

She nodded.

My commuting excuse would only go so far. "I'll let you know by the end of the week when I can return. If you see Linda before then, tell her that there was a ranch emergency." And hopefully, there wouldn't be a real one.

"Okay." She stuffed an especially gooey portion of the roll into her mouth before digging in her purse. She withdrew a key and pushed it over. "So you can get in without knocking."

The amount of trust she was putting in me was staggering. I didn't take it for granted, nor did I take lightly the way she likely evaluated my family's reactions to me. If they had thought I was a bad idea, Lily would've noticed. This whole marriage was a group effort. I wouldn't let any of them down.

"Okay." Good. She was starting to realize I was serious. She acted like she was a burden. I always did what had to be done, and I'd continue to do so. I wouldn't let my wife stand in the way of me caring for her.

Eight

LILY

I'd never been so ready for the weekend. The short reprieve I'd gotten while Eliot was staying with me over the weekend had vanished. Kellan had his worst nights of sleep yet.

"Thanks, Wanda." I led Cali out of the house. "Have a good weekend."

"You, too. Glad you don't have to work."

So was I. I had to catch up on everything in the house. Now that the place was mine, mostly, I could tackle some smaller, less time-consuming projects, like emptying out Grandma's closet so Eliot had somewhere to put his clothing.

The same nerves fluttered in my belly that always did when I thought of him. Why did I have to have a crush on my husband?

Ansen and his brother dropped off several packages

of meat at the vet clinic. A "wedding gift" from Eliot. Grocery bags full of Barron beef.

"What's for dinner?" Cali asked after she was buckled in.

As much as I looked forward to a real meal that wasn't "heat and serve," tonight wasn't the night. I was tired and had a task list a mile long. I started for home. "I say we celebrate Friday night with cereal for dinner."

"Yay!"

I might've gotten married on Monday, but the rest of the week had been normal. Well, my new normal. Eliot said he'd let me know soon when he could return, and that meant I should tackle the subject with Cali.

"Hey, Cali."

She kicked her feet and met my gaze in the rearview mirror.

"I need to talk to you about Eliot."

"I like him."

Same, girl. Same. "Well, he and I... We had to..." What could a six-year-old keep secret? "We like each other and we got married, but it isn't going to be like the traditional marriage I had with your dad."

"You're married?"

I nodded.

"Can I see the ring?"

She'd rather know about the jewelry. We'd discussed why I no longer had the ring her father had given me. Was her question a sign she wouldn't hang her father-figure hopes and dreams on Eliot? "We didn't get them. Listen, I wanted you to know that nothing will really change. Eliot's job is in a different state, and we live in Crocus Valley. We actually might not see him a lot."

"Oh." Disappointment rang in her tone.

Same, girl. "Grandpa or Aunt Linda might ask about him. He's going to live with us, but you know, he might not be around a lot because of his job."

"Okay."

Okay. That was…easy.

We pulled into the garage. I was looking forward to a mellow night at home. Cali unbuckled, and I was gathering the diaper bag and my purse when my phone rang. Mom's name flashed on the screen. My stomach dropped.

When I sent Linda a copy of the marriage certificate, she said she would talk to everyone this weekend. I told her I'd wait for her to inform them of Grandma's will and trust, and then I'd be ready for their call. I might've copped out and let Linda rip off the bandage so I could bask in not worrying about losing my house before I faced my parents' concerns.

"Hello?" I squeezed my eyes shut.

"Lily!" Mom's voice boomed out of the phone. "*You're married*?"

"Now's not a good time to talk about it." Cali didn't think it was a big deal, but if she heard Mom's cries, she would. "How about I call you—"

"You can start by picking us up."

My heart thumped so hard I feared it knocked itself out. "What?"

"We're at the airport in Crocus Valley."

"*What?*"

"Your father used the company jet as soon as we heard. Why didn't you come to us when Linda was going to kick you out?"

They were in town? Now? What about my basking?

I was being selfish. Immature. Learning not to turn to my family whenever I had a hiccup was one thing, but I had to stop hiding from them when things weren't ideal. "What could you have done?"

"You married someone you just met!"

My head was spinning. I pressed my fingers against my temples. The speech I'd rehearsed to explain everything as succinctly as possible vanished from my head. "I'll be there in five minutes."

I hung up. My phone pinged with a text.

Then another. I didn't have to look to know my siblings were the ones texting. Linda was just going to pass on the trust information. Had Mom and Dad told everyone I'd gotten married?

"Cali, can you buckle up? Grandma and Grandpa came to visit, and we have to pick them up."

Cali squealed. At least one of us was delighted.

The drive to the airport was short. The tiny airport was the size of the small grocery store in town and just outside of city limits. It had two whole hangars for airplanes, but it must be big enough for small private jets. It had to, being on the fringes of the oil and coal industry. Top execs like my dad flew in and out for business.

My phone blew up the entire way. Linda must've gotten a hold of everyone. This shitstorm of a weekend started early. There went my quiet Friday night.

My parents were waiting outside the doors of the airport. Dad was still dressed in his black slacks and pewter-gray dress shirt. He'd ditched the tie, and his salt-and-pepper hair was ruffled from the wind. Mom wore short pants with black-and-white Converse. She had a pair in every color. Her dark, curly hair was pulled back, and she looked more pensive than when she had been fretting over me moving.

I parked and got out to help them load the luggage,

but Dad came around the hood and jerked me into a giant hug.

"How you doing, kiddo?"

The comfort of Dad's hug seeped in. His cedar after-shave was the same he'd worn his whole life. I returned his hug. "I'm good, Dad. Really."

"I don't understand what my mother was thinking." His expression clouded over. "Or my sister. We'll see if we can get you out of this."

I should be relieved Dad would use his legal resources to fight the trust, but my anxiousness grew. Could I enjoy being married to a nice, considerate guy for a little while longer?

"It's fine." I pulled away. "Eliot's a good man. You'll like him."

Dad's frown deepened at my sincerity.

Mom straightened from the other side of the car. She'd been bent in hugging and kissing her grandkids. "How can you know him well enough to say that?" She cast a worried look toward my dad.

"He's the brother of my boss. His whole family lives in town, and I guess I have the same last name as them. I'm Lily Knight now." For the next year anyway, the paperwork was still processing.

Dad's brows drew together. "Knight? Does he have a brother named Alcott?"

"Cody? Yes."

A wide smile spread across his face. "Well. That changes things."

"West?" Mom wasn't sold on Dad's change of heart. I was just plain confused.

"If he's anything like his brother, then our littlest girl might just be in very good hands."

"You know Cody?" Of course he did. Cody worked in the oil industry, controlling wells all over Montana and who knew where else.

"King Oil has a deal with Knight's Oil Wells. Come on, let's go get something to eat." He went around to load their suitcases in the back.

Several of the knots along my spine loosened.

"Mom, don't we get cereal?" Cali asked.

"Grandma and Grandpa are taking us out," I said, sliding into my seat.

She clapped her hands. My mom got into the back, wedging herself between the kids' car seats.

"I'd like to talk to this young man," Mom said when we were back on the road.

"Mom, he's forty." My stomach tightened. *Don't scare Eliot off yet. I'm in my honeymoon period.*

"Can he meet us at the restaurant?" Dad asked.

"He lives in Buffalo Gully."

"He's not living with you?" Mom's voice pitched up.

Crap. "Yes, but he still has the ranch. He'll be commuting."

Cali kicked her feet and grinned. "He makes the best pancakes."

A divot formed between Mom's eyebrows. "Does he now?"

Why'd I feel like a teenager caught with a boy in my room?

Dad tapped his fingers against his knee. "He's good with kids?"

"He has nieces and nephews."

"Call him," Mom said.

"I'm sure he won't mind if we call him later." How embarrassing though.

"Now," she said. "While we're still parked."

I shot her an incredulous look in the rearview mirror. *A grown woman does not simply ask how high when her parents tell her to jump.* My former mother-in-law was a bitch, but she wasn't wrong.

But my parents were worried. Rightfully so, after the way Carter treated me. I'd had a month to get used to the idea, and then a few days after announcing Eliot's name. Mom and Dad hadn't processed for a day yet.

"Call him up." Dad pointed to the radio. "You can put him on the car speaker, right?"

They'd continue insisting, and if I didn't, Dad might track down Cody at his house and ask for Eliot's contact info. Calling Eliot was the least I could do to ease their nerves.

I grabbed my phone and groaned.

Violet: Why wouldn't you tell us?!
Alder: Lily. Call me.
Poppy: WTF WTF WTF Is he at least hot?
Clover: Way to lock it down.
Jasper: Call me if you need me to beat him up.

That was the same thing Jasper said when I told him I was getting a divorce.

I let out a sigh. "I was going to let everyone know."

"I thought you might've told them of your crazy-fast marriage. Or that they'd been invited," Mom said pointedly.

I had only thought they'd disapprove and try to talk me out of it. Were they hurt I didn't include them? Of course they were. Hurt, confused, and concerned.

"The timeline was escalated, I'll admit. I hope you understand."

Mom let out a heavy breath. "It's your grandmother

I'm upset with. And Linda. You shouldn't have been put in that position. Not after—" She cut her gaze to Cali and snapped her mouth shut. "You should've called us."

"I know, but you guys have done so much." And that was all I could say. They'd have saved me in a heartbeat, just like they moved me to college. Just like they moved me again when I got into vet school. They'd moved me after a different quick wedding because I insisted I was in love with Carter and everything would be fine. Then they'd moved me back to Billings. Then to Crocus Valley.

At least this way, I was the only one inconvenienced. Me and my new husband. I dialed Eliot.

When he answered, wind blasted over the phone. "Lily pad. I was going to call later this evening."

The way his deep voice boomed through the car was all kinds of soothing. He'd used a nickname and he didn't know my parents were in the car. "You're on speaker and my parents are very interested in talking to you. Is this a bad time?"

Another gust of wind came over the line. "Nah, I've got a few minutes. I'm on my way to get an escapee. She's having a good time at the neighbor's, but I don't need her running into a bull quite yet."

"Hi, Eliot!" Cali called.

"Hey, boss lady."

Cali leaned forward, straining against her seat belt. "Kellan might be teething."

"No kidding? No wonder the champ was keeping us up all night."

She giggled and poked my mom to look at Kellan's swollen gums.

I gauged Mom's reaction. Some of the concern had drained away and not just because she was squashed between her grandkids. The easy interaction between Eliot and Cali was hopefully a good sign in her book. In fact, she might put it in her book. I wouldn't be surprised if she wrote a character named Champ.

"Hello, Mr. and Mrs. Duke," Eliot said next. "Nice to meet you. Sorry it wasn't in person, but ranch life called me back."

"When can we meet you?" Mom asked, leaning forward until the shoulder belt caught her.

My cheeks blazed. Thankfully, Eliot wasn't here to witness my parents acting like I was sixteen and he'd asked me to prom.

"When are you coming home next?" Dad asked.

I tensed. He was home. So was I.

The wind was the only response for a moment. "There's a dance recital at the end of the month that I have some nieces and nephews in."

"The end of the month?" Dismay poured from Mom's voice. My stomach sank.

"I apologize," Eliot said easily. "I've got some interviews scheduled for a new guy, and then I'd like to be around to train him. I know it's not the ideal answer for a newlywed man. It's a good thing Lily understands my work almost as well as me."

I smiled at the way he both answered and ignored all their questions. Even Dad couldn't argue his response.

A faint shout came through the line. "I hate to go, but we've spotted the runaway."

"Don't worry, Eliot. Thank you." I let my appreciation flow through my simple thanks, but mostly, I was trying to suppress the thrill I got knowing I'd get to see him at the end of the month.

"Love you, Lily pad."

I drew in a sharp breath. His words wrapped around me like a warm blanket. *It's for show.* But they didn't sound like they were fake.

This was the most dangerous part of our ruse. I could forget the situation and let my hopes take the wheel. I couldn't allow it. "Love you too, Romeo."

Eliot

I'd been married for two weeks, and I hadn't seen my wife since I said my vows. Other than a few check-in texts to make sure she was doing okay after her parents' visit, we didn't talk. I just returned from running to Miles City. I made an unplanned stop. I was supposed to pick up some horse supplement, and I needed a new pair of pants since I'd torn a pair in the stables when I caught myself on a bent clasp. One of the horses had slammed against her stall so hard she'd twisted the metal. Alexander had about pissed himself laughing when he'd seen me with a gaping hole in the butt of my jeans.

I entered the house. The smell of the pie Chambers's wife had sent with him filled the air. Cherry? My stomach growled. I went straight to the kitchen. The pie already had a slice missing. There was nothing my bookkeeper liked more than fresh pie.

I set my small plastic bag on the island and circled around to get a plate and fork. I was digging a slice out when Chambers sauntered out of the old office I'd renovated to be his. The sweet smell of the dessert wafted up to me. Yep. Cherry.

I'd had too many sweet cravings in the last two weeks after remembering how Lily licked caramel off her lips.

"Hey, there's the mister." Chambers had taken to calling me that since I'd returned from Crocus Valley married. He knew the same story my family did.

"Anything happen while I was gone?"

"Something always happens while you're gone." He pulled up a stool at the island and flipped my bag over. "What's this?"

His next favorite thing was being nosy, and he'd answered my question in an ominous way.

I dug into the slice of pie. "Chambers."

He sighed. "Red Wildfire ripped her cheek open on a fence post."

I groaned and closed my eyes. Another vet emergency. Between colic, arthritis, and regular maintenance, the vet costs were hemorrhaging the ranch. Life had been a different story when Sutton had worked for Knight's Arabians and Cattle Company full-time.

"Alexander took her in. I told him I could report to you."

I took my animals' injuries personally. So did a lot of the guys, which was why they didn't like telling me when something bad happened. I'd get pissed, they'd think I was blaming them, and none of our emotions would treat the animal.

"Doc isn't sure about nerve damage. Won't know for sure until the healing starts. He patched her up real good, said it was a good thing she didn't take out her eye, and of course, there'd be an emergency surgery charge."

I stuffed a huge hunk of pie in my mouth. Our emergency surgery charge would be extra high. The vet in town had hated the Knights for years. Sutton's time with us had been a nice reprieve.

At least the horse got the treatment she needed, and Alexander would stay on top of it. I'd check her out as soon as I finished eating. The horse and the handler could relax for a bit.

I opened the bag and dropped the two silicone rings on the table. Both were black. With my job and Lily's, any other color would get disgusting after a week. "Figured we should have something."

Chambers folded his hands on the countertop and stared at the rings. "Oh?"

I shrugged and shoved another piece of pie in my mouth. The idea came to me, and I'd done it. "People've been asking around town." One thing spread faster than fire in a dry field and that was gossip. "Might as well make it look official."

"It is very much official."

I shrugged again. We'd be married almost a month before I met her family.

Nerves made a tight ball in my gut. Few relationships had gotten serious enough for me to meet the parents. If the girls were local, I already knew them. Technically, Lily's dad knew my brother. He might've talked to Barns before, which didn't make me feel better. "I'll just do an overnight when I go down for the recital."

"Take the weekend, Eliot. What are you going to miss? Putting up hay?"

"The new hire is starting next week."

"The Baltimore guy? I can show him the ropes until you get back. Take the weekend. Meet the 'rents."

"You've got your own family."

"Roxie likes to hang out here. She enjoys the country

without having to do the work." He took a slow drink of his coffee. "You talk to her lately?"

He meant Lily. He was being nosy again. "Not really, why?"

"Just thought you might be checking in on her."

"I do."

"Don't you call her?"

"It's not that type of deal. We don't text every day."

He made a noncommittal sound. "What's she look like again?"

I put my dishes by the sink. "She's a little shorter than Aggie. Her hair's dark and curly. I'm sure she cut it short after Kellan was born. That kid'll take a fistful of anything he can. She's got these really cool eyes. They're like so blue they're purple." Nice tits. Round ass. Cheeks that turned pink in a heartbeat. Made a guy think about what else would get her to flush. I gazed out the window over the sink. It faced toward the drive. "She's stubborn. Hates people treating her like she can't do anything. You can see it in her face. Won't ask for help." Wait. Why'd he care what she looked like? I glanced over my shoulder.

He took a slow drink from his mug, wearing a message in his gaze I didn't care to interpret.

The pie sat like lead in my gut. "I'll go check on the horse."

Before I walked out the door, I changed out my ball cap for the old tan cowboy hat I wore for work. Outside, I tugged the brim down to block the wind and pulled out my phone.

I tapped out a message to Lily. **How's it going?**

Fucking Chambers.

Nine

ELIOT

I pulled into Crocus Valley and turned on the highway that led to Lily's place. I was meeting her parents.

It was no big deal.

My gut churned like there was a paddle inside, mixing the acid. No. Big. Deal.

I was married to their daughter. They had to think we were in love.

That day on the phone was the first time I said I loved someone.

Lily deserved to hear the words for real. Maybe someday— A loop around my stomach tightened. We had to get through the next year.

Once I was on the long driveway to her house, I stiffened.

Did she have company?

Three cars lined her drive. A Cadillac SUV, a BMW, and a regular hybrid more like Lily's.

Please tell me she's home.

I parked behind the stall she didn't use in the garage. A tall man walked out, looking like he came right off the golf course with his khaki shorts and blue polo shirt. The corners of his eyes creased when he squinted at me. Lily's dad.

Barns had never looked that sleek. My father's skin had resembled the leather of the worn Chesterfield he'd sat in to smoke his cigars and drink his whiskey neat. His breathing had rattled long before he'd been diagnosed with cancer. And he'd had so many cancer spots cut off his face that he had looked like he was slowly getting patched together.

When I got out, Lily's dad was staring me down. I waited for the deep, commanding voice I'd heard over the phone, only this time, he'd point out everything I did wrong.

"Afternoon, sir." Mama hadn't done much for me, but she'd taught her kids manners and Cody had ingrained them in us after she'd left.

He grinned. "Weston, please."

His grip was strong and full of warning.

I respected his reaction. My dad hadn't cared about Aggie. Weston Duke was invested in his daughter's well-being. "Is Lily home?"

"I'm afraid you're early."

I was afraid of that too.

"All my other kids are here."

I cocked my head, but no, I'd heard him correctly. "All of them?"

They outnumbered my big family. I was the lone Knight on the premises.

"Like a family reunion," he said. "Don't worry. It's

not just to inspect you. It's been a logistic nightmare passing along information about the trust. My sister will talk to one kid and that kid will talk to another and then information gets warped."

"Like a game of telephone with extra bad reception."

Weston nodded grimly. "This way, we can have everyone in one spot. Linda finally coughed up a copy of the trust, and I had my people look it over last week. Enough of that for now. Come on in."

My stomach was all kinds of twisted going inside. When I entered, I was pinned by several sets of eyes, like I was a bug for a school project. Wariness and tension were woven into the air, and I did not care for that feeling in Lily's warm home.

A woman rose. She was older, closer to Weston's age, with dark wavy hair and a pinched expression. Lily's mom.

"You must be Eliot." She held out her hand. "I'm Magnolia."

I clasped it. "Nice to meet you. Can I call you Mom?" I heard a choking sound from one of Lily's siblings, and I grinned. "Just kidding. Trying to break the ice."

The look I got in return from Magnolia was introspective. What had she been expecting from me?

I was floundering. The country kid in me wanted to go back to work. To get on a horse and find shit that was broken and fix it. I didn't want to entertain Lily's family. I wanted to pick her and the kids up and go somewhere where the air didn't smother me in judgment.

Magnolia put a comforting hand on my back as if she wasn't sure about me, but she wasn't the type to push me into the middle of a creek without a paddle. "This is Alder, my oldest."

She pointed to a stern-looking man with piercing hazel eyes. He resembled Weston the most, but the wave in his hair was from his mom. His nod was nearly imperceptible. He reminded me of Cody.

"And Violet, the next oldest," Magnolia continued, pointing to the woman next to Alder. She had a flashing blue gaze and her black hair was pulled into a tight bun. She reminded me of Cody when he had hidden behind his professionalism. "I'll go in chronological order." Magnolia patted my back again. "Poppy and Clover. Then Jasper."

"If I get tested, can it be multiple choice?" I joked.

Violet clucked her tongue. "He's not taking this seriously."

The verbal slap came out of nowhere. I held my hands up. "Whoa there. Don't misunderstand my nervous humor. Lily might've learned about a deadline for our relationship that hastened our marriage, but I'm serious about her. I'm serious about this place. And those two little ones deserve the best. I'll make sure they get it."

Violet crossed her arms. She wasn't as hostile as before, but her mouth was still set in a flat line. "Carter used to talk a good game too."

"I sure as hell ain't that bastar—" I dipped my head to Magnolia. "Apologies, ma'am. I haven't heard a thing about him that's likable."

Magnolia's militant expression matched her eldest daughter's. "You heard right."

A chortle came from Jasper. He was standing in the corner with his arms crossed. He resembled Alder but younger. Magnolia gave him a hard look, but he raised his hands. "I'm never not going to like hearing Carter shit talk."

"That makes all of us." Was it Poppy who spoke? She and Clover were crammed into the recliner, with one perched half on the armrest. Were they twins?

The Dukes had a real flower-and-tree thing going for their names. The other two sisters' hair and eyes were lighter than Lily's. They were dressed more casually, along with Jasper, but where he was wearing jeans and a loose shirt, the two women were in shorts and blouses.

Weston handed out copies of a document. "We can go ahead and get started."

"Lily's not home." The rustling of paper stopped and attention was on me. I dug my boots in. "You came here to talk to everyone at once, so... We wait for everyone."

"Lily's gotten a head start, or you wouldn't be here." That was Clover. I was ninety percent sure. Whoever it was smiled, and where Violet had an edge, I didn't get the sense her comment was meant to be challenging.

The door opened, and Cali streaked inside. She flung herself at my legs. "Eliot!" She stopped when she saw everyone, eyes wide. The Duke crew transformed in front of me from stern to elated. A chorus of "Cali" rang out. Violet's was the loudest and she flung her arms out, nearly taking out Alder. The guy actually cracked a smile.

Cali's grin had filled in since I'd last seen her. She raced toward Violet, who dropped to her knees on the floor. "I missed you, girl."

I went to the door and held it open for Lily. Her gaze was fraught, and in her bright eyes, she was silently asking me if I was all right. The dark circles were back. Was Kellan fussy again? Teething?

Her dad took the baby carrier from her.

Lily turned her wide gaze to him. "I didn't know you all were coming. Tonight."

Wow. They'd really just helped themselves to her house. In their mind, it was still their grandmother's place, and since she was gone, they'd taken over. I could understand, but also, Lily's overwhelmed reaction was enough for me.

Perhaps events like this contributed to what had alienated Lily's ex. I could understand, but he was still an asshole.

Cali was crowded by her aunts and uncles. Even Jasper had pushed away from the wall for her. Magnolia was freeing Kellan from his carrier. The baby was almost as stunned as his mom.

I rested my hand on Lily's back and leaned close to her ear. "Doing okay?"

"Me?" she whispered. "What about you?"

"It's been a party." I flashed her a smile. She didn't have to know her family intimidated me. "I haven't been here long."

She gave me a knowing look. "Long enough?"

"Now that we're all here," Weston said. "Why don't we get talking?"

Lily slumped against me. I rubbed her back. She was tired, and all the seats were taken. She'd been working all day, and she hadn't expected to get jumped by a family meeting.

Kellan was settled between Poppy and Clover, happily drooling at the women smiling and cooing at him. I still didn't know who was who. Cali was on Alder's lap, and Jasper had squished himself on the couch to get close to her. Lily's family loved her kids. My estimation of them went up.

"I've had a chance to read through the will and trust," Weston started.

"Wait," Lily said, pulling away from me. I missed her heat. "You have a copy?"

"You didn't review the document before you got married?" Alder asked, his tone clipped.

Lily stiffened. "Aunt Linda knows what she's talking about." A flush crawled up her cheeks. "She wouldn't lie to me."

"There's a lot of money on the line for her," Weston said. "She won't get the payout from the estate unless all the terms of this trust are carried out within seven years. One year for each of you to get married before the deadline."

"As if we'd do it sequentially." Violet scoffed. She shook her head, and her disappointed gaze landed on Lily. "You got married, and you didn't ask to see the trust?"

Lily shrank against me. "I…"

"I think we should pick this up later." Lily's ex was spineless. I had no issues setting limits that would work for everyone. Lily was drawing in on herself, and I could see the girl who was afraid she'd never stand on her own. She was exhausted. "How about tomorrow? Or Sunday?" I made a point of asking Lily.

Her expression softened just for me, and goddamn, a guy could get used to that.

Weston frowned. "We're all here. We should go over this—"

"Eliot's right." Lily straightened her spine while sticking close to me like she was soaking up my strength.

"Lily." Jasper was unexpectedly serious. "We really need to discuss this. You only just met this guy."

If Lily didn't need us to lie, I'd feel like shit. Her family clearly cared about her. They worried for her.

There were worse things than involved parents and siblings.

She lifted her chin. "Sometimes you just know."

And I knew from the moment I saw her she was strong but barely keeping her head above water. "Like it or not, my wife's had a long day. You'll need to talk on her schedule. I respect that you're worried about her and you're not sure about me, but I can't prove I'm not some controlling jackass in one night." Cali let out a scandalized gasp. "Sorry, boss lady. I'll watch my language. But I heard Friday nights are Lucky Charms night and I'm hungry."

Lily's lips twitched like she was fighting a grin. "How about tomorrow for lunch? I'll make some hamburgers with the beef my husband so kindly arranged to have delivered. Then, we can all go and support the kids in the dance recital. Cali's been asking about lessons."

I nodded, but that was news to me. Lily and I faced her family. Even the kids were quiet, like they sensed the edge to the air in the room. How would the Dukes take to me kicking them out?

Magnolia rose. She clapped her hands together. "Well, you heard them."

One of the twins cocked her head. "Um...where are we supposed to stay?"

Jasper chuckled. "I think what Eliot's telling us is... not here."

Lily

. . .

Embarrassment swept through me as the last of my family pulled away. Guilt ate at my insides, but also relief. I had barely recovered from my parents' last visit when they came to town like a whirlwind and left almost as soon as the check was taken care of for the meal. Then I walked in on Eliot facing down my entire family.

Kellan was on his play pad, and Cali was right outside the front door, waving at everyone leaving. I might be irritated at my family, but they doted on her.

Eliot was sitting on the couch, his forearms draped across his knees. He was wearing the shirt he'd worn to the courthouse like he'd dressed up for the occasion. His hair was ruffled from the wind or from working part of the day, but he looked as smoking hot as always.

"I'm so sorry." I pinched the bridge of my nose. If he didn't regret marrying before, he would now.

"Not your fault."

"I can't believe…" I shook my head. "You talked, and they listened." It'd been amazing to see. Individually, each of my relatives was formidable, some more than others. But all together?

"It's my giant balls. They can tell I mean business."

I sputtered out a laugh. "Maybe it's all the balls you've taken. You give off big castration energy."

He grinned. Energy sizzled between us. A shiver traced down my spine, lighting up places best left dark. Only they hadn't been dormant. Not since the last time Eliot was in town. "You do not have to eat cereal for dinner."

"It happens to be one of my favorites. Mama always hated cereal. She thought it was too unrefined, and I'm not talking about nutrition. We were too country, too hick, too boring."

His face lit up when he was talking about any of his brothers or his sister. The guardedness returned when he mentioned his mother. "How old were you when she left?"

"Nine. Maybe it should've hit me harder, but Aggie was the youngest and the only girl. Mama doted on her. Aggie was the only one Mama had kept in contact with. The rest of us had been mad at our mother, but Mama wanted to save Aggie from the fate of getting trapped in a marriage." He shook himself like he was waking from a dream. "Enough about her. We have your very present kin to worry about."

The shame from their visit returned, heavy on my shoulders. "I can't believe I didn't think to ask Aunt Linda for a copy." Horror crept up in my throat, making breathing a struggle. "What if you didn't have to marry me?"

His lips turned down, and he thought for a moment. "You know, neither of us asked to see proof. Your aunt didn't strike me as a manipulative lady."

She hadn't been as long as I'd known her. The feeling of foolishness ebbed. "Thank you for that."

"Your dad left us a copy. We can review it with milk dripping down our chins like responsible adults."

I laughed. "How bad is it if I confess that this is turning into the best Friday night I've had in a long time?"

Ten

LILY

I blinked awake. Eliot had taken Kellan again in the middle of the night after I'd fed him. When Eliot had entered the bedroom, I'd been hit with a stark desire of wishing he was coming into the bedroom for me.

Voices filtered in from Cali's bedroom. That girl was on cloud nine. She had her aunts and uncles in town, her grandparents, and Eliot.

I put on a fresh shirt and some shorts and quietly made my way to the bathroom.

"I don't know why my old mommy doesn't want me. My daddy doesn't either." Cali's voice was tiny, more matter of fact than a six-year-old's should be.

"Aw, Cali. I'm sorry. My mama left too. It sucks when the people who should love us the most hurt us the worst."

I stopped at the door. I'd been ready to rush in and check on Cali's state, console her if needed, but Eliot spoke like he knew exactly what she was going through. Cali had never had the benefit of firsthand understanding.

"I know for a fact your old mommy's issues have nothing to do with you," Eliot continued, "and everything to do with her. But it still sucks."

"Yeah," she said, melancholy. "Mommy's a good mommy."

My chest squeezed. I loved that little girl.

"She's the best mama," Eliot agreed.

A smile tugged at my lips.

"She says I'm gonna talk to someone."

"Like, a professional?" he asked.

"Yeah, a consoler."

"A counselor?" The humor in his voice was barely noticeable. "I think that's a good plan," he said quietly. "Having someone to talk to probably helps a lot."

I put my hand on my chest. The image of a young boy with big brown eyes and no one to go to about his big feelings flashed through my head, leaving an aching in my chest.

"Yup. Did your daddy give you up too?" Cali asked.

Tears heated the backs of my eyes. Fuck Carter and his selfish life.

"No, but he wasn't a nice daddy."

Fuck Eliot's parents too. I went to the doorway of the bedroom so Eliot knew I could hear. He was in the rocking chair with Kellan asleep on his chest. Cali had coloring books piled on her bed, and she was surrounded by markers. His gaze flipped to mine. I gave him a small smile, and his eyes heated.

For a heartbeat, I could pretend this moment was real if only to show myself why I had walked away from the marriage with Carter and told him I wanted full custody of the kids. He'd been painfully ready to give up all of his rights.

"My brother Cody mostly raised us," Eliot continued, holding my gaze. "He was a kid himself, but he did a good job. Don't ever tell him I said that."

Cali nodded solemnly.

He rocked slowly. The corner of his mouth tipped up. "Did you catch up on some sleep?"

My body was getting programmed by him. I got sleep because he was around, and I, therefore, felt good. Just seeing him made me more rested. "Only thanks to you. Again."

"Don't mention it. You ready to entertain?"

I let out a slow exhale. I'd be more worked up if Eliot wasn't here. Last night, we'd read over the trust paperwork. It might not have been prudent to trust Linda sight unseen, but she'd told the truth.

"I'm going to clean up, and then I can take Kellan. He'll help me get hamburgers ready." I crossed my arms. "You don't have to be there if you don't want to."

"If you know one thing about me, it's that I don't abandon ship."

"Is that how you ended up managing the ranch?"

He rocked, slow and steady, his expression neutral. Kellan was starting to wiggle. "Someone had to manage it, otherwise Barns would've run everyone off. He got worse over the years."

"Who's Barns?" Cali asked.

"The guy who was supposed to be my father, but he was more of a boss."

She wrinkled her nose like she didn't care for the sound of that at all. I didn't either.

No wonder Cali had taken to him. Yes, she craved attention and validation from adults in her life, thanks to her birth mom and Carter. But Eliot had understood her right away.

I was starting to understand Eliot too. He was a guy who wouldn't leave a frantic mom hanging when she had to marry someone. He did what had to be done. He gave of himself because it was what he thought was the right thing to do. It was the one thing his parents hadn't done for him.

I went into the bathroom, mulling over my thoughts. He was helping me because he was my husband and that was what spouses did. He probably wanted to be a better one than his dad. It was all so clear. Any hints of romance were nothing but my fantasies, misinterpreting his generous actions.

Eliot

"Need a hand?" Alder walked over to the grill with a can of sparkling water in his hand. He was dressed down today, in crisp jeans and a polo, looking more like his dad.

The fact that I'd gotten the old grill Lily found in the garage working was a miracle, but I wasn't about to tolerate stovetop burgers when there was a grill with a heartbeat in the vicinity.

I transferred a burger to a higher rack to keep it warm while the last few finished. "I've got it, but you can find out who wants cheese and who doesn't."

"Can't they just put it on themselves?" Confusion entered his gaze.

"I have a system."

He continued to stare at me, but I didn't sense resistance.

"My family gets together a lot," I explained, only because he wasn't being an ass. He mostly seemed lost at not being in charge.

The Dukes were a lot less overpowering today than yesterday. Violet brought cases of sparkling water. Poppy —they were not twins, but they were only ten months apart—had come bearing chips. Clover supplied the dip. Jasper joked about filling his trunk with beer and got a stern warning glare from his mom. I still wasn't sure if he was joking, but he produced a new cooler with ice that he must've just purchased.

People were gathered on the concrete pad in front of the old shop. Various plastic chairs Lily had found in the garage and shop had been hosed off and dried. Cali was the only kid running around, but she had plenty of aunts and uncles to entertain her. So familiar but so different to what I was used to.

"The grill is kinda my thing," I continued. My brothers knew not to touch the grill unless I handed over the tongs. "I have a process."

Understanding filled his eyes. "You have a large family too. Dad mentioned how many Knights there are."

"We started our gatherings with the big cattle weekends on the ranch. The food was more of a thank-you, but then we just kept doing it. When Aggie moved to Crocus Valley and got married, her wedding kicked off a new tradition. Now, the parties rotate through everyone's houses and holidays. It really doesn't take much for them to get together anymore."

"Them? Not you?"

Alder was sharp. He'd caught that, and I didn't realize how I'd phrased it. "I'm ruled by the job. Depending on the season, I might not be able to get away."

His eyes narrowed.

Shit. "Of course, now that I'm commuting, I'll be around more."

He cocked a dark brow. "Commuting. That can be hard on a relationship."

"Lots of divorces happen when people live together every day."

A dark cloud rippled across his expression. "Too true."

I wasn't sure what I said, but there was a story there. I was surrounded by my new in-laws and I knew very little about them.

Alder stuffed his hands into his pockets. "About this dance recital?"

"It's my sister-in-law's dance school. Pretty informal." I hadn't planned to attend until Lily had talked to me with her parents in the car. I had an employee put in his notice just as the new guy started. He was going back to school. I needed to get to hiring another person before winter arrived and scared everyone off. The new hire from Baltimore would take a while to get the hang of everything. He was a fresh cowboy. He knew horses, but he didn't know about raising them or caring for them each day. He could ride, but every day was a lesson.

"Do a lot of people from Coal Haven go to it?"

I took all the burgers off the grill. "Maybe? I'm sure some of her students are from Coal Haven."

"Right. I won't be able to stay long. I have some work to catch up on."

"Sure." Curiosity rose inside me. As the oldest, he'd lived in Coal Haven the longest. Did he still have connections there? I'd ask Lily later.

Jasper sauntered up to us. Alder's jaw clenched. I recognized that look from Cody. Poor Jasper and whatever his life's choices had been.

"Speaking of work," Alder said to Jasper, "have you found a place—"

"My severance package is—"

"Almost gone," Alder said. Yup, he was a lot like Cody. Even their names were similar.

"I've got an opening." I should shut my mouth, but I found employees in all sorts of places. I'd hired guys I met at horse shows or at the gas station on my way to horse and cattle sales and at those horse and cattle sales. I'd learned to be resourceful over the years.

Jasper studied me, but his expression was serious. "What kind of opening?"

"Ranch hand. Pay is shit, I'm not gonna lie. Most of us do the work 'cause we love it." Or because there was no one left to do it. "What's your experience with horses and cattle?"

Jasper gestured to the land around him. "Picture these pastures filled with cattle and horses."

"And goats," Alder added.

"And goats. We used to help our grandparents as kids. Less often after we moved to Billings, but enough to keep my skills up." Jasper rubbed his lower lip between his thumb and forefinger. "It'd just be until I find something in my field."

"Unless your field keeps downsizing." Alder spoke in a way that said there was more to the story.

I'd ask Lily.

I'd have to touch base with her on a few things after today. How she felt about her family's visit. If she was okay with me offering Jasper a job. It was possible that with him hired on, I'd be able to break away more often. Which would mean more time with my wife.

Lily

"I can't imagine why you're into him." Violet's murmur was laced with teasing sarcasm.

She was holding Kellan. Cali had taken her on a frenetic tour of the place as if Violet hadn't spent as much time running through the yard and buildings as me before I moved in. Now she sat with me and Poppy and Clover while Cali dominated my parents. Jasper had cruised by the food, grabbing a handful of chips or veggies and beelined for Alder and Eliot.

Eliot could handle himself, but I hoped he didn't have to. I liked the way he'd stood up for me. The way he reacted to my family was worlds different than Carter. Instead of being defensive, he'd cooperated. He wasn't isolating me, and he'd made the picnic a success. If I got nothing else from this marriage, other than the house, I'd learn what a true partnership was like.

"Are you saying my husband's hot?" My sister had never had a good thing to say about Carter. She was already more complimentary about Eliot.

"He's not my type, but he doesn't make me want to wash myself like Carter."

"Oh my god, Violet." It was never fun to hear how epically bad my choice had been.

Poppy wrinkled her nose. "Carter did have that Cadillac-salesman vibe."

"No, it's the hair gel that gave him that oily feeling," Clover added.

"He was a mistake, okay? You were all correct about him. Go ahead and say I told you so." I chugged from my can of sparkling water, wishing it had anything more than zero proof. I should've listened to them. Carter had gotten to me by making me feel like I had to be more sophisticated and savvier than a girl from Billings who loved her family and animals.

"We didn't want to be right," Violet said quietly. "We were afraid that we were though."

I gave her a reassuring smile. "I think I was afraid you were right too." I'd fallen in love with Cali as soon as I'd seen her. I'd seen my chance to create a home like what I'd grown up with and I'd seized it, red flags be damned.

Clover clicked her tongue against her teeth. "I don't feel like Eliot will tell you he's fucking his coworker when you tell him you don't like his attitude."

"He's not that limp dishrag, that's for sure." Violet peered at Eliot like she was sizing him up. "Carter would've whined about how mean we were being yesterday."

Clover snorted. "He wouldn't have entered the house."

"Probably would've driven away hoping we didn't see him," Poppy added. "But not your man. He was ready to throw down for you. 'You'll need to talk on her schedule,'" she mimicked Eliot's deep voice.

"He was not." I bit back a giggle. They'd never given me a hard time about Carter.

Poppy flashed me a smug smile. "He was like, 'Lily's not home,' like he was going to demand we wait."

"He did not." But Eliot had told me he was going to put a stop to the discussion if I hadn't arrived.

"He so did." Clover snickered and put her hand to her mouth. "Pissed Violet off."

Violet's eyes flared. "I was not upset."

Clover held her hands up. "I know you don't like the stick up your ass getting twanged—"

"Clover Jean Duke, you do not talk to me like that." Violet's voice got lower the angrier she grew. "You never give Alder a hard time about being an uptight prick."

"Because we all know how he used to be."

Violet snapped her mouth shut, then sighed. "Fair. But someone's had to watch out for you three and your bad decisions, and I'm not talking about cutting bangs yourself."

Poppy ran her hands along the brown strands framing her face. "Hey, they're almost grown out."

Violet eyed Clover. "The tattoo."

Clover winced. "It's classy and I stand by it."

"Is that why Jasper asked me if there was a place in Billings that did cover-ups?" Violet challenged.

"Why don't we do this?" I blurted out before Clover could answer.

Poppy blinked. "What?"

"Just hang out and give each other a hard time for no other reason than because we're sisters?" I glanced at Eliot and stroked my gaze over his broad back to his impeccable ass. "The Knights are always hanging out, and I know I've heard them say they haven't always been that way, but... I just want sisters I can talk to. Brothers too."

"Well..." Poppy continued to pull at her long bangs. "We don't live close like you said they do."

"I know." I shouldn't have brought it up, but after the Fourth of July, I couldn't quit wishing for what I didn't have, which included a sexy husband who made my panties wet while he cooked hamburgers on the grill.

Violet dropped her chin down and studied the concrete. "I think you underestimate how much we worried about you with Carter. We could all see the wedge he was putting between you and us."

"It didn't help that I felt like he wasn't all wrong." That was the rub. His and his parents' catty remarks had held a lot of truth. "You guys were always taking care of me, and I never wanted to upset anyone."

"Carter was different," Violet said. "He was a sentient red flag, Lil. He treated you like shit."

"He treated me like a queen until I wasn't necessary." That was how he fooled me.

"Yes," Violet replied, "but there were several red flags under his bravado. Look, we were all supportive of you marrying him so you could adopt Cali. But dropping out of vet school? That douche could've found a way, but he wanted a free babysitter."

He could've, but he'd dangled exactly what I wanted in front of me. My own family. "At least I came out of it with two amazing kids."

"They're the only reason Alder and Jasper didn't kill him and hide the body in the oil fields," Poppy said.

I might be bloodthirsty for the way I liked to hear

that, but so be it. "Carter's out of my life, and I'm better for it."

"Don't you want to go back to vet school?" Violet asked. Of all of them, she would be the one ruminating over why I wasn't trying to finish what I'd started. She'd have clawed her way to the top no matter what.

"Actually, no. I like being able to do my job and leave. I've worked in clinics enough now to see the stress. Plus, I get to deal with the animals more than the people. The vets don't get that."

My sisters peered at me for a moment, then Violet nodded. "It's your life."

"It is," I agreed, grateful they seemed to understand that I didn't need to be at the top of my profession to be happy. I wanted a job I enjoyed and a house full of love like I'd had growing up. I was also ready to move on from the topic of me. "So, when are you all getting married?"

Violet blanched. "Can you imagine if I dragged Willis to North Dakota?" She scoffed.

Was I brave enough to say what was on my mind? I glanced at the tall man with the nice ass who was my husband. Yes. I was. "Willis has always reminded me of Carter."

Poppy was in the middle of a drink when she sputtered. Clover turned like she was trying to see where Cali was playing with our parents. She most likely wanted a reason to get away from the conversation.

"You can't be serious," Violet said in a haughty tone.

"As serious as Carter's love for hair product." If I didn't feel it was important to open my sister's eyes to her crappy boyfriend, I'd keep my mouth shut.

Clover swiped a hand over her face, but her smile

stayed in place. "What have you done with our timid little sister?"

"I think you're asking the wrong person." Poppy jerked her head toward Eliot. He was putting a plate of burgers on the table. "What's he doing to her?"

"Ten bucks if you give me the good details," Clover said.

"Clover!" She'd be scandalized if I listed everything I wanted him to do to me. She'd be even more appalled if she knew that the final answer would be nothing. Eliot and I were doing nothing together but pretending to be in love.

Violet shook her head, back to being an impervious older sister. "It looks like it's time to eat. I'll get Mom and Dad."

Poppy nudged my shoulder. "Thanks for having the balls to bring up Willis. He's the reason she never comes to visit. Montana is too hick for his California ass."

"He can stay out of Billings, then," Clover said. "I can't believe she left him long enough to come here."

I watched Violet turn on her chipper voice to let our parents and Cali know it was time to eat. "As long as she's here and he's not."

Poppy threaded her arms through mine. "You're right, though. We need to get together more. It's been too long." She snorted. "I'm just not getting married to do it. But you've been through a lot, and you deserve the sexy cowboy who fell into your lap."

<h1 style="text-align:center">*Eleven*</h1>

ELIOT

I finished the dishes left from lunch. There weren't many, but after we ate, Lily and I listened as Weston rehashed everything we knew about the last will and trust of Annie Duke. Lily's aunt was in charge of it all, but she and Weston had the authority to determine if we were a real couple or not. They both had to agree and sign off. Weird stipulation, but Annie Duke must've been in love with the idea of love. Then we'd had to rush to the recital. There hadn't been time to introduce Lily's family to mine before everyone had to return to Billings. From there, they'd travel to their respective homes. Jasper would come out to the ranch in September.

After the recital, the rest of Lily's family cleared out of town.

Lily leaned against the counter. "Did you offer Jasper a job?"

It was close to ten, and the kids were already sleeping.

Usually, I was sending her to bed first, but we had some time to ourselves. The house was quiet around us. My place was always quiet, but this was different. This was a home.

I hung up the dish towel. "Technically, Alder made a joke, not joking, about Jasper's lack of a job, and I happen to have a legit opening."

"Jasper used to love helping Grandma and Grandpa. He spent summers working for them."

I rested a hand on the counter. We were facing each other, and I wasn't inclined to move away from her. "He'll fit right in." I had a sense about the guy. The way his interest took over when he realized I was serious was a good sign. "Until he gets married and claims his own slice of heaven."

"And there's the kicker. You might only have him for six years."

"That's a good stretch for this kind of work. He also might get married earlier."

Mirth danced in her eyes. "I'm going to have so much fun watching them scramble."

An easy silence fell between us. I dug in my pocket, and my nerves fired up in my stomach. I retrieved the two little silicone bands I'd been carrying around all day.

"I thought we might need these." I handed her the smaller band, and my heart scooted right into my throat. Both my boots were planted on the floor, but I felt like I was proposing. I wasn't, but suddenly the bands were too cheap, too flimsy, too plain. Lily might not wear a lot of jewelry, but she deserved nice things. Did she like diamonds? Emeralds? Plain gold bands? Platinum?

My heart rate increased, and I had a hard time drawing in a breath.

She frowned at it like she didn't know what she was looking at. "Is that a ring?"

"Yeah. So creeps leave you alone. Like that fucking Dr. Jake." I'd heard too much about the veterinarian over the years. He'd been the lone vet in town until Sutton opened her clinic.

She laughed, then grimaced. "His reputation precedes him. Don't worry, if I need a house call, I'll phone Sutton's Animal Care."

"You'd better," I growled. Jealousy clawed its way into my chest. I did not want that man around Lily. He was too much like her ex.

She put her ring on. "It fits. How'd you know the size?"

"I just did." I slid my ring in place. The weight was light but noticeable. I'd never worn anything other than a watch. I flexed my hand. It felt good.

She brushed a lock of hair behind her ear. My fingers itched to do the same. "I think the kids were worn out." She smirked. "I'm going to need your family to have a dance recital and party every weekend."

"We love recital weekends. Too bad you're missing the street dance. We usually go to that afterward."

"Oh." Her expression went blank. "You can still go. I highly doubt my aunt does street dances. You shouldn't have to worry about her seeing you."

I drew back. I'd given her the impression I was missing out. "I'm not going to a dance and leaving you here."

"Your brothers and sisters are there?"

I nodded.

"Then..." She swallowed. "Married guys still go to street dances without their wives."

Not this married guy. I dug my phone out. "I've socialized all day. Believe me. I'm peopled out." I clicked on my music and a slow country song filled the silence. I held my arms out. "Care to dance?"

"Eliot. You don't have to."

I tugged her into my arms and started a slow two-step. She fit perfectly in my hold. Her hand was dainty in mine and her other hand was warm on my shoulder. "If you don't know how to dance, just say so."

"I do!" She dropped her gaze. "It's been a long time. And most of those days were in a college bar. Or a right-after-college bar. Okay, it was line dancing."

I laughed. "I'm just as guilty of being able to line dance to 'Cotton Eye Joe.'" I twirled us around, and she held on tighter.

"I don't look like it now, but I had my share of wild bar nights." She screwed her face up. "I'm not sure if I should admit that, much less sound proud."

"I'm sure I've got a story to match each of yours." Mine probably outnumbered hers. "There's not much else to do in Buffalo Gully." The more members of my family left, the less there was to do. "It's barely a map dot."

"I think towns that are barely map dots are the best," she said softly.

The song ended and switched to another slow country ballad. I had a playlist for the quiet times when I just needed to not think of the future and how monotonous it was. The times I was stuck carrying out the obligations required of a Knight so my family could have some freedom. Having her in my arms certainly accomplished the same thing.

"Why aren't you married, Eliot?" When I lifted a brow, she rolled her eyes. "You know what I mean."

"'Barely a map dot' towns don't have a lot of options. I mean, there are plenty of decent women there." Plenty might be stretching it. Buffalo Gully was small. "But none who wanted to give up civilization to live in the middle of nowhere around a bunch of cattle and horses and strange men."

"You breed strange men too?"

I chuckled. "Some days, it feels like it. I have a high turnover. Between the pay, which is competitive in an overall low-paying field, and the isolation, guys move on. They go to different ranches, they find their piece of heaven to buy, they settle down and want to be closer to a larger community. Mostly, I get guys who want to learn the ropes but have their own aspirations."

"They don't want to work forever for the guy with the aspirations."

The bleakness rose in my chest, creating that gaping cavity I toed dirt into. Someday, it'd fill. "Exactly."

"No. Not exactly." She peered into my eyes, hers jumping back and forth. "I said something not quite right."

I steered us around the table. How'd she guess? My family never did. I made comments, they ignored them, we got on with our lives. That was how it worked. I wasn't used to being heard. "Aspirations is a strong word. I prefer to think of myself as the guy with the obligations."

We danced and she waited, her gaze warm on my face.

Damn, she wanted me to continue. "I guess when I was a kid, I would've said I wanted to be a cowboy when I grew up, but I also wanted other experiences."

"Like what?"

"I dunno. I mean, I travel for horse shows, but we never go that far." And I'd backed off those. Our Arabians were so established by now I didn't have to do a lot of ground-roots marketing. It was word of mouth and online advertising these days.

"Where would you go?"

"Hell, anywhere." Again, she waited. I wasn't getting out of this conversation. Maybe I should've gone to the street dance. But then I'd miss having her in my arms. "Some of the guys who come out to intern with me, or even to work for a few seasons, are from the East Coast. I've never been out there. I can't get away for that long. I do these weekends, but I'm close to home in case anything happens."

"Boston? DC?"

"It's not the place, it's the ability." I ground my molars together. In the time of one song, she'd dug into the heart of my frustrations. Barns's words streamed through my head. *What are you fucking whining about now?* "I just get a little wistful. I'm not like my mama."

"How was that?"

I clenched my jaw again.

She tipped her head. "You don't have to talk about her."

"No, it's only fair." I didn't usually like to discuss Mama. I'd been less to that woman than I was to Barns, and that was saying a lot. "She felt like she missed out on life. She resented us. And when she had a chance, she left. I'm not like her. I might want to travel, but it's not a compulsion. I'm not a prisoner." Those words rang empty. "I have a good life."

"Doesn't mean it's wrong to want something different. Something you chose."

"Sometimes being forced into things makes life interesting."

She blinked. Shit.

"I'm so sorry." She stopped and horror dawned in her expression. I kept my arms around her. "You can't leave your home or your career, and now you can't leave this marriage."

I grinned. "Not for eleven months."

A flash of hurt ran through her gaze so fast I should've missed it.

"I trapped you, I know I did. I promise that as soon as the time is up, I'll have divorce papers drafted."

My stomach clenched. The thought of those papers landing on my desk as just another task to finish left a thick, oily feeling in my gut. "It's fine."

"I can even get them done earlier, and you can sign on the day of. Aunt Linda doesn't have to know right away. By then, it won't be your business."

"I'm not talking about—"

"If we find a loophole, I'll definitely let you know. Alder and Violet won't let up—"

I pressed my lips against hers. Lust rose like a flame on a dry day. I couldn't blame my long stretch of solo nights. My desire was on a constant and inappropriate smolder around Lily. She was curvy in a way that gave a guy ideas, thoughts about how soft she'd feel under me or how those tits of hers would overflow in my hands. She was oblivious to her sex appeal.

I was not. She dug her fingers into me. She wasn't pushing me away but pulling me closer. I continued kissing her, licking along her plump lower lip. Her mouth would've held me rapt for weeks if I was weaker, but I'd been determined not to pant around her like a stud ready to mount.

I lost that battle. I tightened my hold. She whimpered in a way that made me think of naked bodies and rumpled sheets.

Being taller than her made it harder to palm her ass, but when she twined herself around me, she fit perfectly. I could bend over her, keep my mouth on hers, and get a good grip on those ripe cheeks. When she opened her mouth for me, I groaned. Hot and wet. My mind filled with other areas of her I could explore, but I was content for now. She answered each stroke of my tongue with her own. Then she tunneled her hands through my hair, and fuck, that was my kryptonite. She massaged my scalp. If my eyes weren't closed, they'd roll.

I brushed a hand over her jeans and up her shirt. When my fingertips touched skin, electricity sizzled between us. Christ, we'd light the sheets on fire.

I tasted her as I trailed my fingers higher to her breast. Her bra was lacy but lined. Thick. A warning bell went off in my brain. There was a reason why I shouldn't do this, but I didn't stop. She was responsive. Her greedy tongue licked against mine, her demanding hands tilted my head at just the right angle, and her body—

Kellan's cry echoed from down the hall.

Lily stiffened, and I jerked my head up. *Fuck*. She was a mom. I was supposed to be helping her, not feeling her up.

"Oh god." She pushed her fingertips against her forehead. "Eliot, you don't have to do that."

"Do what?"

Kellan let out another cry. She rushed around me.

Her face was as red as a cherry, and her bouncing butt cheeks didn't help temper my arousal. My erection strained against my jeans. I pushed at it, trying to make it less obnoxious.

Did I go after her?

Did she think I gave her a pity kiss?

I huffed out a breath and planted my hands on my hips. Staring at the floor, I slowly gained control of myself. It was getting late, and I couldn't have her hiding in her bedroom and going to sleep thinking I only kissed her because I felt sorry for her.

The bedroom door was closed, but Kellan was still fussing. She might be changing his diaper before she fed him. I knocked lightly.

A few tense seconds ticked by before I heard, "Yeah?"

I squeaked the door open. Her hair was hanging over her face as she changed him on the bed. Kellan glanced over at me, stopped crying, and gave me a two-toothed grin. I smiled back at him before zeroing in on his mom.

"Let the record state that kiss was not out of pity."

She faltered snapping his onesie. "You don't have to worry about it."

"But I do. I'm here to help you. I'm not here to maul you. You don't need that pressure."

Finally, she turned her head enough that her curtain of hair fell back. "You feel like you're pressuring me?"

I lifted a shoulder. "You've got a man in your house who you don't know well. You're in a tight spot."

"You're right." She snapped more buttons together. "I was forced to kiss the impossibly handsome cowboy who reads books to my daughter and takes the baby so I can sleep. Oh, and he dances."

I leaned against the door frame. "Impossibly handsome?"

She scowled at me, her mouth twisted like she was holding back a smile. "You're the best-looking brother."

"Dang. You're making me blush. Can I record you saying that?"

Her lips twitched. "No, because you'll play it back for them."

"A few times." I pushed a hand through my hair. My body was buzzing with the memory of her against it, her mouth on mine. She was soft and the way she'd opened for me—damn. I would not get a wink of sleep tonight while trying to keep my erection under control. "It's getting late, and that little guy doesn't believe in sleeping in. I'm not going to come onto you anymore, but it's not because I don't find you attractive. I've always thought you were cute, but I put you so far in the off-limits category I can't just change the label and have it be okay. It's important to me that you trust me."

Her eyes had narrowed at the word cute. Did I fuck up trying to make things right? "Okay. Thank you."

Goddammit. If I kept trying to make her see that I would fuck her in a heartbeat, I'd delve into creeper territory. She already couldn't get rid of me for eleven months. I'd go to her grandma's old bedroom, now my room, and try not to stroke one out on a floral quilt with a snake as a witness. "Night, Lily pad."

"Night, Eliot."

Lily

· · ·

I was in the middle of cleaning out the dresser and closet from Cali's room when I heard laughing and splashing. I pushed off the floor and peered out the window.

Could that guy get any more perfect?

I held out my left hand. A ring. Unnecessary and practical. I squeezed my hand into a fist. I loved it. More laughter filtered in.

Eliot had found an old plastic pool in the shop. My grandparents had probably used it for watering some of their animals, but Eliot had scrubbed it out and filled it with water from the spigot, thanks to the hose he'd also found in the shed. He'd already mowed the lawn, which took him all morning, and then he'd trimmed the weeds. Since he was doing the outdoor chores, I'd taken advantage of the time to make headway clearing out Grandma's things.

Neither of us mentioned last night. Kellan had only gotten up once to nurse after the time he cockblocked me.

Would Eliot and I have gone that far? I feared I would've stripped my clothes off and told him to call me a lineman because I had been ready to climb him like a telephone pole.

The hot wave of embarrassment swept through me, only it left behind a steady beat between my thighs. Nope, that wasn't embarrassment. That emotion didn't make my nipples hard.

Oh god, I was so turned on. My hormones had made a big return in the last month. I felt like I could get pregnant by looking at Eliot.

I tied my hair up to get it off my neck, but I continued to spy out the window. Eliot had come in after he cleaned and sanitized the pool. He took Kellan back out with him. I thought he was kidding when he said he'd fill it, but he squatted by the pool and held Kellan up so only his legs could whack at the water. Cali was on her belly, bodysurfing.

Glancing behind me, I assessed the room. Cali now had space for more clothing when we could get to the store, and her closet was emptied out of old shoes, belts, and Sunday dresses Grandma hadn't been able to get rid of and had stored in the guest closet. Cali's new bedding was almost done in the wash. Tonight, she could go to sleep with the room feeling like hers. I owed Eliot just for getting her over the obstacle of sleeping in her own room.

Grandma's room was next. I had made room in the closet. He said he hung a few shirts and pants up. I'd do the same in case we got inspected, or however Linda wanted to validate our marriage.

That was enough for today. The lure of outdoorsy fun trumped cleaning.

I went to the kitchen and made some lemonade. I found three big plastic cups that were probably older than me and poured them full. Then I shouldered the door open to go outside.

Eliot's deep laughter carried through the yard. When he looked up, his eyes filled with heat, and he trailed his gaze down my legs. I was in old pink shorts and an even older college T-shirt. "I thought you could use some refreshment."

He rose. Kellan kicked his legs, searching for the water. "Thanks."

He downed his glass, his throat working. With his arm bent, his biceps bulged. Yeah. I'd have shed every stitch of clothing if he'd been into it last night. But he hadn't. Despite what he claimed, I latched on to what he'd said before the kiss. He was a man who did the right thing for everyone else. Not for him. He didn't want me to feel bad about rooking him into marrying me.

But hey, he thought I was cute.

Men had thought less of me, and I hadn't been fazed. Carter had called me gorgeous, but then he called everything with boobs the same thing. When I heard him call Petunia the potbellied pig his gorgeous girl, I'd quit pretending that the endearment was special to me.

"Want a refill?" I asked when I took the cup from him.

"I'd better not, or I'll be stopping every few miles to pee." He smiled at the way Cali giggled and splashed around. "I told her we'd have to drain this in an hour before I leave."

Cali popped her head up. "Can't have a mosquitoes beading ground!"

"No beading grounds," Eliot said solemnly and winked at Cali. "I breed enough animals. Mosquitoes don't need any help."

He was leaving in an hour? My good mood from the day dipped. I'd survived my family swarming the place. This weekend had turned into exactly what I wanted. A quiet day at home where I wasn't drooping with fatigue. I'd been productive, and the kids were having fun.

I'd have to keep up after Eliot left. I couldn't rely on him. He might sense it and feel like it was his duty to provide the life I wanted.

It wasn't. Even if I was starting to want him in my life for more than a random weekend.

Twelve

ELIOT

Chambers was sipping his coffee at the island. He'd taken the last piece of his wife's juneberry pie and was sifting through photos I'd gotten sent from Lily.

"And this is Cali's first day of school," I said of one with Cali and a backpack that was half her size.

Chambers peered through his readers at my phone screen. "She's growing like a weed."

Pride puffed out my chest. I had nothing to do with it, but that girl's grin on her first day of school made everything feel right. I'd marry a thousand strangers to keep her in that house where she could go to a school with a teacher she adored. "She really is. Lily just sent this today."

The next photo was an image of Kellan with a sloppy grin in a new pair of overalls his grandma had gotten him. Lily and I messaged back and forth. It was mostly about the kids. I liked seeing them, but I also suspected I was a safe person to message. I didn't quiz Lily on their health and well-being—or hers—like her family would.

I was dying to know. I had to be sneaky. Almost six weeks had passed since her family had bombarded her. I missed them. I missed her.

I should've been back by now. But with the changeover in personnel, training them, and getting everyone through their vacations and time off over the Labor Day weekend, I'd been needed. Jasper would be starting in a couple of weeks, and the ranch would be full of new people. New people made mistakes. I couldn't go away every weekend.

The problems were nothing new. Each season was like Groundhog Day. I woke up, did chores. Sometimes, I'd iron out a conflict between my employees, many times, they'd tell me about an issue on the ranch. Then we'd fix shit, train animals—sometimes fix them, too, and then do evening chores.

To change things up, I could go to the bar.

"When you going back to see her?" Chambers sipped his coffee like he didn't just ask a leading question.

I did the same with Lily in our weekly texts. Is Kellan sleeping through the night yet? Translation—how are you sleeping? Some weeks, he was fussy. Others, he let her get some rest.

I stuffed my phone away. "I should've gone this weekend." Lily hadn't asked. We'd never established if I'd be at her place for holidays, or should I try once a month? Her family had given her space while they figured out their own inheritance plans, and her aunt had been giving them all space. I hadn't been needed. And maybe Lily needed a little time and distance between us.

We'd gotten too close to playing husband and wife

the last time I was there. Dancing in the kitchen. The kiss. I'd gotten carried away. Was she cautious of me? We parted on a good note. I'd hugged Cali and they'd waved at me from the stoop when I drove away.

"How's everyone else?" Chambers asked innocently when he was really prodding me to go. "Cody and the others?"

"They're slowly prepping me that they won't be around for fall work."

His eyes widened. "None of them?" It wasn't easy to surprise Chambers.

"Wilder can't leave Sutton's side. Since Vienne can't do all the work on the house she used to, Austen has more on his plate. Cody said the kids really want to come visit, but with Tova pregnant, he won't be able to put in the long days he used to. Aggie and Ansen have their rescue to cover. My brother-in-law's family usually looks after their animals, but they're going on a family trip to Texas."

The times were changing, but I was staying the same.

"It's gonna be quiet around here, then." Chambers scooted around the island to wash out his coffee cup. "It's Friday. You can make a quick weekend of it."

I'd get there around Cali's bedtime. Kellan might already be asleep. What was I thinking? I couldn't pop up on her doorstep. "We just recovered from me being gone last time."

He harrumphed but didn't say anything.

I leaned on the corner of the island near the oven and glowered at his back. "We're not married for real." I wasn't the only one who needed reminding.

He peered over his shoulder. "Not saying nuthin'."

"You're saying a whole damn lot, Chambers," I said dryly.

He lifted a bony shoulder. No one could tell by looking at him that he could haul a fifty-pound bag of feed like it was a sack of feathers. "You like the girl."

"She's cool."

He gave me a look, and for a heartbeat, I missed having a normal dad. A guy who shot me these expressions when he thought I was full of shit.

I wasn't, for the record. Lily was great. I liked dancing with her more than any partner I'd been with. I didn't have to come up with forced conversation. She was easy to be around. But that was the thing. It wasn't hard with her because there was nothing between us. I wouldn't wedge myself into a life she was trying to build for herself and those kids.

"Must be something exciting keeping you in town for the weekend," Chambers drawled.

"It's called work."

He snorted again and started for the front door. He parked in front of the garage, usually by my pickup, since I used the garage as more of a workshop.

Irritation crawled up my spine. Yes, it was Friday. I'd be working like normal all weekend. But I wasn't pining away at the house like he thought I was. I'd prove it. "I'll walk out with you."

"Going out?"

"Yup."

Fifteen minutes later, I wanted to go back home. I'd rather play cards in the bunkhouse with the guys than sit alone at the bar with my old math teacher whose wife left him ten years ago because he never left this bar outside of work hours. On my other side, a few stools down, was a lifelong bachelor who'd gotten kicked out more than once for "bumping into" a woman's ass or boob. Repeatedly.

I took my hat off and scrubbed my face. A beer was slid in front of me. My old math teacher drank the same thing.

Fuck.

A wave of soft floral perfume puffed around me. "Hey, stranger." An old high school sweetheart of Wilder's slid onto a stool next to me.

"Hey, Jodi." I was happy to see a friendly face but also acutely aware of the silicone band on my finger. It wasn't like she was interested in me, and besides, I didn't date my brothers' exes. The rule took out a huge chunk of the dating pool in Buffalo Gully, but I already lived where my brothers didn't want to. I worked the job they didn't want. I didn't need a woman they didn't want either. Harsh, but there it was.

"Oh my god." She tapped my ring finger, her fingertip warm. "The rumors are true."

"Yep."

"Congrats." Her eyes glittered as she studied me. She wasn't enthusiastic.

"Thanks."

"Did she move to Buffalo Gully?" Confusion mingled with curiosity in her voice. She looked around like she was waiting for a strange woman to shoo her from her seat.

"We're figuring out the living arrangements." I wasn't going to explain our situation. There was no reason I couldn't, but I was keeping the information close to my chest. Lily was no one's business.

"How's Wilder?"

"Living the dream for real." Did I sound wistful?

"Yeah?" This time, her happiness sounded genuine. "You know I briefly entertained the notion we might get back together." She laughed. "It was clear that night I ran into both of you here that I thought, nope, he's not getting over her."

"Good thing he won her back."

"Good thing he didn't win her back to Buffalo Gully. Look at how beneficial it's been for all of you to get out of town."

My stomach twisted at the thought of moving Lily to the Knight ranch. Or of isolating her like Sutton had been when she and Wilder lived in town. And seeing her in the house among all my worst memories.

What the hell was I thinking? Lily wasn't moving. We'd married so she wouldn't have to.

Jodi grimaced. "It's worth the drive for me from Sidney every day to help my parents instead of buying the house on the end of their block."

"I'm pretty sure that place is haunted."

Her laughter rang through the bar. To other patrons, we might look like we were flirting. I should go home.

The idea sounded better the more I thought about it. "I'm gonna take off. Nice talking to you."

Disappointment filled her eyes. "I almost didn't believe you tied the knot."

Me neither. I wiggled my ring finger. "Like you said, it's good that I got out of town."

My phone buzzed, and I pulled it out to look at it. Lily. A jolt of electricity went through me just seeing her name. "Excuse me." I popped up and went toward the exit. It'd be quieter outside.

"Talk to you later, Eliot," Jodi called after me.

The call dropped just as I stepped into the cool night air. I frowned at the screen. Lily's number registered as a missed call. Another call lit the phone, then disconnected. Worry ignited the knots in my gut from earlier.

I called Lily.

A little girl's voice flowed over the other line. "Hello?"

"Cali?" There was crying in the background. Alarm drowned out the drone of the cars driving by.

"Eliot?"

The burn in my gut grew stronger. "What's wrong?"

"Mommy's puking."

I started for the pickup. The crying on the other end didn't die down. "She's sick?"

"I think so. I puked last weekend. So gross." She dropped her voice to a whisper.

Lily didn't mention Cali had been sick. "How long has your mommy been throwing up?"

"I dunno. All day, I think."

For fuck's sake. Why wouldn't she call me? "How's Kellan?"

"He's in his swing."

"Is he okay?"

"He's hungry. His bottle's on the counter."

But Cali couldn't feed him without supervision and Lily was likely in the bathroom. Had she called her family? My gut said no. She'd try to do it all herself.

Lily

·   ·   ·

The room spun. How could such a tiny bathroom go in circles like this? Should I call Mom?

I should've called her this morning when I worried I wouldn't get Cali to school or Kellan to daycare. I had called in sick from work.

So damn glad I had sick days.

At least I'd gotten Kellan fed and to bed—with Cali's help.

I should've called Mom. This wasn't a pride issue, it was a safety matter.

Cali was in her bed, probably with her tablet and watching a show. She might fall asleep watching a movie, but I'd have to take the Mom of the Year entry tonight.

A bark sounded in the house.

Shit. The dog was going to wake Kellan up. I pushed away from the wall. Another surge came and I draped myself over the toilet bowl.

Another bark.

He'd have to wait. Another heave racked my body.

How was there anything left?

The barking cut off. Did Cali let the dog out?

Panic tried to take over, but I kept my breaths as even as possible and listened. I didn't hear doors opening and closing, and Cali wouldn't be subtle. As long as she stayed in the house.

I hung my head over the toilet bowl. God, I needed a bath. I barely had the energy to drag myself to my bedroom. Cali had brought me a sippy cup full of water and a sleeve of crackers. Just looking at them turned my stomach.

I heard the front door shut and claws skitter on the floor.

"Cali?" My voice was hoarse. I couldn't yell very loud.

There was no way she controlled that dog. Though he was getting better at listening to her.

I needed to check on her. And Kellan.

I flushed the toilet. One step closer to getting up.

The bathroom door opened. The comforting scent of leather and sandalwood surrounded me as the handsome cowboy filled the opening.

I choked on a sob. Relief or humiliation? I was too sick to tell. "Oh, god, Eliot, what are you doing here?"

"I was about to ask the same thing about Bug."

Talking about the dog sapped all my energy, but it was better than noticing how the bathroom stunk, how I smelled, and worse, how I must look.

He squatted next to me. "You should've called."

I nodded and closed my eyes. I only caught his long legs in my periphery. I didn't have to see how devastating he looked. Yet his presence soaked into my bones, unknotting my shoulders and soothing my sore abdominal muscles. Without the stress of wondering how I was going to do it all, my body was readying itself to collapse.

"Eliot?" Tears streamed down my cheeks.

"Yeah?"

"I'm really sick."

"I know. Cali accidentally called me. You want a hot soak?"

Had it been an accident? Cali had been worried about me. Chalk up another time I should've called for help. The tub was full of the kids' bath toys. The thought of removing those had been exhausting. I nodded. "So bad."

He moved away, not far, but I missed his heat. Within seconds, the bath was running.

I gasped. "The kids."

"I peeked in on them when I was walking through.

Both are asleep. I shut Cali's light off, and I'll get the tablet out of her bed later. Want a bubble bath?"

"Yes." Anything to replace the smell of sick.

The smell of berry-scented soap filled the air. He dug out a couple of towels and a washcloth. I snuck a look at him through my dank hair. I wasn't ill enough not to appreciate how fine his ass was in those jeans or the way his muscles flexed through his shirt as he arranged the items on the counter.

He turned, and I didn't have the energy to pretend I wasn't staring. He held a second towel in his hands, and his gaze softened. "Need help getting in?"

Yes.

No. This man's first glimpse of me naked was not going to be when I was a disgusting mess.

First glimpse? Like there was going to be one at all?

"I got it." I could get out of my sweats and roll into the tub.

He set the towel by the base of the tub. "I'll come back to check on you. Use this to cover yourself if you don't want me seeing anything."

I nodded and then he was gone.

Thirteen

ELIOT

I roamed the kitchen and living room, waiting for Lily to get into the tub. Christ, she looked like she was barely conscious. Her eyelids were hooded, and she was as gray as the tile floor. It'd taken all my restraint not to sit next to her and pull her into my lap.

Only the horror in her gaze kept me from doing that. But the stark relief was also as apparent. She would've been in trouble on her own. That dog could've dragged her across the county.

Why didn't she call someone?

Because she was stubborn as hell.

I stopped at her fridge. There was a child safety lock on it. For the kids or for the dog? I found a kids' electrolyte drink. I poured her a glass of that and a cup of water. She hadn't touched what looked like crackers that lay by the wall, but fluids were probably more important.

I'd taken care of enough sick cattle and horses in my time to know that.

On my way back to the bathroom, I stopped in Cali's room and took the tablet out. She was starfished across the covers, her limbs splayed, but she was in pajamas. I got the throw blanket from the living room and covered her.

Kellan's monitor showed he was still passed out.

I knocked lightly on the slightly ajar bathroom door. "Ready?"

"Yeah," she croaked.

I took a second to run through the rules. No looking. No trying to catch a glimpse. No ogling if I saw something. This wasn't the time. She needed help, not a horny man at her side.

I stepped in. The toothpaste was sitting at the edge of the sink. She must've brushed her teeth. She was in the tub and had her head leaning on the back wall. The towel I'd left her to cover herself with was draped down her body and half-concealed by bubbles. Her flesh was visible, but the wet fabric did nothing to hide her tempting curves.

Nope. Not going there.

I got a hand towel from the cabinet, folded it, and handed it to her. "For behind your head." I set the drinks on the tub's ledge.

"Thanks." She took a tentative sip. We both knew she had to try.

The smell of vomit had dwindled. While she drank and rested, I gave the toilet a quick wipe down and washed my hands.

"You didn't have to do that." The cups were back on the ledge and her eyes were closed.

"Hard to feel better when everything's dirty from

being sick." I sat on the toilet lid. "How'd you end up with Bug?"

She opened her eyes. They were already clearer. She looked tired as hell but not quite ready to waste away. "His owners moved and dropped him off to get euthanized."

"That sucks."

"It does." She let out a gusty breath. "It's like that though."

"You sound like Sutton."

"She worked with the family a lot, we all did, but they just weren't prepared for that amount of dog."

"Why didn't you say anything about him?" Or about how sick she was?

"I didn't want you to worry. Cali told Mom and Dad, and they asked if I knew what I was getting myself into." She pursed her lips. "As if I haven't worked with dogs for years. But you've seen Bug get away from me."

She wanted to prove she could do it before anyone had a chance to question her. "Has he been too much?"

Her chuckle was faint. "He'll be too much for at least two more years. Maybe three. But he's improving already. Cali's become his human, and she's serious about training him." She exhaled and shut her eyes as she rested her head on the folded towel. The bubbles were slowly dissipating. I fought to keep my gaze off the growing visible area around her breasts. Wet fabric did nothing to hide the swell of her tits.

I was losing the battle. I dropped my gaze to my hands.

"Cali's been a big help as we train him on the boundaries of the property. At least he's used to other animals. The barn cats will eventually get used to him."

"Any other animals you've collected since I've been here last?"

Her smile was faint. "Your sister saved the two baby goats that lost their mama."

"Or you would've?"

"I'd have only needed some new fence."

I chuckled. "You collect animals at an alarmingly high rate, Lily pad. You started with a snake, and now you've got Pebbles, Bug, and several barn cats."

She opened her eyes. "I grew up the baby in a chaotic house. It's my norm."

"Your home must've been full of love."

"It was. Annoying and smothering, but yes, it was full of love." A shiver racked her body.

"Do you need more hot water?"

"Yeah, but I don't want to move. I think I could finally sleep." Her eyelids were getting droopy.

I rose and grabbed the towels. She clocked my movements, some color finally entering her cheeks.

Holding the bath towel by the edges, I turned my head. "I'll close my eyes."

A couple heartbeats went by, then water sloshed. The sound of the drain squelching filled the bathroom, then splashing as she rose.

I kept my eyes shut. My brain was happy to fill in an imaginary image of her wet and naked. I suppressed a shudder of desire. I could not get an erection when she'd just been puking.

The towel was plucked from my fingers. "Just a minute," she said.

I felt her move around me. I didn't have to look to know she was being careful not to touch me.

"Okay."

I peeled my eyes open. She was mostly dried off, and she had a smaller towel wrapped around her head. The pale-blue towel was around her body, covering most of her cleavage and falling to her midthigh.

"How are you feeling? Steady?" I tracked every goose bump covering her body and stuck on a cute little mole by her right shoulder. Then another farther along her clavicle. How many more could I find?

"I think I'll be fine."

Not good enough. I opened the bathroom door. She was full-on shivering and ready to cross to her bedroom, but I didn't let her get far.

"Hold still." I picked her up, cradling her in my arms.

"Oh my god." Her complexion paled, went gray, then turned a shade of green. She clutched at the flap of towel holding everything together.

Shit. Swinging her into my arms was the wrong move. "I'm gonna walk slow, okay?"

She swallowed hard and nodded.

With deliberate movements, I navigated down the hall. Her bedroom door was open and the light in the hall was enough to illuminate the inside.

"Can you see all right?" I asked in a low voice. Kellan's even breaths filled the room.

She nodded. "I just need to grab a pair of shorts and a shirt before I get into bed."

"Let me clean up the bathroom, and I'll come back to check on you."

I did as I said, leaving her to dress. I returned to her room with the drink and water. There was a clean puke bucket on her nightstand. She was tucked under the covers, but in the faint glow of the night-light, her shivers couldn't be hidden.

"You're cold." I set the glasses down.

"It's the bath. I'm sure I don't have a fever. I'll warm up in a minute."

That wasn't good enough either. My boots were already off, so I climbed into bed right behind her.

She stiffened and rolled to her back. "Eliot!" she whisper-shouted. "What are you doing?"

"Warming you up. Sorry. Shoulda asked first. Want me to leave or lend you my body heat?"

She blinked, and I heard her swallow. "You are really warm."

"A damn furnace, honey."

She sagged into the mattress. I crowded behind her. She was warm already, but her shivers lessened the closer I got. I wrapped an arm around her waist and pulled her against me while strategically angling my hips back. My dick had taken notice of the woman in my arms, and it didn't care that she'd been hunched over the toilet bowl less than an hour ago. She was soft in all the right places.

"Get some rest."

"Mmm." She sounded skeptical. "I don't know if I can."

"Want me to sing you a lullaby?"

Her soft chuckle shook her body. "Sure. I'll be on the receiving end of one for once."

The only song that came to mind was a country song about a toxic relationship, but it was a good one to sing acoustically. My shower would attest to that.

I started singing, my voice low, only for her ears. She was stiff at first, but eventually, her shivers subsided. Soon enough, her breathing grew steady.

I should go. She was warm and asleep. My work here was done. I could take the monitor and go to the other bedroom so I could get some sleep before Kellan woke up.

But I didn't move. I relaxed around Lily, buried my nose in her sunshine-smelling hair, and drifted off.

Lily

I woke up in the snuggliest of cocoons. I was warm, my stomach wasn't pitching in all different directions, and the fatigue from yesterday was fading. I wasn't full of energy, but I could stay in this cozy nest for eternity.

My mind was sluggishly trying to wake up. A giant weight was pressed against my side—or was I pressed against it? A big, warm presence was in the bed.

Wasn't I divorced?

Since when had I woken up this comfortable with Carter? He'd always complained about how much I wanted to cuddle with him. He'd said I was needy.

This wasn't Carter in bed. I was divorced. I had also remarried.

I blinked my eyes open. Enough light backlit the shades to make everything clear. My gaze landed on a stubbled jaw, gone a little slack in sleep. His lips were slightly parted, and his eyes were still closed. The dark sweep of his lashes on his cheeks matched the shade of his stubble. A lock of hair fell over his forehead.

Memories from the night before crashed back. I had been throwing up. He had cleaned up the bathroom and ran me a bath. He sang to me before bed. What a nice voice. I had my very own singing cowboy.

For a little more than nine more months anyway.

I stayed where I was, not moving. Was it wrong to enjoy this while he was sleeping? Was I crossing a line with my husband?

But he'd stayed in bed last night. A small tendril of hope wound around my heart. If I let it cinch tight, it'd cleave the organ right in two.

This guy could break my heart.

My divorce had devastated me. I lost my job and my home and I'd had to embark on a journey of single parenthood. But losing Carter hadn't been what got me down. His betrayal, yes. The idea that I didn't have the marriage I wanted, that I knew it had fallen so short of what I had dreamed of was what had throttled me. Moving home. That had kicked me while I was down. But ending my relationship with my husband? No. Of all the issues I'd gone through at that point, every one of them ranked higher than the actual breakup.

This man was dangerous. He would be so easy to fall for.

I could feel myself drifting...spinning...

Oh shit—was I going to throw up again?

I sat up. The room spun. I pressed my fingers to my head.

The bed shifted and he rose. "You feeling okay?"

Oh god, the morning roughness to his voice was all male. A complete turn-on.

"No," I croaked. The mix of emotions inside of me was at odds. My stomach wasn't protesting. I was unbalanced, but it had nothing to do with the illness that had swept through the family last week. "I'm better."

My hormones were going wild. It didn't help I was in bed with the hottest man I'd ever seen.

A glass of water appeared at my elbow. "I can get you cold juice, but maybe try a few sips of water and see if you can keep them down."

I nodded and took the water. "Thanks."

Kellan grunted, his little sleeper rustling against the sheet in his bassinet.

"I'll grab him when I get back," Eliot said.

"Why don't you find something to eat?" I took a sip of water. "I'll feed him and clean up. If I make it through that, then I should be fine today. I'll probably just watch movies with Cali all day."

I glanced over my shoulder. His eyes were hooded, but he was watching me. Was I imagining the hurt in his eyes? Did he think I was kicking him out?

I licked my dry lips. I'd need more than a few sips of water to feel normal again. "We've all had a rough week. If you feel like you've missed out on all the latest Disney movies, you're welcome to stay." I summoned a weak smile. "Cali would be delighted."

His answering grin sent my stomach into another somersault. "Since she's the one who called me, sure."

"I'd like you to stay, too, but I'm afraid I'll get you sick."

"After last night, I've already tempted fate. Don't worry about it. It's been a while since I've had more than the bottle flu."

"You're missing work."

"I wouldn't say I'm *missing* work, Lily pad." He stood and stretched with his hands high above his head.

I practically pivoted on the bed to watch the way his shirt crept up beyond his waistband to reveal the bronzed flesh of his back. His butt was clenched and his legs were strong posts.

I should not be filled with this much desire after being so sick. He'd taken care of me. He'd cuddled with me without grumbling. He was still making sure I had what I needed. Of course, I wanted to finish what started with that kiss in my kitchen all those weeks ago.

Wasn't it that very mini make-out session that had kept him away for a month and a half? He was busy, but he'd also made those other times work.

The confusion didn't help my dehydrated brain.

He brought his arms down and rolled his neck from side to side. "I'll get some grub for Cali too. Take your time." He pinned me with a firm stare. Did he catch me staring at his marbled ass? "And call for me if you think you're going to be sick."

I nodded, feeling absolutely and utterly cherished. I was the spoiled one, according to my siblings. The girl who took on too much and needed to be looked after because there were so many older brothers and sisters who made me their responsibility.

Yet, with Eliot, I didn't feel smothered. The way he treated me made me feel precious. I'd soak up his presence while I could.

Fourteen

ELIOT

I was cleaning up lunch. Lily didn't look as wan as when I'd arrived or even this morning after she woke.

I would not think about what it was like to wake up and have her right there. To see the way she eyed my body when she thought I wasn't looking. If she hadn't been sick only hours earlier, I would've crawled back into bed. But there'd been a baby in the room. And we weren't a real couple.

Weekends like this made it hard to remember.

I started the dishwasher. Lily was feeding Kellan, and Cali had laid herself down for a nap. She'd been thrilled to see me this morning, but she'd been mellow all day. It must've been a helluva week with school and stomach bugs.

When I was done, I went outside. At some point, since she'd had Bug, she found time to erect an enclosure for the dog to run around in until he got used to living in wide-open country. I let him out. Since I was in the yard, Lily said he'd stick around. It was when he was bored and alone that he got into trouble. I picked up a ball and tossed it. He darted off.

Lily could clearly handle herself. She was a single mom with a house and forty acres, two kids, and several pets. Strong women like her intimidated weak men. Her ex had undermined her confidence to the point of hyper-indepedence. Would she ever trust me enough to tell me what she needed?

My phone rang. Cody.

I answered. "Hey."

"Eliot. When do you need us this fall?" Cody always got right to business.

Hadn't he been preparing me for a lack of familial help this fall? "I haven't looked at the dates yet. You know I like to see what the weather's going to be like." Barns used to have us moving cattle—rain, sleet, or snow be damned. The work would get dangerous for us and for the animals.

"Yeah," he said, resigned. "I wanted to get this planned around baby appointments and football games. Ivy's in basketball now too, and that's in the fall for her age."

A thread of envy twined around my neck. "You can sit this one out."

"The kids love going. It's good for them." He sounded more like he was justifying the trip. "We'll figure something out."

"Don't worry about it." My ever-present bitterness crept out. Cody always figured his shit out. I just never pointed out that it was for himself. I'd be a selfish asshole to do that, but I was also left holding the bag, or in this case, two hundred and fifty head of cattle and twenty horses.

"Any chance Chambers is around? If he's working today, I wanted to catch him."

"I don't know, but probably. I have better internet than him." Chambers's wife didn't like old westerns, and shootouts were all I heard coming from the office during the day.

"You don't know if he's there? Where are you?"

"Lily's." I stubbed the toe of my boot into the ground. Bug returned with the ball, dropped it, and ran back and forth, anticipating the next throw. I lobbed it again. "She got really sick, so I came down for the weekend."

He grunted. "My first thought was that you were with some other woman."

Anger dripped hot in my veins. "What'd ya take me for, Cody? I promised her I wouldn't."

"It's just... You're acting like you're married."

Annoyance made me grind my teeth. "I am married."

"Yeah, I'm gathering that."

"Her family has to believe it." Bug dropped the ball and raced away before I had a chance to throw it. I tossed it with extra force. Cody's tone chafed.

"More than her family might be believing it. You like this girl."

First Chambers, now him. "Of course I like her, or I wouldn't have helped her out."

"Sure. That's all it is."

Lily's full breasts underneath a wet towel did not flash through my mind. Nor did the way she fit against me in bed. "I'll let you know when I have some dates in mind. It'll be around the middle of October, as usual, but like I said, don't worry about it. You've got a lot going on."

"Are you coming back at Halloween?"

Since when did I plan a thing for Halloween? I didn't have kids, and I lived too far out of town to get trick-or-treaters. "Why?"

"Lily's got kids." Amusement rang in his tone. "Cali's going to be all about trick-or-treating. You guys can always join up with us. Ivy loves being a mother hen."

Ivy was bossy in the best ways, like her mom had been. "I hadn't planned on it."

"You're married now."

"Until next June."

"They're welcome regardless, but it'd be fun to have you out."

How'd he know to yank at the string that wanted to experience domestic bliss so badly? "It's not my decision to make."

"True. Send me the dates and then I'll expect to see you in costume." A kid's holler came over the line. I couldn't tell which niece or nephew it was. "Gotta go." He disconnected.

A thud landed at my feet. The ball. This time, Bug paced instead of running after the ball before I threw it. I stooped just as he ran by, licking my cheek in the process. "Ah, gross."

I was laughing just as Lily stepped out. She put her hands in her green hoodie's front pocket. The front had the logo of the Billings Zoo. Her skin was no longer pale, and her eyes weren't glossy. A whole different Lily than last night. "Both kids are napping."

"Do you need to lie down too?"

She shook her head and dropped to sit on the step.

Bug raced toward her, got some ear scratches, and ran off. I wandered to sit next to her.

"I think fresh air will do me some good." She stretched her legs out. "I feel almost normal."

I tucked my phone back into my pocket. My brother's roundabout invite was in my head. I shouldn't plan to be away from home during a busy time of the year, but I also didn't want Lily to miss out on something I'd never been a part of. "Cody said you could join them for Halloween. Ivy would love to lead Cali around for trick-or-treating."

Surprise lifted her brows. "He wants us to go with him?"

"He thought I was coming down, but yeah, you're invited along regardless."

"Oh." She curled her arms around herself, a slight frown on her face. "I haven't thought that far ahead. Cali has. She wants to be a witch this year."

If I was waiting for an invite, I was left disappointed. My throat grew scratchy, and I cleared it. I would be busy. By then, her brother would be training with me, and I would have to be around to train him.

I scratched the back of my neck. "What are you going to dress Kellan as?"

"A baby who sleeps through the night."

I laughed. "He did last night."

"I think that was the magic of you being there." The prettiest blush filled her cheeks.

"I never thought a woman wanted me in her bed so her baby would sleep through the night."

Her laughter chimed across the lawn. "You might find yourself inundated with interested ladies. Good thing you're married, or you'd be getting a lot of proposals."

I grinned and rested my arms on my knees. Bug was chasing after a yellow cabbage moth.

"What will you be doing?" she asked hesitantly. "For Halloween?"

I ignored my thrill at her interest. "Dunno. We work cattle in October and move them to the winter pastures. We used to move horses, too, and we still do, but it's a lot easier with less of them. Jasper's starting soon."

Surprise made her eyes a brighter purple, almost blue. "He's really going through with it?"

"You didn't know?"

She shook her head. "They expect information to funnel up, not down to me. Besides, we've all got our own lives."

I was intensely grateful my family had populated Crocus Valley. Lily would have them if not her own.

"Thank you for helping Jasper." She leaned in until our shoulders brushed. Heat wicked down my neck, traveling south. I clamped down on the inside of my cheek. A shoulder touch shouldn't feel that erotic.

But damn. It'd been a long time since I'd been inside a woman. And the need to bury myself in this one grew stronger.

"I think he's felt a little lost since he got laid off," she said. "At least that's the impression I got when they were all here. He thinks he hides it well."

"As long as he didn't lie about being able to ride a horse." I smirked at her. "It won't matter. We'll teach him everything. I can't afford to be that picky."

"He's in good hands with you." That blush returned. "I can tell you're a good boss."

"I've had worse." I shrugged. It was my father, but I didn't say it. The sympathy that lit her eyes told me she'd heard it regardless.

"You and your siblings turned into amazing people."

"We've had our rough patches." I rested my arms on my thighs. "We also saw how Barns treated Mama. Don't get me wrong, she didn't treat us the best, but what she had to deal with in a husband?" I shook my head. I couldn't imagine behaving like that around Lily. Making her stay with me because she had no choice.

Wasn't that the position she was in?

Men are poison to women, Eliot. Mom's haughty voice haunted me. I hadn't understood her words at the time, but I sure as fuck remembered them as an adult.

"I'm sorry for what she went through." Lily saved me from starting a comparison chart between my marriage and my parents'. "If the silver lining is a guy who'd drop everything to drive three hours and clean up vomit, I guess there could've been a worse turnout."

"Anytime, Lily."

Her smile wavered, and she licked her lips like she was nervous. They glistened, not quite as plump as after I'd kissed her. How easy would it be to dip my head down and capture that mouth again?

"I'm sure I pulled you away from something way more interesting," she said. "I mean, I'm sure Cali did."

"I was at the bar."

"Oh." Those ripe lips of hers stuck farther out. "I'm sorry. You were out having fun—"

"No, Lily. I wasn't having fun. I was chatting with an ex of Wilder's about how in love he is—and always has been—with Sutton."

"Maybe she was scoping you out."

"Doesn't matter." I wiggled the finger with the ring on it. "Married. Remember?"

"Hmm... I seem to recall something about that."

"Last night sucked for you, I have no doubt. But it's one of the most interesting Friday nights I've had in a long time." I stared into the distance to avoid her gaze. Bug was trotting around the yard, ready to investigate any moving thing. The breeze was growing colder, and I didn't want Lily to catch a chill.

I rose and held my hand out to her. "What movie is next on the list?"

The awe and disbelief in her gaze could give me a complex. I wasn't her hero. But if she left this marriage knowing how a man should treat her, I'd consider that the biggest success in my life.

Cali opened the front door, blinking. Her hair was messed up on one side. She must've slept hard. "Mom, Flakes isn't in his cage."

🐎

Lily

Flakes was found curled up inside a cabinet his tank sat on. The door had been left cracked open. There had only been thirty minutes of panicked searching. Eliot had blanched like he'd never sleep in that room again. If he didn't like Flakes, he'd never said, and he'd helped look for him without hesitation. Kellan had awakened when Cali started calling Flakes like he was a puppy.

My heart rate had finally returned to normal.

I was cuddled on the couch with Cali between me

and Eliot. Kellan was in his swing, his eyelids droopy. We'd already eaten dinner, and his bedtime was soon. Eliot had made us his special pancakes and eggs for supper.

We were on our second run of *Snow White*. Cali wanted to dress like the poisoned apple lady for Halloween. Not quite a witch, but different enough to satisfy her requirements. If she caught wind that Cody had invited us to do the Halloween thing with him, she'd talk about little else until then.

I might have to take Cody up on the offer. It'd keep my mind off Eliot's absence.

"I think she's asleep," Eliot murmured.

I peeked down. Sure enough, her eyes were closed, and her head was tipped on his shoulder.

"Poor thing is still recovering from the week. School and being sick takes a lot out of her." I was about to move to carry her to bed, but he shifted to stand while keeping her from falling to the side.

"I got her."

The sight of him carefully picking her up and carrying her to her bedroom would stay with me forever. Her dad had never had time to just sit and enjoy the evening. I knew if we were at Eliot's place, he'd probably be working until sundown and even later. But when he didn't have to be here in the first place, this was nice.

The sight of his broad back in full flex was sexy. A flush fired across my skin, and it had nothing to do with being sick. I'd felt great all day.

When he returned, he dropped into Cali's spot. We weren't touching, but he was close.

"Think it's time for something that's not animated?"

He grabbed the remote, and I tugged half the blanket over his lap.

"Sure. What do you like?"

"You should know by now that I'm fine with whatever you like."

He was always spoiling me, but this time, I wasn't delighted at the way he coddled me. The smallest favor I could return was picking a show he liked. "What do you like to watch?"

He slid his gaze toward me. "Anything."

"When you have the chance to watch TV, what do you pick?"

His eyes narrowed slightly, like he couldn't figure out why I wouldn't just choose something I enjoyed. "I like a superhero movie as much as the next guy."

"DC or Marvel?"

He straightened the blanket over him. "I dunno. I guess I like them all."

"Is there one you haven't seen and you want to?"

He twisted to face me. "What's this about?"

"I want to know what you like."

"No, you don't."

Now my irritation was notching up. "Yes. I do."

"Just pick a show."

"It pleases me to do something you like to do."

"You don't want to know what I like to do."

I rolled my eyes. Stubborn man. "You can say it, you know. It's okay to let others know what you want—"

"I like to fuck, Lily."

I snapped my mouth shut. My pulse kicked up faster the more his words sank in. I heard him wrong. That was it. "I don't know if that's DC or Marvel."

Incredulity widened his eyes, then he laughed. His

Adam's apple bobbed with the deep, pleasing sound. "I haven't seen the latest DC, but I don't recall seeing sex, or even tits, in either franchise."

Lust rammed into my belly. I clenched my thighs together. "Then you haven't been looking. Those costumes don't hide a lot in the females."

He held my gaze. "I've been looking, just not at theirs."

I sucked in air. Did he mean...mine?

I gazed up at him. He was still turned toward me. At some point in our conversation, I pivoted to face him, like I was a sunflower and he was the sun.

I ran my tongue along my lower lip. His gaze lowered to watch, then lifted back to me.

My heart skipped at least two beats. "I don't think mine are—"

"That's where you're wrong. I like them very much."

He hadn't seen them. Last night, they'd been covered. By a wet towel.

His gaze was still glued to mine like he was waiting to see what I'd do.

I had no idea what to do. I wasn't a femme fatale. I'd been a harried, easy target for a man who had wanted a housekeeper, a cheap employee, then a mom. "I like your muscles," I blurted out.

A dark brow lifted. "My muscles?"

"You have a lot of them."

He nodded, thoughtful. "You know what else I like?" He had my rapt attention. "The way your lower lip is bigger than your upper lip. It gets nice and plump when you lick and nibble it, and Christ, Lily, I want to taste it again."

"Why don't you?" I could groan. The answer was obvious. "Never mind. Last night—"

A low growl rumbled from him, then his mouth was on mine.

Desire raged through my body. His lips were firm but gentle. He was tense until I ran a hand through the dark locks of his hair. I clenched a fist in them. I'd only put my hands and mouth on him, but I knew I'd never get enough.

He relaxed as if he'd been holding himself back. I was slowly pushed backward until I was underneath him. I stretched my legs out around him.

God, his weight over me, pressing me into the cushions? I could come from that alone. Had it been that long since I'd gotten off?

Yes. But also, it was him. I was never this responsive.

I wound my arms around his neck. He licked against the seam of my mouth, asking for me to open. He didn't have to. I'd do anything this man wanted. I widened the cradle my legs made until he was settled between my thighs. I rocked up into him, and a low groan vibrated through his chest. I did it again, and he went taut.

He released my mouth. "Goddamn, you keep doing that and I'm going to come in my pants."

"Me too." I rolled my hips into him again. Electricity radiated out from the juncture between my thighs. I could feel that I was wet.

He nibbled a path from my jaw to my ear. "Do you need to come, Lily?"

The way his voice rumbled straight into my eardrum sent shivers across my body. The shudder added to the way I was thrusting my hips against him. There was a perfectly large ridge in his pants, and it was the exact place

I needed it the most. A ton of pesky clothes were in the way, but the promise of a climax was in sight.

Part of my brain said that wasn't possible. I could not orgasm with all my clothes on. Dry humping was never enough.

My pussy didn't care. My clit was too starved to listen to reason. And when he gripped my ass and pulled me hard to rock against the monster erection his jeans were holding back, I wrapped my legs around his waist. My mind was no longer invited to the party.

He nibbled a path down my neck. The moan that left me sounded like it was right from a phone sex call. I wouldn't know what that sounded like, but it wasn't a sound I normally made. Just like being this close to a peak wasn't something I did without a ton of stimulation and some impatient grumbles from my partner.

He braced himself on the armrest behind my head and ground into me. Another ragged moan left my body. "Eliot," I groaned.

"Are you going to come for me?" He dug a knee into the cushions, keeping himself anchored while I rubbed myself all over him.

"Yes," I gasped. "Oh god, yes."

"I want to taste that little clit of yours."

I couldn't make a sound. My desire clogged around my vocal cords, building into a giant bank of thunderclouds that were ready to unleash every spark of energy they'd collected since the last time I'd orgasmed, months and months—a year?—ago.

"Eliot," I said on a whine.

"I bet it tastes as sweet as this pouty lip." He nipped my mouth, then licked where his teeth had been. "Come for me."

I did exactly as he asked. I shattered. I arched into him, my head digging into the armrest. I couldn't move him, which only kept me in place to ride out the tsunami wave of ecstasy that crashed over me.

He kissed up my neck and placed a sweet peck on the side of my mouth. "That was fucking beautiful."

"I don't usually— I don't." I couldn't catch my breath, but embarrassment was also starting to sink in. "I'm not like this."

"Like what? Expressive?"

Yes. "I usually have a hard time...you know...finishing." Maybe the baby hormones fixed something that was broken? But with his solid weight over me and his large erection trapped between us, I didn't think so. He could get a granite statue to climax. "It's new. Thank you."

His chuckle lightly shook both our bodies. "Anytime, Lily pad." He lifted his head to study me, his expression questioning.

Anytime. We were married. We were adults. I swallowed. The afterglow from my peak washed away in the onslaught of nerves. He said he wouldn't fool around while we were married. He must be feeling the strain. "We could, you know. Do it anytime."

The muscles in his jaw flexed, and his gaze stroked over my face. "We are married."

"Just what I was thinking." I dragged a hand through his messy locks. "Seems a waste to abstain if we both want to."

"I do want to," he murmured, easing my anxiety that his desire stemmed from having no other option. His gaze softened with an almost smile, then concern took over. "I don't have condoms."

Oh. Shit. "I'm not on birth control."

"I can bring them next time."

"When is that?"

He thought for a moment, then kept thinking. "How many weeks away is Halloween?"

Weeks. I wanted this man inside me now. But I'd taken on a large dog that was still in his puppy years. I couldn't add another baby. I wouldn't make this man feel baby-trapped after what his mother went through. "Six weeks."

He groaned. "Dammit, Lily. That's a long fucking time away."

"We have to make this work for a year. I'm not burning you out with traveling in the first six months."

"Wilder and Sutton made it work when they had the same living situation. We can do this."

"And I can tell my aunt that if she stops by, we're still newlyweds, and we were so swept away that we had no idea the logistics would be such an obstacle."

A shadow flickered over his expression. "Yes. Your aunt. She hasn't seemed to care so far."

I didn't want to talk about the reason why we married. I was already tired of that being the motivator between us. The fantasy was getting sapped out of this moment.

"We'll make it work when we can." I slid my arm between us and curled my fingers around the hard line behind his zipper. "But right now, I think I can help with this."

Fifteen

ELIOT

My mind was getting fucking blown. I gripped the sheets on the bed I normally slept in alone. I was sitting on the edge of the mattress with my jeans around my goddamn ankles. She hadn't waited for either of us to undress. She ripped open my fly, and as soon as her warm hand gripped my shaft, my brain shut off.

She was kneeling on the floor in front of me. I'd never be able to get a second of shut-eye in this room again with this memory.

Her dark hair framed her face. The room was dark, but her hollowed cheeks were visible. I wanted to hold on, to make this last, but it'd been a long time since I'd gotten off. And then there was that earth-shattering experience on the couch.

So fucking amazing.

Now, the tables were turned. She had me at her mercy

with the way she kneaded my balls while pumping the base of my shaft. Then she did a swirl with her tongue.

"Fuck, Lily. I'm going to blow." I said it as a warning, but she took it like she had my permission to increase suction.

She had all my permission, but the energy coiling at the base of my spine grew impossibly stronger, more charged. How the fuck was I going to stay quiet while coming?

Another tongue flick at the crown of my erection and fuck— I was done. "Lily." Her name came out strangled.

She didn't back off.

Electricity shot through my body and exploded down my cock. My release shot out, but she didn't let go, drinking all of me in, working me with her tongue and her hands. Sheer ecstasy filled me to overflowing, and I had to close my eyes and clench my teeth to keep from roaring her name.

"Fuck. Lily." I had only two words left in my vocabulary. "Fuck."

She finally released me. I dragged her up to the bed with me before I fell backward. She drew her legs up while mine hung down. My dick was probably bobbing in the air, but the door was closed and locked.

If we both got our way and a box of condoms, my cock would be out around her behind closed doors whenever possible. "Christ, woman. That was amazing."

"I'm glad you liked it," she said in a way that made me think her prick of an ex was an ass about that too.

"Fucking unforgettable." I stared at the ceiling. There was no looking at the clock and wondering how best to leave. "And it's not because it's the first time I've had a snake for an audience."

She giggled. "Flakes isn't a prude, and he doesn't gossip."

"Good to know."

"I can move him so you don't have a roommate when you stay over."

"I'm not a snake guy, but after being afraid he was lost, I warmed up to him." I pressed a kiss to her temple. "I kind of like having you next to me in bed."

She rolled up to an elbow and traced her fingers down my shirt. "I like it too."

"You wanna sleep in here tonight?" I was more nervous asking to have her in my bed than asking her on a date. I hadn't done that yet either.

She chewed on the corner of her lip. "Each kid has their own bedroom. I was going to move in here eventually." Her brow furrowed. "Cali knows we're married. And it'd be more believable if others came over."

Believable. Right. But if that meant she wasn't leaving my side, then I was good with it. I didn't have condoms, but I had a lot of ideas. "Hey, Lily?"

"Mm?"

"Get those pants off. I'm not done with you yet."

♞

Eliot

A ding woke me. I cracked an eye open. A round bottom was pressed into my side, and I did not want to move. When had I ever woken up this comfortable? I usually didn't linger in bed. There were chores. Guys to touch base with. A full day of work.

Another chime sounded through the house.

The warm body next to me shifted. Lily.

She'd put on a shirt and pajama shorts before bed. I was in a pair of basketball shorts in case Cali walked in.

"Mo-om!" Cali called as if summoned. "Someone's ringing the doorbell."

Kellan let out a cry. It wasn't an *I've got to eat now* sound, but he wouldn't last long.

"Who's visiting this early?" Lily groaned and sat up.

Exactly what I'd like to know. I could've been ensconced with her for a few more minutes. The kids might've slept in.

I checked the time on my phone. It was after nine. Oh. We all slept in.

Lily rolled out of bed. She wasn't wearing a bra, and I was captivated by her chest. Unbound tits, full and—

Knocking resounded through the house.

"I'll get it." My morning wood was flagging enough to hide with a loose shirt. I threw on the same one I'd been wearing last night. Lily's sunshine scent was all over it and goddamn. I might never wash it.

I snuck down the hall. Pebbles meowed and rubbed against the entry to the kitchen. "Cali, can you feed the cat?" I asked as I made my way to the front door. I didn't bother to check who it was when I opened it.

Linda stared back at me. Her brows lifted. "Oh. Eliot. You're here."

The surprise in her voice was like sandpaper on my eardrums. "Why wouldn't I be?" I asked with more heat than intended. I didn't appreciate her reminder that I woke up with Lily because it was best for appearance.

She blinked rapidly. "I talked to my brother. He said

Jasper was going to work for you. You still work in Montana?"

She might not have heard about the specifics, and she didn't know about my workforce issues. This was an organic time to play them up. "I'm not around as much, so I need another employee. We're still trying to figure out the commuting. Having Jasper might help me get away more."

More freedom wasn't the reason I'd hired Jasper. The ranch needed me as a full-time employee more than anyone else. I didn't like faking that I was living with my wife. I hadn't needed to officially change addresses. Everything I did was under Knight's Arabians and Cattle Company.

"Hmm." There was a crease in her brow. She looked past my shoulder. "Good morning, Lily."

"Aunt Linda? Hi." Lily appeared next to me. Kellan was getting louder. She must've seen her aunt and come to rescue me. "Do you want to come inside?"

I should've offered, but I was still cranky about feeling like I'd lied to her.

"No, it's early. I'm sorry to bother both of you. I was just doing a check-in to satisfy the requirement of the trust." The corners of her eyes pinched. "Darren and I are heading out of town."

"No problem." Lily folded her arms. She'd put on a bra. Another reason to be cranky about the intrusion. "Going anywhere fun?"

"To Rapid City. Just a little getaway." She let out a heavy exhale. "I've been inundated with questions and inquiries regarding..." She waved a hand around. "All this."

Sympathy filled Lily's face. She had a big heart. I didn't feel sorry for Linda.

"Who's been hounding you?" Lily asked.

Linda's mouth tightened. "Your father, of course. He's not used to not being in charge. And Violet. She keeps double and triple-checking my interpretation of the stipulations."

"I hope that's a sign she doesn't want to marry Willis."

Linda snorted. "I would never sign off on them after a year. I doubt West would either."

Lily hugged herself tighter. "You wouldn't? You'd really attest that Violet and Willis didn't meet the requirements?"

I heard our names instead of her sister and her boyfriend. At the end of our year, would Linda really claim our arrangement was bullshit? My pulse thudded. I didn't intend to give her a reason to think Lily and I weren't legit, but Linda had six relationships to sign off on before she got her own inheritance. Most people wouldn't look beyond the dollars.

"Of course." Linda blinked owlish eyes. "I care about all of you, and I know your grandma wanted the best for you." She hesitated. "May I come in after all?"

I stepped back. Lily had already invited her inside. "I can get some breakfast ready for all of us."

"I won't be long. I just—"

Kellan started crying again. Cali came out of her room, fully clothed in a ball gown and a tiara. She scooted behind Lily and eyed her great-aunt.

"You can attend to the baby," Linda said with a stiff tone. "I don't have long, but I don't want to rush what I have to tell you."

Lily exchanged a worried glance with me. I gave her an encouraging smile. We were doing nothing to make Linda think we weren't a real couple. She went to the bedroom.

"Have a seat while I get Cali something to eat." I gestured to the recliner. Cali tucked her hand into mine. "Want some toast, boss lady?" That earned me a smile.

By the time I was done making toast and Cali was at the table where we could see her, Lily was in the living room with Linda. Kellan was strapped into his bouncy chair and willing to wait a few minutes before he nursed.

I sat next to Lily on the couch. I took her hand in mine. The gesture wasn't for show. She was tense, her mouth set in a line. She should be as content and relaxed as she'd been in bed next to me.

Linda glanced at us both. She folded her hands. "Before you were born, I was married to someone else. Darren is my second marriage."

Lily straightened. "Really?"

I was mildly surprised, but Lily hadn't known?

Linda nodded. "I thought it was true love. Quick and impulsive but pure." Sadness infused her eyes, and she looked older than her sixty-some years. "On my end, maybe. He just saw an easy life. The oil boom was happening, and we had wells on our land. Both Weston and I drove new cars. I didn't have loans from college. He thought he was getting a free ride."

"I'm so sorry, Aunt Linda."

I was, too, but I could see where this was going. Linda had been deeply hurt by this man, used, and she'd make sure that didn't happen to Lily or her siblings. It was why she was in charge of the trust and not her brother.

"When I learned the real reason why he married me"

—she squeezed her hands into fists—"I was devastated. I can't describe the pain. And the divorce." Her laugh was full of scorn. "We spent so much money fighting him. In the end, I had to pay him spousal support. For years. If his bad decision didn't cut his life short, I'd probably still be paying it." She made a disgusted sound. "He had a good lawyer. Poor Darren had an ironclad prenup slapped in front of him as soon as he proposed."

Lily's fingers twisted around mine.

"This isn't easy." She circled her hand like she was talking about everything around her. "Having to decide if the man you married really loves you. But I will. No one will take advantage of a Duke again. And since you left that worthless piece of trash, you are a Duke again."

I didn't want to like Linda when she had so much influence on her niece, but the way she spoke about Carter put us on the same side.

"I'm a Knight now. You were ready to kick me out," Lily said flatly. "All because I wasn't married."

Linda's features tightened. "Like I said, this isn't easy. I was tempted to call your bluff that day in the office, but I thought worst-case scenario, it gave you time to move."

"You didn't believe me?"

That had made two of us that day when I first heard about Lily's situation.

Linda nodded. "Not at first, but here you both are. After all I went through, and all my divorce put my parents through, my mother trusted me with this legacy. She knew West and I would do our best to make sure you all are seriously happy before we sign off. Do I want my share of the inheritance?" Her laugh was barely more than a breath. "It'd make retirement more comfortable, but I take my duty seriously. Both your father and I do."

"Lily shouldn't have had to worry about being homeless." My tone was harsh, but I didn't care. Lily gave my hand a reassuring squeeze. "Now we have to stress that you'll kick her out again because I'm not here enough."

Linda lifted her chin. "I acknowledge this is just as hard for you. But if you're truly in love, then I can live with you having to rush the wedding."

Rush the wedding. Lily's grip would've been painful for a lesser man. I was losing feeling in my fingertips.

I couldn't move in permanently, but I had to do what I could to put Lily's mind at ease after her aunt's visit. "I trust you won't hold it against us that I run a business three hours away, and this transition might take longer as I'm entering my busy season."

Linda didn't respond right away. Lily's grip grew impossibly harder.

"You can trust that I'm not looking at that *alone*." She sucked in a breath and let it out slowly. "I really do want you happy, Lily. You were always such a precocious child, and I know West worries about all of you."

"I appreciate that," Lily said rigidly. "As long as you appreciate the pressure this puts on me. On our relationship."

On our fake marriage. What Linda said made sense, it made her the guardian in her eyes, but Lily and her siblings shouldn't have had constraints on any inheritance left behind. It created a lot of stress for the recipients.

"I do respect what you're going through. I was glad to see Eliot open the door." She smiled, and it softened her features. A whole different woman. "You two look happy."

"We are," I said without hesitation.

"Good. Well." She looked around like she was making

sure she had everything, but she hadn't had a thing when she entered. "I should get going. Darren wanted to leave an hour ago."

Lily walked her to the door. After Linda was gone, she closed the door and slumped against it. "Oh my god, that was close. If Cali hadn't called you…"

I wouldn't be here.

Lily needed more of an effort from me. "I'll come back in two weeks."

"No."

Had I imagined the weekend? Was she second-guessing everything that had happened between us and deciding we needed more distance?

"No," she said again. "You've been worried about how busy you'll be. We can make it until Halloween." Her smile was shy. "But I'll miss you."

"I'll miss you too." I sauntered closer to her. "But know that when I land on your doorstep again, I'm going to have a big box of condoms."

LILY

It was only the beginning of October. I had to go through the entire month before I could see Eliot again.

I clicked the TV off. The house was quiet. The kids and the dog were asleep. Pebbles was snoozing in her cat tower in the corner. She was not a fan of the snake aquarium that I'd moved next to the tower along the wall, but she didn't protest enough to sleep somewhere else.

I was sleeping regularly in Grandma's old bedroom. Safe to say, it was my bedroom now.

Eliot had only stayed over three weekends, but the house was empty without him. I couldn't look at the kitchen on nights like this and not picture us dancing. This bedroom was a mindfuck. I'd gotten new sheets and bedding, but none of the memories with Eliot were attached to them. So I hadn't put them on yet.

New mattresses would be arriving soon. I couldn't very well leave them in the hallway. They wouldn't fit, and I had arranged for the deliverers to haul out the old ones.

If I got any more pathetic, I'd be in the closet, sniffing his shirts. Thankfully, I hadn't done that. Yet.

I trudged to bed and set the baby monitor on the nightstand. Kellan had been sleeping mostly through the night.

Before I crawled under the covers, I shot off a **Good night** text to Eliot. We'd been texting more, but despite what happened between us in this very room, the messages hadn't been more than check-ins. I refused to seem needy.

The neediness inside me was not just emotional.

How are you guys? From him.

Doing well. He slept through the night! I didn't tell him when Kellan was fussy.

Way to go, champ!

I was staring at my phone. With a sigh, I crawled between the covers.

Jasper had started working with Eliot. Should I text him and make sure everything's okay?

What was I worried about? That Eliot realized I wasn't worth the wait and was at the bar? Was Wilder's ex hot and interested in him?

Gah! I was never like this.

But then, I'd never gotten the butterflies in my stomach like I did with Eliot. I'd never gotten off like I did with Eliot.

My phone buzzed. I should be ashamed of how quickly I scrambled for the phone.

Eliot: You awake?

Me: Yes

I kept staring at my phone. When it vibrated, I nearly dropped it on my face. He was calling.

I answered with a "Hey."

"Hey. Did I catch you at a bad time?"

My breathlessness was from my scramble to answer. "No. I'm in bed."

"I wanted to hear your voice."

"Oh." I did a little wiggle. Pure giddiness. "Well, here I am."

"You sound as sexy as ever."

I didn't recognize my giggle. I didn't make those sounds. "So do you. The first thing I noticed about you was your voice."

"The first? I need to work on my ass."

More laughter. "I was a little distracted the first time. I could barely look at you."

"I noticed. I thought I had cookie on my face, but I didn't even have one because Bug knocked them over and ate them."

"I was a mess that day."

"A cute mess."

Cute. There it was again.

"You weren't a mess," Eliot reassured me. "Or was it the cute that silenced you? Oh shit, it was cute. I said it the night we first kissed, and you got quiet."

"No, cute's fine."

"I can't quit looking at your tits. How about that?"

I grinned. "I like that."

"You're sexy as fuck, Lily."

"You don't have to—"

"You're adorable. You're cute. But I can't quit thinking about how much you'd flush once I buried myself inside of you and got you off again. If that's not sexy, I don't know what is."

Heat coursed through my veins and a throb hummed between my thighs. "When you put it that way…"

"Trust me. I'd put it a lot of ways if we were in the same room."

"What exactly would you do?" Horror flashed cold into my lungs. I did not just ask that.

"You really want to know?" His voice was deep and rough.

"Yes," I whispered, afraid he'd keep going but terrified he'd stop.

There was a rustle of clothing on the other end. "You said you were in bed? Are you alone?"

"Yes."

"Slide that hand of yours down your belly and tell me how wet you are."

Shivers of arousal rippled over my skin, but I did as he asked. I closed my eyes, moved my sleep top out of the way, and imagined it was his calloused fingertips running over my abdomen.

I delved into my slick seam and let out a moan.

"How wet are you?" he asked, his voice low.

"So wet."

"I bet that clit of yours is as puffy as your bottom lip."

I licked my lips like I had to verify what he said.

"Rub it for me, Lily pad."

The nickname did it for me. Hearing it in his low growl? I could get off without touching myself.

I traced a finger around my swollen nub. "Eliot."

"I bet it's so fucking wet. Make circles and imagine it's my tongue."

I widened my legs, my hips pumping. I could feel his weight over me, his hot breath in my ear, and his groans vibrating through me. "That'd feel so good."

"Christ, you're probably so hot I'd sear my skin. Do you know what I'm doing?"

"No," I said on a gasp, lost in the fantasy. All I had wanted was a good-night text, but I was getting way more. He couldn't be in the same bed, but this was a close second.

"I've got my hand around my cock, and I'm fisting it tight. I can feel how wet and hot you'd be, gripping me so fucking hard."

I whimpered. He made me so needy, and he never seemed to mind.

"Can you get a finger in?"

"Yes." I adjusted my position and pushed a finger inside. He'd be so much bigger, so much harder.

"Ride it, Lily."

I did as he asked. "I wish it was you."

Another growl came over the line. "It will be. Soon."

"Eliot. I'm close."

"Me too, Lily."

"Eliot?" I didn't know what I was asking. Permission? Acceptance? I'd never had phone sex before.

"Let go. Let me hear you."

I had both his permission and his acceptance. My detonation was hard to keep silent. Whimpers and gasps came out of me. I dug my teeth into the lip Eliot seemed obsessed with.

"That's it. Ride it out. Fuuuck." He made similar sounds to me. Grunts and groans. Heavy breathing. I loved every second. He got off on the phone with me.

He'd said I was sexy and then he'd proved it while I was in a different town. A different state.

"Eliot?"

"Yeah?"

"This was my first time." I rested my hand on my abdomen. If he was here, I'd roll into him and cuddle. He hadn't pushed me away yet.

"Since you have two kids, I'm going to assume you're talking about over the phone."

I giggled. "I didn't give birth to Cali, but yes."

"Get used to it. I'm gonna have to call you every night."

"I'm gonna have to answer." I'd go to bed early if I knew this was waiting after I crawled between the sheets.

"I have to be as quiet as you. Your brother is across the hall."

"Seriously?"

"Yup. My half-retired bookkeeper doesn't have to take on extra duties when I'm gone. Jasper can be up here answering the phone and teaching Chambers how to use new apps."

It was nice to hear my family could help Eliot as much as his had helped me.

A gusty sigh came over the line. "Halloween ain't gonna come fast enough."

"No, it's not."

"I like you, Lily. I know we're married, but this, what we did when I was there last, it's not because I'm trying to convince your aunt about a damn thing."

"I know." My response was heavy. I didn't really know, did I? He told me he wanted me, so why was it so hard to believe him?

"My hand is full of cum because of you, and I'm alone in my room. No witnesses. But next time I see you, I'm going to prove it. Maybe I can take you on a date."

"Mr. Knight, are you asking me out?"

"Yes, I am, Mrs. Knight. Now I'm going to let you go to sleep because I know those kids get up early. Then I'm going to call you tomorrow night, and I want to hear those needy little moans again."

Eliot

I sat at the kitchen island, tapping into my phone. Jasper was usually out most nights and I had the house to myself. I thought the kids would be in bed, but Lily had sent me a picture of Cali and Bug playing in the early October snowfall they were getting.

The jumbo box of condoms I had bought sat unopened in my bedroom by the duffel I usually packed when I went to see Lily. Three more weeks and I'd get to see Lily again. Phone sex with her was on another level, but it was nothing like having her come apart in my arms.

As much as I looked forward to calling her in the evenings, I enjoyed our messaging throughout the day. The guys gave me shit for looking at my phone so much.

Me: Who's having more fun, Cali or Bug?

Lily: No contest—both. The dog and the girl are fast asleep.

Me: Kellan too?

Lily: I have a quiet house. Even the cat is in Cali's bed.

Me: What are you wearing?

She sent an image. She'd held her phone high and shot a picture of herself giving me a sultry smile while also showing off her kitty-cat pajama pants and a top that had a saucer of milk.

I laughed. She didn't have to explain her clothing. She was still nursing and would think having a milk graphic on her shirt was hilarious. I did too, and I liked that she was comfortable enough around me to be herself.

Lily: Before you get taken over with lust, I should tell you we have a fish now.

I was taken over with lust regardless, but I had to hear about the fish. And I wanted her voice in my ear.

"How'd that happen?" I asked when she answered.

A soft chuckle gusted over the line. "We went snow pants and boots shopping in Bismarck. In the pet aisle, we saw this little betta struggling. He's so pretty, but he wasn't doing so hot in his little container. So…"

She'd never have left that fish behind. "You bought everything he needed, and now he's in his new palace."

"He visibly started doing better right away. You should see him. He's got the prettiest blue fins."

"I think you're going to outdo Aggie on the rescue front."

"I do have room for a horse or two and enough veterinarian connections to mitigate the cost. Cali's been asking about riding lessons. A lot of kids in her class do 4-H and rodeo."

If I was closer, or hell, lived in the same zip code, I could teach Cali how to ride. I could even provide the horse. I'd know its lineage and have all the records of its training and temperament. But I wasn't there. "Whenever you're ready, I could talk to Aggie and Ansen and see if they had a good lead on a pony for Cali to get her started."

"That sounds nice." She paused. "What are you wearing?" There was a slight teasing note in her tone.

I snapped a pic of myself. I had all my clothes on, and my hair was crushed from wearing a hat all day, but I sent it anyway.

"Hot stuff."

"That's what an older lady at the grocery store said the other day. I think she was the mom of a classmate."

Her laughter was music to my ears. "You're telling me I have competition?"

"Nah, Lily. There's no one else with tits that fill out the saucer of milk on your shirt. In fact, I think you need to slide your hand down those pajama pants."

"I've never gotten off so many times in my life as I have this last month."

That was exactly what I wanted to hear. I'd make this year of marriage worthwhile for her. "Are you wet for me, Lily?" I asked her that each time, and each time, I lived for the answer.

That earned me a small gasp. "Yes."

"Then I'll have you coming in no time." I had to shift positions on the stool. My zipper was biting into my erection. I could go to my bedroom, but I liked talking her through an orgasm, out in the open, like I could do it anytime I wanted to.

"Circle that tight little bud with your finger." I kept the phone to my ear, propped my other elbow on the island, and sank my head into my hand. I widened my legs to take the pressure of my pants off my dick. It didn't help, but I liked the intensity. I could pretend it was her pressing against me.

Her moan came through the line and went straight to my cock. I could imagine pumping in and out of her. I knew how her walls rippled when she climaxed, how she'd squeeze me.

"Do you need more?" I asked, my voice rough.

"Yes," she said on an exhale.

"Push one finger inside and ride your palm."

Another ragged groan. Fuck, she did everything I asked. I curled over the phone like it was my lifeline. My heartbeat thrummed in my erection, but I was focused on her. "Pump in and out."

"Eliot." There was the needy whine I loved so goddamn much.

A door banged open. "Hey, the new man of the house is home."

Fucking Jasper. Her yelp was a bucket of water to my libido.

"Is that my brother?"

"Yes," I said tightly.

"Oh, hey." Jasper appeared from the hallway. He'd come through the garage dressed in clean jeans and a flannel. Why wasn't he at the bar? "Any chance that's Lily on the phone?"

"Yes," I answered him with all my irritation.

He continued into the kitchen, oblivious to his massive intrusion, and went to the fridge. "Hi, Lily!"

"This is so embarrassing," she whispered.

"She says hi," I told him. He was clueless about my glare stabbing him between the shoulder blades. He'd been sleeping his way through the single-women population of Buffalo Gully, or so I assumed since he was gone most evenings and was a bleary-eyed mess in the mornings. I could've gone to bed with the sounds of her orgasm in my ear. I'd be fresh as a daisy in the morning, thanks to my Lily.

"Did he catch you with your pants down?" she asked.

With my dick in my hand? Thankfully not, but I couldn't say that out loud. "No. I'm sitting at the island." I continued to glower at Jasper. He turned from the fridge. His hoodie said King Oil and had a giant oil well in the middle. When he'd arrived, he'd dressed for the job like the other guys. I couldn't place him in an office working on a computer all day. "And he's raiding my fridge."

Jasper leaned back to peer at me. "I bought groceries last week. Why are you so grumpy?"

Another light chuckle came over the line. "Cock-blocked by my brother. I'm going to bed, and I'm going to finish what you started."

I made a choking sound. Could I ask her to record it? Send me a picture? Dammit! I would miss out. "Don't you dare."

Jasper narrowed his eyes at me like he was afraid I was talking to him.

"Don't what?" she asked innocently and damn if that didn't get my blood flowing to all the wrong places when I was in the same room as her brother. "Don't come really hard while thinking about you?" she purred.

"I didn't know you had a mean streak," I growled into the phone.

Jasper let the fridge door fall shut. "Did I walk in on something I shouldn't have?"

I ignored him. "Lily—Halloween." I said it like a warning.

"I look forward to it. I might even show you what I'm going to do to myself in bed tonight. Good night, Eliot."

She disconnected. Who knew when I met that girl she'd be the ultimate tease?

I squeezed my eyes shut. How the hell was I going to last until Halloween without taking three showers a day and jacking off? I hadn't even been that bad in high school.

I clicked my phone off and buried my face in my hands. I could not hurt my wife's brother. He was my family, if only until the summer, and he was my employee.

"I don't want to know, do I?" Jasper asked.

"No."

He contemplated me. All that rummaging in the fridge and his hands were empty. "So you two are actually a thing?"

Crankiness was setting in. Yes. No. Sort of? "We're married."

"On paper. But come on, man."

The arousal from earlier was doused as thoroughly as a week-old campfire. "Come on, what?"

"I love my sister, but we all know you caught her when she was a train wreck."

I bristled at his description.

He just shrugged. "You can't convince me that a freshly divorced mom, with a newborn no less, a house that still smells like my grandma, with vet school debt that her douche of an ex made sure stayed in her name before he married her was exactly the kind of woman you were looking for."

"I wasn't looking."

He gave me a steady stare.

What would they think if they knew we'd gotten physical? Neither of us wanted to hear that maybe fooling around when we were supposed to be married in name only wasn't a good idea. Lily wouldn't want her family to know. Mine did, but we understood, and my siblings would stay out of her life.

"I like her."

His gaze stayed steady. The most serious I'd seen him. "You like her, or she's convenient?"

If he wasn't looking out for his sister's best interest, I'd want to deck him. "I like her. And it's none of your business."

"But it is. She's my sister, and I care about her."

"She's my wife, and I care about her."

"And when the year is up?"

That goddamn deadline. This was why I'd been happy with no one knowing. "I can't move."

"Can't or don't want to?"

I pushed away from the island. At least my erection was gone. "Like I said, it's none of your business."

"Don't hurt her, or it will be."

"Yeah, and what'd you do to Carter?" I was being a dick, but it seemed like her family only butted in when she called them desperate.

"Just so happens the IRS might be taking a hard look at the books of his vet clinic, and the soon-to-be ex-husband of the woman he left Lily for might've been sent time-stamped photos of the two cheating assholes that'll only strengthen the settlement he gets in the divorce."

I sputtered, "Holy shit."

He grabbed a banana from the counter next to the fridge. "Lily hates when we interfere, and Carter did his best to make her feel like shit for it. But that doesn't mean we're going to sit back and do nothing."

My respect for him grew stronger. "If I do anything

remotely as damaging as that prick, you have my permission to destroy me."

His gaze turned appraising. He seemed pleased. "As long as we have an understanding. Just don't tell me what I walked in on. I'd like to keep this banana down."

Seventeen

LILY

Snow was still on the ground. We'd gotten more last night, and today, the wind picked up. The roads were icy in the western half of the state, stretching into Montana.

Eliot: No travel advised.

He wasn't going to make it.

Disappointment ripped through me like the cold wind outside, leaving a chill behind. I'd been so excited. I had shaved everywhere and even bought some new bras and underwear. I was wearing them under my thick knit sweater and jeans. They would be lost on Halloween, but I could enjoy the effort. I'd wear them tonight when he called.

I adjusted Cali's black cloak over her winter coat. "Are you sure you don't want a stocking hat under the witch hat?"

I'd had to rig a tie for the hat to keep it from blowing

away while we trick-or-treated. Kellan was tucked into his car seat.

"No hat." She shook her head. With the way she was bundled up underneath her costume, she looked like an abominable snow witch.

"I'll pack one, just in case."

The roads weren't bad enough to shut us in. I lived close enough to town that the deicer and gravel had been judiciously used.

"Why can't Eliot come?" Cali asked as I slid into the driver's seat.

"The roads are too bad." I coasted down the driveway.

"Ivy's Snow White." Cali brandished an apple from her cloak. She managed to coordinate the costume with Ivy at school.

"I heard."

"Will we get to see the babies?"

Sutton and Wilder had their twins. I'd seen a picture of the boys—Alex and Drew. Eliot had mentioned something about them being named after game show hosts, which made sense with the different sayings Sutton would utter.

In the photo, there were two blue car seats with little babies strapped in. Their cheeks and lips were puffed out, and both were sleeping. We'd been planning to visit them tomorrow when Eliot was with us. "Another time."

I met Cody and Tova at the grocery store. They were driving the van they used for Tova's mom's wheelchair.

Tova poked her head out the large side door. The wind buffeted the strands of hair sticking out from under her cream-colored stocking hat. "Come on in. We have the heat cranked and everyone can sit in the back and the kids can run to the houses."

Cali dove in while I grabbed Kellan's seat. He grinned when all the kids greeted them.

Tova wiggled between the front seats and sat in the passenger seat. She twisted around as much as she could when she was due in a month. "We couldn't go get Mom. The roads are too bad."

"Eliot can't make it tonight either," I said.

Cody glanced in the rearview mirror. "I was hoping he could make it since none of us could help move cattle. How'd Jasper do?"

"My brother had a good time. Said he felt like a kid again." Jasper had actually been messaging me about his adventures.

Cody coasted up and down neighborhood roads. The kids would dart out on a gust of cold and pile back in, jabbering about the candy they scored. I shot a picture of Cali, Ivy, and Ivy's brother, Grayson, to Eliot. After an hour, we were dropped back off at the car. I didn't get a response from Eliot.

At home, I got Kellan to bed while Cali was counting her candy. I stopped to send another text to Eliot. **Happy Halloween.**

I frowned at the screen for a while. Was he upset he couldn't make it? Did I do something to make him angry? Carter used to ignore me when I did something to piss him off.

Eliot was not my ex. He wasn't out messing around because I wasn't enough. Still, it was hard to shake that old anxiety.

"Bedtime, Cali."

She stuffed all her candy away. We read a quick book and then I tucked her in.

She snuggled into her blankets. "I miss Eliot."

I kissed her forehead. "Me too."

"I'm glad you married him. He's a nice daddy."

"Oh, honey." I smoothed her hair off her face. Eliot had hardly been around, and he took precedence over Carter. While I was grateful he was far better to her than Carter, I dreaded next summer when Eliot and I divorced. She should be in therapy by then. The therapist might not believe my story, but I'd cross that bridge next summer. I gave her another kiss and left her room. I didn't know what else to say.

Outside her door, I pressed my fingertips to my forehead. *"You've got to think things through."* My mother-in-law's voice mingled with my mother's. *"Always so impulsive."*

Was this marriage the right thing? Was having Eliot be a part of my kids' lives for a year and then saying goodbye to him a smart idea? Did I have a choice?

They had often said similar things. But where Mom's was advice, my mother-in-law's had been condemning. In this case, I had to be impulsive. I wasn't sleeping with Eliot to make sure he didn't serve me divorce papers before the year was up. But what about after? Should I have thought of that more? I liked him, dammit. I wanted to have sex with him. And I didn't want to worry about the future.

I went to the living room. I had an hour before bed, and I had the weekend off. I picked a movie and snuggled into the couch. Once or twice or four times, I frowned at my phone. No response from Eliot.

Should I message Jasper and see if he mentioned Eliot?

Too pathetic?

What if Eliot and Jasper were making the best of a guys' Halloween?

What if my single brother was showing Eliot that he missed the unmarried life? Jasper wouldn't purposely lead Eliot astray, but would he lead by example?

I needed to shut my mind off.

When the credits rolled, I went to my bedroom and stripped down. Then, I went to the bathroom and started a playlist. A little speaker in my bathroom pumped all the naughty country songs I couldn't listen to around Cali. I stepped into the bathtub and under the shower spray. Warm water surrounded me, and I soaked it in.

Today had been chilly, both at work and while trick-or-treating. Could that be why I was on edge?

I had just finished rinsing my hair when the bathroom door cracked open.

"What's wrong, Cali? Can't sleep?"

The door quietly clicked shut. I pulled the curtain back and yelped. Eliot had his arms crossed and was leaning with his back against the door. His hair was flattened from a ball cap he was no longer wearing, and his eyes were dark and promising. He was like an apparition the steam conjured up.

"Oh my god!" I held the curtain in front of myself. "You're here?"

He arched a dark brow, his gaze leisurely dropping down my concealed body and roaming back up. The curtain wasn't opaque. "You don't have to hide yourself, Lily pad. I promise that what I can see is even better than I imagined."

Beads of sweat broke out on my brow. The bathroom was suddenly way smaller than it'd ever been. He was here. He'd driven on roads that probably shouldn't have had a vehicle on them, and he'd come to see me.

My pulse kicked up, and I looked my fill of the rugged man in my bathroom. "You're overdressed."

The corner of his mouth kicked up, and he reached behind his head to yank his sweatshirt off. That magnificent chest of his was on display. His pecs rippled as he hung the shirt up on the towel rack. His boots were already off, but he didn't yank down his jeans. He stuck his hand in a pocket and withdrew several condoms.

"That's a lot." Did he plan to use them all this weekend? A shiver traveled over my skin.

"I've got more." He flicked open the fly of his pants and shoved his jeans down.

I clutched the shower curtain closer to me. Oh my. A scattering of hair trailed down his stomach, farther down to... *Wow.* The last time we did anything, it'd been dark. Now, the light in the bathroom only acted like a spotlight. He was definitely better than my imagination. I hadn't pictured this, and I'd even seen him without a shirt before. He was long and thick and so damn hard I ached. I wanted that inside me.

"Keep staring like that and I'm going to think you want to taste it again."

"I do." Having him at my mercy, with nothing but my hands and mouth, was a powerful feeling.

"Nah, Lily. It's my turn." He prowled toward me and stepped into the tub.

I looked up at him. The water was hitting against my back, and droplets were getting tossed around. Many landed on him.

"Hey," he said, like I'd just answered the front door to him.

"Hey. You made it."

"The roads were shit. I had to take a longer route. Sorry I missed your messages."

My hands twitched. He was too close, and we were both naked. I had to touch him. I flattened my palms on his chest. "You shouldn't have risked it."

He ran a thumb along my lower lip. "It was worth it." He lowered his head and his mouth was on mine. I opened automatically for him, and when he thrust his warm tongue inside, I groaned.

He gripped my upper arms and carefully turned me until my back was against the far wall. The shower curtain closed us in. This was our own private cove. When he broke the kiss, he reached behind him and flipped the water off. Without the noise, I could hear my needy breaths.

His focus turned back to me. Normally, I'd want to shrink, to hide, but the desire in his eyes went straight to my head. A flush spread down my body.

He traced the path of a water droplet with a finger. "This time, I'm going to find out for myself how wet you are."

Every night he called, he asked me. And every night, I answered. But he was here. In the bare flesh.

He kissed me again, but he didn't linger. He worked his way down my neck. Down to my pebbled nipples. The cadence of his kisses matched the thrum between my legs. He continued down, lowering himself to his knees.

My breathing was unsteady. Self-consciousness was setting in. Had I shaved well enough? Were my stretch marks a complete turnoff? Would he lose interest?

But he gripped the insides of my thighs and gently eased my legs wider.

"You're fucking glistening." His hot breath wafted over my damp skin. A shiver racked me, but I wasn't cold. "So damn wet."

He placed a kiss on the inside of one thigh. I was ready for him to dive in. We didn't waste a lot of time on the phone. Once we were done catching up about our day, we got to business.

He placed a kiss on the other thigh.

"Eliot," I groaned. I would start trembling and lose my footing. My arousal, my anticipation—I wasn't going to survive it.

"I'll give you what you need." He ran a finger down my pussy, delving into my seam.

My knees turned rubbery, but I fought to stay in place. I would not ruin this moment by falling on my ass. I needed to be steadied, so I fisted my hands into the damp strands of his hair.

He held my gaze and pushed his finger inside. My legs trembled, and he scooted closer until I had to lift a leg to drape on his big shoulder.

He slowly pumped in and out of me. He brushed my clit with his thumb, and I vibrated with nothing but sheer electricity. Energy coursed through my veins, looking for an outlet, needing an explosion to release it soon.

"So fucking responsive," he murmured against the skin of my belly.

I thought I came fast when his voice was in my ear, but when it was him touching me? I was skyrocketing toward my peak.

He removed his thumb and I almost whimpered—until he licked me.

"Oh god." The intensity was staggering. I couldn't move, or I'd fall down or fall on him, but I didn't want to move in case I messed up his rhythm. Yet I was afraid to hold still. The onslaught of pleasure was more than I'd ever experienced.

This man on his knees in front of me made me feel things I hadn't thought were possible. He was my own personal fantasy.

"Eliot?"

He answered with a grunt and continued attacking my clit, pumping his finger in and out of me.

There was no more holding back. I rammed into my climax. Stars detonated behind my eyes.

"Eliot!" His name echoed off the walls. I rode his hand and his face and I cried his name some more. I'd never come so hard or for so long in my life.

When I finally started coming down from the peak, he was there, licking and kissing his way up my body.

"Goddamn, Lily. That was so fucking worth the wait." He nibbled up my neck.

I was limp but somehow still standing. He anchored me with one hand while he shoved the shower curtain aside and stretched to the sink to grab a condom.

He brought the packet to his mouth to rip open. My body was coming alive, anticipating having that glorious cock of his inside me.

A baby's cry rent through the air.

Eliot

.   .   .

An hour had passed. Kellan was still fussing. After I got dried off and dressed and rerouted enough blood to my brain to function properly, I had popped into his room. He'd gotten big since I'd last seen him.

A sense of loss tugged at my chest. It'd only been six weeks, but his dark hair was filling in, and he had two more teeth poking out. I'd gotten a sleepy grin and a coo.

Lily had looked regretful, but I gave her a kiss on the head.

Now I was stretched out on top of the bed. Lily had gotten new blue bedding, changed out the blinds, and moved the snake tank to the living room. When I walked in, I could smell her sunshine scent instead of old perfume. I had wanted to be buried deep inside of her for the third time by now, but I'd rather be under the same roof than separate.

Fatigue dragged at my eyelids. If I had been responsible, I wouldn't have driven. Many of the county highways on this side of the state were all marked "no travel advised" on the online road map, and only more had been added after the sun went down. But there were enough that were still labeled as just "icy." Still not a good idea, but at least I could see the road. It was enough to get me to Lily.

I was dozing off when the door creaked open. The light wasn't on, but the steps weren't right for Lily. I cracked an eye open. A short shadow was making its way to Lily's side of the bed.

"Mommy?" she whispered.

"No, boss lady, it's me."

"Eliot!" she said in a delighted whisper. "You're here." Then she groaned. "My tummy hurts."

Oh shit. Did she need a puke bucket? Water? I'd taken care of Lily, but I didn't have much experience with sick kids.

Lily stepped into the room. "I think he's finally—Cali?"

"Mommy, my tummy hurts."

"Oh no." Lily put her hands on her hips. She wore a T-shirt and shorts like me. She'd taken the towel off her hair, and it hung around her neck.

"Too much candy?" Lily asked.

"No?"

I grinned at Cali's lack of confidence.

"Can I sleep with you?" Cali's voice was small.

I couldn't see Lily's exact expression, but her dismay radiated across the room. It matched my own, but there was nothing that could be done. The kids came first.

I rolled up. "I'll take the couch."

Cali was already scrambling onto the bed.

"Thank you," Lily said quietly.

I put a hand around her waist and tipped my head down. "Don't mention it. Get some rest." I placed a kiss on her hair, not sure what Cali could see or what Lily would want her to see.

I gently closed the door and went to the living room. The snake tank was dark, and the cat was in her tower bed. "Looks like it's you and me, guys."

Once I was sprawled on the couch with the two throw blankets across me, I stared at the ceiling. I was tired, but sleep was evading me. I'd seen the sexy red bra and underwear when I'd changed while she was getting

Kellan. I'd never been cockblocked so much in my life. I would laugh if it wouldn't disturb everyone.

Was this what my brothers and Aggie went through now that they all had families? I gave Cody shit when he'd wanted Tova when she was his nanny, but seriously—how did he and Tova manage to hook up at all with kids around?

I didn't know how many minutes ticked by, but I was finally starting to doze when I heard muffled footsteps.

I opened my eyes to the outline of Lily in the hallway night-light.

She came straight toward me and tossed a packet on my chest. "She's asleep, but we should hurry."

My cock instantly woke the fuck up. I fumbled with the condom. "Are you sure?"

"No, but I'll leave my underwear on, and I'll keep the blanket over me."

I...had never been this turned on. She'd snuck away for me. Her trip out of the bedroom was almost as treacherous as the drive on icy roads.

I yanked my shorts down far enough to free my erection. I tossed the wrapper on the floor and rolled the damn thing on. Lily's shorts were on the floor, and she was already crawling over me.

Finally, she straddled me. Blood pounded in my dick, and I was so close to heaven I couldn't see straight. I wanted to have sex with this woman, but some things were paramount.

"Not so fast," I said quietly. I slid my hand between her legs, pushing her underwear to the side. This didn't feel like the fancy red ones, but I couldn't give a fuck. As long as she let me get under them.

She was wet, but I wanted her good and soaked. "Christ, Lily. You're as soft as satin and always so fucking wet for me."

She groaned and rocked on my hand. The blanket was wrapped around her waist and she leaned over me. I toyed with her clit and pushed two fingers inside. She bowed her back and tilted her face up. The moan was pure reward.

I could get her off again, but we were risking interruption. I gripped her hips. She kept her underwear pulled to the side, and I notched myself at her hot entrance. She took over from there, sinking onto me.

"Jesus," I hissed. "So fucking good."

"So big," she whispered and lifted herself an inch and then lowered herself again.

She did that until I was seated fully inside. We both held still. Need pounded at my brain, demanding I thrust, thrust, thrust. I just needed a moment to savor this, to feel the full connection between us. Yes, we were sneaking in a quickie, but she wasn't just a quickie.

This woman was... Only mine for a year.

And then?

She moved, and my thoughts gladly derailed, giving way to the ecstasy coursing between us.

"I can't believe I can come again." Her words were almost lost in the quiet living room.

I held her hips, slowing her pace, or I'd blow before she did. "If we had time, I'd make you climax three times."

She popped her head up and the disbelief was apparent in the dark.

To prove my point, I put a thumb back on her clit.

The shudder that racked her body went straight through my cock. She pressed her hands into my chest and rode me and my thumb.

I wasn't going to last. I didn't need her in a spotlight to see the way her lips were parted as she panted or how her eyes were closed. She was so fucking beautiful. This woman was mine.

Her walls convulsed around me, and she buried her face in my shoulder. When she went taut and silently screamed her release into my shirt, I finally let go. My climax shattered behind my eyes. I clenched my teeth and tried like hell to smother any noise that came out.

Fuck. We bucked together until we both went still.

"That was...damn, Lily."

Her giggle was soft. She lifted her head. "Yeah. It was." She placed a kiss on my lips, paused for a moment, and then straightened. "I should clean up and get back in case she wakes again."

I wished I could cuddle her to me, curl around her, and fall asleep to the sound of her breathing. I slid a lock of her hair through my fingers. There'd be time for that later. I'd make sure of it. "I know. I'd like you to stay, but she's got dibs on you."

She gave me a curious look. "You don't mind cuddling?"

"Why would I? I get you in my arms."

She dropped her forehead to my chest. "You're so perfect."

"Far from it."

"Trust me. You are." She wiggled off me, and just like that, I was ready to go again. She lifted the blanket higher. "Seriously? Again?"

"Don't underestimate how much I want you."

"You say things like that and you like to cuddle? You make it hard to be a good mom and snuggle with a little girl who has sugar belly." She leaned down to kiss me again, then I watched her ass wiggle all the way to the bedroom.

It was going to take me another hour to get to sleep.

Eighteen

ELIOT

I was holding a baby and so was Lily, only it wasn't Kellan in her arms. My tiny nephew Drew was safe with her, and I had Alex. They weren't the tiniest babies I'd held, but they were close.

Sutton and Wilder were out having a lunch date. They might not have entrusted me with two babies this small on my own, but I had an expert with me.

Cali was sitting between us, reading a book to the babies. They were both fast asleep and had snoozed through the first three stories. Kellan was on a blanket on the floor, happily practicing his rolling.

Cali finished the book about bunnies. Magnolia was the author, and it was one of the gifts Lily had gotten for the twins. She'd also given Sutton a new-mom present that had home spa products like hot and cold face packs, lotion, and gourmet chocolates. Cali had read each of the four books—two for each boy—and the bunnies was the last.

"I can't believe how well you can read," I said. Since when could first graders blow through four baby books like they were nothing? "That's amazing."

She beamed.

Wilder opened the door to the kitchen. Sutton entered, still moving gingerly. Wilder shadowed her the whole way.

She grinned at us as she made her way through the kitchen and into her living room. "Thank you so much for that. That was my first outside meal since I was put on bed rest."

"You're most welcome." Lily smiled. "Do you want them in their cribs?"

"Sure." Sutton carefully sat in the recliner. "Hopefully, they'll take the same three-hour naps they've been taking all week."

Wilder took Drew from Lily. "Eliot and I can lay them down. You two relax."

Cali snuggled into Lily. The sight always melted my damn heart.

I followed Wilder upstairs to the nursery.

"How's Sutton doing?" I asked.

"She's still sore, and she can't wait to sleep on her side. One of her stitches popped open the first week, but it's been a smooth recovery from surgery since." He lifted a shoulder. "As much as you can recover with two newborns anyway. We're tired but content. Glad I could be around for it all."

I was glad he'd finally chosen Sutton over his deputy position too. "No clock to punch."

"No kidding." He set Drew in the middle of the crib

and gazed at him with pure adoration. When I settled Alex, he did the same. "It's just so unreal. Neither of us thought we'd ever reach this point, and now we're here. Some days, I'm scared I'm dreaming. Until I change the diaper bin. Then it's real enough."

A weird spike of envy speared right into my chest cavity. I tried to brush it off. "I'm happy for you." I was. The idea that he could be miserable and alone in Buffalo Gully gave me an ulcer.

His attention was on me. "How about you?"

"What about me?" I was being obtuse, but nothing had changed in my life.

"You're different with her."

Not him too. Everyone I encountered had to tell me their thoughts on me and Lily, and it was the ones who knew there could be no me and Lily. "Well, I've never been married."

He gave me his cop look, the one I was sure he'd used on drunk drivers who told him they'd only had a couple of drinks. "Why aren't you figuring out how to lock this down?"

"Did you forget—"

"No, Eliot. I remember every damn thing, including how bullshit obligations can steal everything I have."

Didn't he realize how well I knew all that? My irritation crept up my neck. "My 'bullshit obligations' are helping you keep all this."

"Nope."

"You're going to wake your boys."

He didn't move. "They're used to us talking when they're sleeping. It's getting them to stay asleep when it's quiet that's hard." He folded his arms. "I don't need the inheritance."

He'd gone from a family of two to four in the last month. Of course he needed the money. "We all know the business has to stay afloat."

"We all know you hide behind that ranch."

"What the hell's that supposed to mean?" When one of the babies made a grunting noise, I clenched my teeth. Wilder was a new dad, elated and exhausted, and I didn't want to crap all over his day with this argument.

"It's been nothing but a convenient excuse to justify why you haven't done a damn thing you've wanted." He faced me like he'd bicker over this topic all day.

The heat winding around my throat turned into anger. "And why would I do that? You're talking out of your ass."

"One, I'm going to teach my boys to swear, not their uncles, so watch your mouth."

"I'll teach them to swear better."

"Two, I can't answer that for you. Only you can. We all had baggage we had to get over or that we still carry with us. Ask Cody. Or Austen. Aggie."

No the fuck I wouldn't. "What was yours?" I shot back.

"I wanted to please a father figure who I wished was my father so bad that I didn't realize he just wanted me to live out his lonely fucking dreams."

I snapped my mouth shut. He actually answered. A response that made all the sense in the world. I'd even told him once he'd picked his old boss over his wife. Yes, we all had baggage, but mine wasn't history. I was living and working it every day.

Wilder's expression grew more determined. "Austen almost moved to California because he wasn't going to fight for Vienne and be like Barns."

"I'm not Barns either. Which is why I'm not making Lily feel like she has to stay married to me after the year is done." He opened his mouth, but I gave my head a sharp shake. "And when the year is done, I'm going to keep the ranch going."

"Her brother's doing a damn fine job, from what Cody said."

Chambers and his big fucking mouth. "He's temporary. An IT guy isn't going to give up everything to run someone's place at a quarter of what he could make in the corporate world. Not to mention, he's got his property he'll probably marry for."

"He'd buy you time though."

"No."

"Fuck's sake, Eliot. You're going to lose her."

Fear tore through my body, making my chest tight and my throat constrict. I could not lose her.

Men are toxic, Eliot. They'll poison a woman with lies to get what they want. They'd do it until her passion dies and the rest follows. And I gave birth to four of them. Mama's words screamed into the void of my mind.

If it wasn't for Lily's first husband, she wouldn't be a single mom with a ton of school debt. I was better than him, but she was still dependent on me. I wanted her to have a choice. I would never pressure her for my own selfish wants. I was an adult. I was a better man than my father. So I had to be ready. The best thing for Lily might be to let her get away.

Lily

. . .

I gawked at the restaurant around us. The dinner rush in Purple Petal was in full effect, but Eliot and I were at a high-top table in the bar. We'd already ordered, and I had a virgin cosmopolitan in front of me.

Eliot had a mug of beer and promised I could drive his pickup.

"I can't believe you found a sitter." Anxiety continued to surge. I had left my kids with a teenager. Eliot vouched for Vienne's daughter, Catherine. His entire family did, and while I'd met the girl, I had rarely had someone watch the kids who weren't my parents or daycare.

"Catherine has babysat for all the Knights and I'm including Aggie in that. If the girl didn't play so much volleyball, she'd be able to have a full-time job with just my relatives."

"She seems like a good kid." I took a sip of my cosmo. The strawberry slush was like candy and since there was no alcohol, I could drink ten of them without worrying about nursing Kellan. "When I was her age, I was full of the same confidence, but I wasn't as mellow."

"You're mellow now."

"Necessity. My mom always accused me of not thinking first, but she doesn't understand that gut feeling, you know? She'll sit in front of her computer and rework four lines of rhyme for her kids' books. She'll go through a hundred different words and turns of phrases, and she'll do the same thing in her regular decision-making. It used to drive me nuts."

"And now?"

I could ramble like I was on my third adult beverage. Eliot was easy to talk to, and Carter had never wanted to listen. "I can see the wisdom of her ways. They thought I should work a few years and then go to vet school if I was still interested, but I was applying as soon as possible. If I had worked a few years, I wouldn't have gone, and maybe I sensed that."

"Do you think you would've felt like you missed out?" The way he scrutinized me spoke of a different motivation for asking than curiosity. He'd been quiet since we'd left Sutton and Wilder's. He'd gone upstairs with his brother, and when he came back down, he was subdued. Almost angry. Wilder and Sutton had exchanged glances, and I had remained lost.

I had thought Eliot would talk to me, but he hadn't opened up yet. None of it was my business, but I'd also been told everything in my last marriage was none of my business. Yet many of the decisions made had hinged on the efforts I put into the relationship.

I wasn't diving down that rabbit hole. Eliot and I were only dating. Our marriage was not part of whatever was going on between him and Wilder.

Or maybe it was all of it.

I should've had a real drink. What was his question? Oh, right. "I don't know if I would've felt like I missed out. Sutton's clinic runs really well. She designed it with a lot of support and flexibility. Carter's is a money mill. He didn't care about animals, he cared about upselling. The vet's jobs were more about how much they could siphon from a family, and I saw the mental toll it took on the vets, on top of the normal stress of the field. Did you know veterinary medicine is often cited as one of the most stressful occupations?"

He shook his head. "I assumed my dad was the reason Sutton had a lot of stress when she worked for the ranch."

"I'm happy being a tech. I wish I could get a do-over

and not take out those loans or see the prenup for what it was—a tool for Carter to use me with minimal risk to himself. But...it happened, and I moved forward. I'm just going to keep going."

"You roll with the punches and collect more animals while you're at it."

I grinned. "You have to admit that Bug is turning out to be the goodest boy."

"I suspect he thinks there are cookies when I'm around."

I laughed. I barely remembered there were cookies in the break room Bug had been after. I'd been so shocked by the sight of a sexy cowboy. "I wouldn't have met you without him."

"We'd have crossed paths."

"I wouldn't have named you as a potential husband, Romeo."

His gaze flickered. "Why not?"

"I'd have probably accepted my fate. But you tried to help then and then you were so nice at the party. I don't know. It's not like I know any other single guys."

The server arrived with our food. We started eating, but he was drawn in on himself.

I ate half my club sandwich, but my appetite was lacking. Something was bothering him. Was I the cause? "Eliot. What'd I say?"

"Nothing." He shoved a fry in his mouth and kept chewing. His throat worked when he swallowed. "I'm just reeling over my brother being a dad of twins when he was just divorced from that same wife a few years ago."

That wasn't it. I should quit asking, but why wouldn't he open up to me? We were getting closer. Or I was letting sex cloud our circumstances. "You can talk to me. I know we're not…"

He arched a brow. "Husband and wife?"

"That's on paper." He was showing me how things should've been in my first marriage. It wasn't all fake, was it? I let my food sit. I needed to hear his answer first. My heart pounded against my ribs. "What's going on between us is more."

He scooted another fry through his ketchup, then ditched it on his plate. "It's more, but at the same time, we both know what it is."

Maybe what I was asking was whether he wanted it to be more? We'd gotten married. Then we'd slept together. Now, we were on a date. Our process was ass-backward, but couldn't it still lead to somewhere?

"I care about you, Lily, and those kids. But at the end of the year, we're each still going to have our own life. If we still want to keep seeing each other, this is what we have."

If we still want to keep seeing each other… "Long distance?"

His gaze darkened. "Long distance isn't good enough for you."

Surprise crashed through me and shifted to irritation. I was tired of people deciding what was best for me. My in-laws made it seem like their mean words were for my own good, but it wasn't. They said what was in their best interest. "Don't I get to decide what's good for me?"

"One year of pretending won't be enough for you to decide. I can't even live under the same roof." He deliberately pushed his drink farther away. "You have time, Lily. Your only requirement is the year. Nothing in those documents said you have to stay married the entire seven years."

He made it sound like he was thinking of me, but he was coming off like he wanted us to be as temporary as the nuptials. Wow. Hurt resounded through me like a gong strike. Temporary. I had known it, but when he'd driven through a winter storm to be in my bed, I had convinced myself it was so much more. That he meant what he said.

In reality, he wasn't looking for more than what Carter had wanted. Only Carter had sought out the marriage to solve some of his issues with Cali and his clinic. I was Carter in this case, but the thought only made me feel more foolish. Carter could keep his wits about him. I was falling hard for Eliot.

I wanted him to be the man who wanted to be by my side for no other reason than love. Not obligation. Not for a trust. Not for his own needs. I wanted him to be a man who would change more than a weekend to be with me. Meanwhile, he was a man whose goal was to become my second ex-husband.

Eliot

I was in the shop, making sure all the snow removal equipment Lily inherited was working. Cali had played outside for two hours and then she'd gone in. The sun was high, and the temperature had swung back up to be unseasonably warm. Melting snow could be heard dripping off the roof and trees.

Being gone from the ranch wasn't as nerve-racking as it used to be, but it was time for me to go. Jasper had called. We'd lost a mare. There was nothing that could've been done. Sometimes, an illness took hold of an animal before we saw any signs. He and Alexander had handled the situation, but I needed to leave before dark, or that melt would turn to ice on the highways. I wouldn't be as driven to get home in time as I was to get to Crocus Valley on Halloween night. If I could spend every weekend like this one... That was a reality that wasn't mine.

Lily entered the shop. The big doors were open. I washed my hands and dried them, turning to enjoy the view. She was looking around the building. I had straightened and organized tools, separating old junk that wouldn't be useful, like spare engine parts from equipment that was no longer on the property and tires. Why so many tires? I piled all that in the corner to haul to the dump if I was ever around during open hours.

You could make that happen.

Maybe I would. It couldn't be a regular occurrence. I had a job. And she hadn't argued about not filing for divorce and finding a guy who could take a load to the dump. A guy who could make her feel desired every day instead of when it was convenient for him.

I nearly sneered at the thought. Fuck that guy. But no. I wasn't selfish with women, and I sure as hell wasn't going to stand in Lily's way of happiness. She'd been thoughtful after our date, but as soon as I got her home and got her clothes off, we were back in sync. Deep down, she likely knew I was right.

She shoved her hands in her hoodie. The shop's interior was cooler, with the concrete floor radiating cold, but she'd be fine if she kept moving. The outline of the baby monitor and her phone were visible in her hoodie pocket.

"Is Cali napping again?" I asked.

She smiled and it was a punch to the gut. The serene, content smile she got sometimes when all was right in her world made me a satisfied man. It didn't happen often enough, but I'd seen it more the longer she was settled in the house that would soon be hers.

"Running in the fresh air for a couple of hours tuckered her out. I have the third handset in the living room. She's passed out on the couch." She set the monitor on the shop bench and put her phone beside it. "You've really cleaned up in here."

"Your grandma hadn't done much in years. Understandable. Besides, cleaning and organizing is almost all it needed." I lifted my chin toward the junk pile. "Check for anything you might want to keep."

"I will." She tipped her head and studied me. The indigo of her irises nearly blended with her pupils in the shadows of this place. "When will you be here next?"

I lifted a shoulder. A hard question to answer when leaving was starting to become the last thing I wanted to do. I'd come next weekend if she needed me, but I also had to keep space between us. I would never be the man Mama thought I'd grow up to be, and I didn't want to create more loss for myself when we parted ways. It'd be easier if I was used to seeing her less than once a month. "We'll have to see what the weather's like."

Her brows pinched together like she didn't care for my answer. "Of course." She licked her lips. We'd had sex last night, but seeing her tongue was an instant turn-on for me. My dick remembered what she could do with it. "Do you have Thanksgiving plans?"

The holiday was less than a month away. "I haven't done much the last few years. I'll probably stay at home so the guys can be with their family." Unmarried employees still had parents, siblings, and close friends they needed to connect with. "Sometimes, I can sneak up for the day, but all my siblings are going to be having babies or home with newborns. I doubt there'll be any feasts getting prepared."

The furrow between her brow deepened. "You shouldn't spend the holiday alone."

"It's happened before." Admittedly, not as much as one would think. Not until the rest of my siblings had moved away from Buffalo Gully.

She pushed her hair back. "My mom just messaged and told me not to worry about making it there. It's a long drive with small kids." She rolled her eyes. "So I told her I'd already gotten a pet sitter."

Her mom had a reason to be worried. "It's a six-hour drive." A long drive for a woman with two young kids.

She leveled me with a stern stare. "It's shorter than driving from Kansas to Billings with a fraction of my worldly possessions, morning sickness, and a five-year-old who doesn't understand why we're leaving everything she knows. Although I'll grant you that Cali switched between my car and my parents' on the way to Billings."

And she didn't want me treating her like that time in her life, like she couldn't take care of what needed to be done on her own. "I worry, that's all."

"Cali will be in the back seat to help entertain Kellan. If Catherine can't pet sit, then I can ask someone at the clinic."

I shook my head. "You don't have a pet sitter lined up yet?"

She smiled, and I caught a glimpse of that impulsive girl who'd worried her family. "You're welcome to join us. The drive is about the same for you."

I'd be working so Jasper could go to her family gathering. "I don't want to say I'll try and then disappoint you."

"No, you definitely make sure I know what to expect." The tension in her voice was a warning bell.

She had the same stiff set in her shoulders when I'd told her I wanted her to have a choice. Telling a girl that on our first official date wasn't romantic. Mama wouldn't have been surprised. *Your dad would rather get me pregnant again than buy me flowers. That's his idea of romance.*

"I don't want to disappoint you," I told Lily. "It's important that you know where I'm at in this marriage."

She focused on me, but I couldn't read her expression. Several moments ticked by. "I understand," she finally said.

Did she? The skepticism in her voice said otherwise. "Lily—"

"I think we have a short window where both kids are napping and you have to leave soon." She closed the distance between us and tucked her hands underneath my sweater. Her cool fingers wrapped around my waistband, but I'd warm them up soon enough. "Think you can keep me warm?"

Sex would be a distraction. But it was her using it, not me, and I'd let her do whatever she wanted as long as she knew she always had an out.

Nineteen

LILY

My parents' house was loud and chaotic. I came down the stairs, taking in the scene. Alder, Jasper, Poppy, and Dad were yelling at the football game on TV. Violet's boyfriend was stuck deep in his phone, antisocial with our group as always. Violet was next to him, pretending to be engrossed in the football game, but I suspected she'd rather be in the kitchen with Mom and Clover. Willis didn't like it when she left him alone with the rest of the family.

Cali and Kellan were in the kitchen. We'd arrived late last night, and they'd been getting spoiled all day.

Mom and Dad had tried to talk me out of driving. They'd even offered to move the shindig to Crocus Valley, but I told them it would be nice to be home.

I hadn't been lying. There was a comfort within these walls I couldn't deny. Yes, I might've been smothered at times, the worst was right after the divorce, but there had also been a lot of freedom. This was my home, and I'd let Carter and his family make me feel ashamed about it.

I was enjoying my visit and Mom's food. There were no memories of Eliot associated with the house. I wouldn't be watching TV tonight, hoping he was secretly driving in the dark to be with me. In our last message, he'd said he was packing breakfast sandwiches to go do chores.

Jasper had confirmed that Eliot would be too busy to go anywhere. *"He gave everyone the weekend off. Hope there're no emergencies, but I guess he can call Chambers if nothing else. And I can get there in under four hours."*

I didn't feel any better hearing Eliot was alone. Tova and Aggie had their babies a week apart, and Vienne was hoping she'd have her baby before Christmas. None of them were surprising Eliot with a visit.

When I entered the massive kitchen with an island big enough for me and all my siblings to sit behind, Kellan waved his hands toward me. I picked him up from the high chair and pressed a kiss into his dark curls. Cali was cutting shapes of sugar cookies on the other side with Mom and Clover.

"Are you getting a jump on Christmas cooking?" I asked Mom.

"We sure are." She beamed at Cali. "I'm sending several tins home with you."

We'd have more cookies than Cali and I could eat in a year. I'd make sure Eliot got a ton. Would he want a picture of Cali baking? I snapped one to send later.

Violet entered and immediately took Kellan from me. Willis also didn't like kids, so she hadn't been holding Kellan if she was sitting next to her boyfriend.

"You sure Willis is okay out there by himself?" I asked.

She scowled at me. "He's fine. Why?"

Clover snickered but pressed her lips together as soon as Violet shot her a glare.

Jasper wandered in. He stopped next to Violet and leaned down. "You'd better warn that phone that man is taken. Whatever is on it is going to seduce him away."

"We can only hope," Clover muttered. Mom shushed her. Thankfully, Cali was too ensconced in cutting her Santa shapes just right to be paying attention.

"Stop it," Violet hissed. "No wonder he's not comfortable around any of you."

"No, that's not it." Jasper went to the fridge. He nodded at me before he opened the door. "Her husband jumped right in."

Eliot did, but he was used to a big family. He was also amazing, and Willis was not. I might be biased.

Violet narrowed her eyes at him. "It was his first and only time meeting us." She blinked at me, the epitome of innocence. I had enough time to stiffen before she spoke. "Speaking of, where is Mr. Knight on this fine Thanksgiving Day?"

"Giving me the weekend off," Jasper said.

"Mmm." Violet wasn't going to let it go. It wasn't like her. "He couldn't take a holiday off to spend time with his new wife? What's Aunt Linda going to say?"

"She's going to think it's as thoughtful as I do that Eliot took the holiday weekend so our whole crew can be together." I didn't care about my aunt's opinion of my relationship. Mom and Dad hadn't invited her for Thanksgiving since the uproar over the trust was still fresh. Nothing was Linda's fault, and we all knew that, but we needed time.

Though it would've been an excuse to get Eliot to Billings. Resentment built like a brick wall around me. Aunt Linda wanted me to stay married. She wanted me happy. Sure, it might contribute to her own chance at gaining her inheritance, but she was more invested in the long-term outcome of me and Eliot than Eliot was.

"Thoughtful?" Violet's challenging gaze was still on me.

As the youngest and oldest sister, we could have a volatile relationship. Yet I was closer to her than Poppy or Clover, so I wasn't afraid to turn the tables on her. "Aunt Linda is waiting to see which one of you is getting married next. Maybe the one with the boyfriend?"

Violet managed a nonchalant shrug that didn't match the hope deep in her eyes. Did she realize she settled for Willis? I couldn't imagine what was so redeeming about him, but I wasn't his girlfriend. Therefore, it wasn't my business.

But I worried about her.

"I've gotta go potty." Cali darted out of the room.

"You never know," Violet said once she was gone, back to sweetly innocent. "Jasper or Clover could meet someone tomorrow and be married by the New Year."

Jasper pulled a face. Clover shuddered.

Mom cast an exasperated look at all of us. "Just how a mother loves to see her children react."

"Not all of us want to be trad wives," Clover said.

"What's a trad wife?" Mom asked, exasperated.

"You," Clover explained. "A wife who stays at home, cooks, and cleans."

Clover smirked at me. "Not all working ladies land a hot guy running the grill at big family picnics."

"He makes great pancakes," I said. He'd made them the morning before he left. And I'd wondered if I should ask for the recipe. At this time next year, he didn't plan to be around and making them anymore.

"He really does," Jasper added. "The guy can cook like no one's business."

My sisters stared at him.

He let the fridge door close and chomped into a dill pickle. "What?" he said around his mouthful.

"Maybe you can marry him when he divorces me," I said. Horror dawned once every pair of eyes in the room landed on me. Good thing Cali hadn't returned yet. Why didn't I watch my mouth?

Concern shone brightly in Mom's eyes. "Is there trouble between you two? You did marry so fast."

"No," I said quickly. Of course they'd blame my impulsiveness. "I was just joking."

Violet studied me, concern in her eyes.

Clover went back to rolling out cookie dough. "Lily swung in with the dark humor. That's usually Poppy's role."

Violet's phone dinged. She looked at the screen and aimed a disgruntled stare toward the living room.

"He beckons," Jasper taunted.

Violet smacked the back of her hand against his stomach. "Shut it, jackwagon." She handed Kellan back to me.

"Mo-om, Vi hit me." Jasper's grin was unrepentant.

Cali danced back into the kitchen. This was the perfect moment to make my own escape. As long as she was busy, I'd take Kellan to the toy room Mom and Dad had made in the lower-level family area. He could crawl around. Then, I could get away from any more follow-up questions.

The lower level was cooler and quieter. A balm to my nerves. I hated that Eliot was alone, and I was trying not to wallow in my hurt that he hadn't tried harder not to be. I set Kellan down by a bin of giant building blocks. The mess of my emotions wasn't sorting itself out.

Footsteps pressed into the plush carpet. Jasper dropped to sit next to me.

"You two really going to cut ties after you fool Aunt Linda?" he asked.

"No, I was just jok—"

"I figured it out and asked him."

My heart leaped into my throat. He knew?

Was that an issue? All of Eliot's family had been informed. When we'd told them, we hadn't been married yet. Jasper didn't start working for Eliot until later in September. Eliot hadn't tried to convince Jasper otherwise? Were his feelings about me so clear that my brother had noticed?

Jasper leaned closer and bumped my shoulder with his, something he'd done my entire life. "He likes you, but he also didn't lie to me about your arrangement. Though I have to wonder, wouldn't it be weird if, after a year, you two didn't stay together?"

Leave it to my laid-back but analytical-minded brother to nail what bothered me about all this. "I don't know. He's dead set against being a family man. His parents had issues, and I guess after being raised by Mom and Dad, I can't relate."

"Mom and Dad's perfect marriage can shine glaring lights on weaker relationships."

"Yeah. It's one of the reasons it was easier to stay away when I was married to Carter."

He bumped me again. "We all knew that. It's why we bugged the shit out of you."

"You guys nagged me."

"Because you're stubborn."

I mock glared at him. I had been that stubborn with Carter. "I was used to everything working out, and suddenly it wasn't, and I had more than myself to consider."

I sighed. I was never this open with him or anyone else. But the fact that Jasper knew Eliot, and he guessed the real foundation of my relationship with him? Well, I needed a friend I could talk to and that was my brother.

"I can't believe you bought Carter's shit."

I rolled my eyes toward him. "There are little ears around."

Jasper gave me a *really?* look. "You don't want him to hear us talk shit about the guy who gave up being his *dad*?"

True. "Carter was very charming and persuasive. He's good with animals. I didn't notice he was so poor with humans. I was overwhelmed in vet school, there was Cali, and he dangled a good life in front of me. Trust me, I didn't see his cheating coming. Or the end of my marriage."

"But you do now?"

I shoved his muscled shoulder. "Ouch."

He laughed. "So you and Eliot are just having some fun until you get the house?"

"I guess so. He's really being a perfect husband."

"No one's perfect, and clearly, he's not if he's not doing everything he can to win you forever."

I appreciated my brother's faith in me as a partner, but Eliot had gone out of his way many times. "Maybe he's not perfect for me. He needs to be free to make his own choices too, and I kind of cornered him."

Jasper reclined on his side and stretched his legs out. "I've only worked with the guy for a couple of months, but Eliot doesn't do shit he doesn't want to do. The whole place has been set up Eliot's way."

"No, it's—"

"Not you. Okay? If he doesn't want to stay married, that's his issue. It's not yours. Just like Carter being a selfish prick shouldn't have been your problem."

Kellan started crawling in my direction. I held my arms out. Kellan bypassed me for my brother. Instead of being jealous, I was pleased. My kids were surrounded by people who supported them, just like I had been my whole life until I got married. Now I was again. Jasper had my back.

"How'd you get so wise?" I asked.

"I was born that way." He lay still while Kellan babbled and patted him. "So, are you going to take a detour on the way home?"

I puffed my hair out of my face. "I'm not planning a detour."

"Hear me out. You can go hang out with your boo and get him to make those noises I try not to hear at night in person."

Embarrassment flooded me. We could get loud. "He does not make noise."

"Ugh. I didn't need the confirmation. I steered clear of your room last night because I was afraid of what I'd hear."

I gasped. "Jasper! The kids are bunking with me."

Besides, Eliot and I texted most days, but the phone sex wasn't as frequent since we'd had real sex.

"Anyway," Jasper continued, "the kids can ride with me to Buffalo Gully on Sunday."

Friday to Sunday? With Eliot and without kids? "He's not expecting me."

"Surprise him. It'll at least show you how he reacts."

The decision took me no time at all. I wouldn't be shorting the kids time with their grandparents, and I could be the one reaching out to Eliot for once. He wouldn't be alone for the entire holiday weekend. The year would go fast, and maybe he'd realize the flame that was growing between us was worth fanning. "Are you ready for three and a half hours in a car with two kids?"

Thanksgiving and today had been full of sunshine and minimal wind. It was like fall had made a resurgence before the winter solstice in a few weeks. I'd been prepared to stop and turn around at least three times on this trip. What was I doing? This wasn't a case of making plans and the weather getting in the way. Eliot had a valid reason for not spending the holiday weekend with me.

I'd come too far to turn around. I drove around Buffalo Gully and turned off on the gravel road. Jasper had given me directions.

I shouldn't have come. Eliot was going to be really busy, and now he'd have to entertain me.

What if he already had someone to entertain?

I shook my head. Eliot was not Carter. Jasper spoke highly of him, and my brother was the cynical one. People thought he was more casual than Alder, but Jasper just kept it to himself better.

I drove, my stomach crawling higher into my throat as I got closer. Eventually, the peaks of a log cabin came into view.

"Oh my..." The place was sprawling, and while it was old, it had a character that couldn't be missed. It was stately yet rugged, but I wouldn't say it was inviting. Whoever had built this wanted something that screamed money and the Western lifestyle and then they hadn't paid any more attention to it.

The flower beds out front didn't have old stalks poking up from the almost melted piles of snow. The grass had been trimmed, but it grew over a walking path from the garage to the front door.

Eliot's pickup was parked in front of the garage.

I parked next to him. It was too late to back out. He might've seen me pull up already. I checked my reflection in the rearview mirror. My face was the color of a tomato. Damn my blush. My eyes were almost panicked, but at least my curls weren't frizzed out everywhere today. I'd actually put some product in this morning.

I left my belongings in the car, grabbed only my purse, and scurried to the front door. The wind this far out in the country was stronger and had a colder bite. I hadn't grabbed my jacket either. I rang the doorbell and huddled in on myself.

No answer.

I knocked.

No answer.

Another doorbell ring.

This was such a bad idea. I took my phone out and texted Jasper. **He's not answering.**

Jasper: He's probably in the barn or stables. Or shop. Or out in the pasture. Go through the garage door.

I was not feeling good about this. Eliot was busier than ever. I'd be a nuisance.

My phone buzzed. **IT'S FINE.**

I looked around like Jasper was right behind me, watching how indecisive I was.

I tucked the phone away and walked around the garage. The entry door was on the side. I stepped in and smiled as familiar scents surrounded me. The garage had the oil and grease smell of Grandma's shop.

Gingerly, I entered the house and crept farther inside. I took my athletic shoes off and ran clammy hands down my jeans. At least I wore a nicer sweater than a hoodie. Might as well interrupt someone's workday in style.

"Eliot?"

His name echoed down the hallway. I passed through a laundry room, then by a bedroom and bathroom. They were pretty plain for a log cabin. Then I emerged from the hallway.

"Wow." The vaulted ceiling had wooden beams arching across it. Large picture windows overlooked the Knights' property. I could see a big red barn, two sprawling shops, and mucky pastures and pens from the melted snow. Cattle grazed farther out. I couldn't see the horses, but Jasper had mentioned a stable.

No wonder he didn't want to leave. He had all this, and I didn't even officially own the house I was living in.

Behind me was the kitchen and island. They were both dated. My footsteps were barely audible on the hard floor. It was warm under my feet. Inside wasn't uninviting, but it screamed bachelor from rafters to foundation.

The decorations were simple and mostly prints of various Montana landscapes. The place had been freshly painted, maybe in the last few years. As for furniture, the main area had more of a ski lodge feel than a home.

"Eliot?" The place was empty, but my nerves needed an outlet.

How much did I snoop?

I left my purse on the island and continued down another hallway. If the large windows in the living room and kitchen didn't let in so much light, this would be a disconcerting walk. Doors lined each side.

I passed an office with an imposing desk, but there was a comfortable-looking recliner parked in front of a large-screen TV. On the end table next to the chair was a simple laptop. From what Eliot had said about his bookkeeper, I could guess a lot of work was done from that chair.

The rest of the rooms were likely bedrooms, all nice-sized, judging from how deep the hallway was. I turned around and retraced my steps.

I heard boot steps and they were growing louder.

I was about to call Eliot's name, but I clamped my lips shut. Jasper lived here with him, but there were other guys who worked on the ranch. Was I in a strange house with a strange man?

I emerged from the hallway and my gaze landed on Eliot and his long-legged strides. He wasn't wearing a hat, but he was running his hand through his hair like he'd just taken one off. He was looking down and he let out a heavy sigh.

"Hey," I said timidly and stuffed my hands in the back pockets of my jeans.

He jerked his head up and stared, coming to a stop by

the island. "Lily?" He blinked like I might be a hallucination.

"Surprise," I said weakly. I continued toward him. "Is it okay that I just popped in? The kids are staying with my parents, and Jasper will bring them Sunday." If Eliot wanted me to stay.

He gawked at me. Then he closed the distance between us with one step and crushed his mouth to mine.

I circled his neck with my arms. Okay. This was a good sign.

My body came alive pressed against his. Heat spread through me, and I inhaled the smell of fresh, cold air mixed with his sandalwood aftershave.

He spun me until my ass hit the countertop. He traced a path to my ear with his mouth. "You're telling me that I have you to myself until Sunday?"

"You sure you don't mind?"

He took my hand in his and pressed it to the front of his jeans. "Does it seem like I mind?" He released me and nibbled a path down my neck.

I tipped my head back. "I know you're busy." My zipper was down and my jeans were unbuttoned. When did he do that?

Passion was making me dizzy, and I hadn't been in this position before. I was overcome by the man I was with, and I didn't have to strategize how to make it happen. We had the house to ourselves.

Light shone in from the giant windows, and the island was like a stage, but no one was around to see us.

He yanked my jeans and underwear down. I stepped out of them, and he kicked them to the side. "All my condoms are at your place, but, Lily, I'm going to fucking devour you."

I didn't have a chance to say anything before he dropped to his knees and parted my thighs. I was steadier than I had been in the shower when he'd first done this, but my legs went molten regardless.

When he licked through my seam, I was lost. It'd been a month since we'd had sex, but I yearned for him like an eternity had come and gone. My only support was him at my pussy and my elbows on the counter.

"Eliot," I said with a whine. My climax was building, pressure closing in where he was circling my clit with his tongue, threatening to explode outward and take me out with the force. "It's not going to take long."

"Be fucking loud. I wanna hear you scream." He delved in again, and this time, he pushed a finger inside. He pumped once and then added another.

The feeling of being filled by him was too much. I slammed into my peak, my head dropping back, and I let out the longest, loudest cry that I'd ever uttered in my life. My voice echoed through the house. Eliot continued lapping at me, thrusting in and out, and I just came and came and came.

"Oh my god." I could barely breathe. I sagged. My legs weren't going to hold me up.

He rose, crowding me between him and the counter. There were chairs on either side of us. He gazed down at me, his expression smug but his eyes full of need.

"You're going to lose your voice before morning."

A shiver raced down my body. He was fully clothed, but our bodies were lined up. All I had to do was free that magnificent cock of his and he could be inside me in seconds.

I reached for his jeans. He put a hand on mine.

"Lily, baby, I have to go buy more protection. As

much as I love your mouth, I'd just bury my face right between your legs again if you touched me."

I patted the island, reaching, searching for my purse. When I found it, I jerked a small box out from the inside. "I came prepared."

His stunned gaze was on the condoms in my hand. "Since I had to stop anyway on the way to Buffalo Gully, I grabbed some supplies while I was there."

"Well then." He flicked open his jeans. "Have I ever told you I like a prepared woman?"

Twenty

ELIOT

I had the condom and was pushing inside of her, afraid I'd blown all my restraint. I feared I'd moved too fast, and once I thrust into that wet heat of hers, I'd be done.

My fears might be founded because as soon as she wrapped her legs around my waist and she was positioned just right on the edge of the island, I pumped with abandon. I pumped and grunted. She kissed my neck and up to my mouth. Her hands and mouth roamed over me.

It'd been a long few weeks, capped by an eerily quiet Thanksgiving holiday that would've made a lesser man feel sorry for himself.

I might be a little selfish at the moment, taking what she'd give me.

Lily was in my house.

I'd walked in well past lunchtime, my stomach twisting because I hadn't had more than quick sandwiches for days, and I'd seen her. An apparition conjured by my fantasies.

I was no longer alone in this big, empty house.

Men are so selfish.

I blocked out old memories. They had no place in this moment. Lily drove all the way from Billings to see me. I had her to myself. I had a fuckton of work outside these doors, but it could all wait.

I just wanted more time with her before I let the world creep back in.

My climax was climbing higher. She stuffed her hands into my hair, and I was done.

No. Not yet.

But I couldn't stop the rush of ecstasy. My arousal had been too strong, too acute. I needed to release inside of her more than I needed my next breath.

My orgasm hit and I clenched my teeth together. I couldn't yell her name, everything was too strong, too much, too urgent. I clutched her to me and rode the wave. Her body gripped mine, clamping around me as I came down from my high.

I was barely coherent, but I was aware enough. "Fuck, you didn't come again."

She continued to tunnel her hands through my hair. "I felt like I was still coming from the first time."

"Not good enough. I should've—"

She silenced me with a kiss. When she pulled away, she blinked those big indigo eyes at me. "I orgasmed literally within minutes of you. Sometimes, just being with you is more than I need."

My traitorous stomach chose that moment to rumble.

She grinned. "Hungry, Romeo?"

I eased out of her. "I only grabbed a quick breakfast sandwich before I went out this morning. I was just coming in for lunch." I'd had the best snack instead. Walked right into a dream. If only I could take her to bed and spend the rest of the day there.

"Wait here." She gently pushed me away so she could bend and grab her pants.

I gave her ass a little swat. The jiggle of her butt cheeks was going to make me hard again. She had more condoms—we'd still need to buy more—and I could so easily bend her over the island.

She grinned at me and rushed down the hall toward the bathroom by Aggie's old bedroom. "I need to run to the car, and I'll be right back."

While she was cleaning up, I did the same in the bathroom on the other side of the house. My stomach continued to be a noisy jackass. I prided myself on handling everything alone while the guys got real holidays, and I stayed at home to keep from bugging my siblings and their growing families while I'd sat in the new chair I'd gotten to replace my father's old Chesterfield chair, and I reveled in the fact that I wasn't like him. He'd have never given everyone the weekend off and taken on all the work himself.

But I had also thought about the food I was missing. I wasn't going to cook a turkey for one. I wouldn't be around to keep an eye on it, nor would I have time to make pie. Chambers's wife would likely send one on Monday. The thought had been some consolation to my empty stomach. But then I'd think about Aggie's mashed potatoes. The way Cody deep-fried at least one turkey for the holiday. Or how Sutton and Wilder had made home-made stuffing last year.

I went back to the kitchen, pressing a hand to my gut. I was just hungry.

I opened the fridge and groaned. More sandwich material. If I could go back to the day I bought groceries, I'd bitch-slap myself. But I'd known how busy I'd be all weekend.

Lily scurried in with a large tote. She put it on the counter. No, not a tote. It was some sort of carrier. Then she unzipped it and revealed the cooler inside.

"When I told Mom my plans, she insisted I bring you leftovers. Thanksgiving dinner was an absolute feast."

She took out a container. I was so hungry I opened the lid while she was digging more out. A turkey leg was on top of carved turkey meat. I started gnawing on it.

She smiled. "I'll heat the rest up while you take the edge off."

I mowed down the meat on the leg. It was goddamn delicious for being a cold bird. Gratitude for the food was my first inclination, but then I grew increasingly humbled with each dish of home-cooked food.

"Did your mom make all this?" I asked around a mouthful. There was everything I'd been dreaming of and more. Some sort of corn dish. Cranberries. I usually didn't touch the stuff, but I'd eat every bite because Magnolia Duke thought to send me food.

Maybe she was worried I wouldn't provide for her daughter in my bachelor pad. She would've been right.

"The rest of us helped." She shot me a knowing look. "Mom makes sure it's equal opportunity in the kitchen. My brothers don't get out of cooking."

After Mama left, cooking became a necessity. Either we learned, or we didn't eat. Barns would make us work harder until we were so hungry we'd boil rocks for dinner.

Meanwhile, he'd head to town, grab some bar grub, and find a bed for the night.

She withdrew a baggie of sugar cookies. "Cali helped with these."

Cali was probably the cutest little baker ever. I studied the shapes with the red frosting. "Christmas cookies?"

"There's more. Mom had all her kids and grandkids under the same roof, and she wasn't wasting time."

She busied herself around the kitchen, getting plates and heaping one of them until there was no room. I didn't have to ask if the other was hers. She heated them up in the microwave and then dug around the cupboards.

I liked that she was comfortable enough to not ask for permission. I liked that she was taking care of me. Here I was, being selfish again, but maybe for a bit longer, I could repay her in orgasms.

Still, it bothered me she'd cut her holiday short with her family. "You didn't have to leave early for me."

"I wanted to." She opened the microwave and stood on her tiptoes to stir the food. Then she shut the door again.

"Don't get me wrong, I'm happy to have you—for more than sex." I put lids back on containers and started loading them into my half-empty fridge. "But I'm afraid I won't be good for much more."

"I know." She crossed to me and put her hands on my shoulders. "I didn't like the thought of you being alone, and it drove me crazy to be passing so close to your house and not stop in."

"You made a special trip."

She shrugged. "The kids get solo grandparent time, and let me tell you, Cali is delighted. Jasper is catching up with buddies. Alder went back to his house. Violet and Willis left last night. I'm honestly surprised Violet's boyfriend came at all. Poppy and Clover are catching up with friends."

"What about Kellan? Don't you need to..." I indicated my chest.

"I weaned him."

"You did?"

She nodded. The microwave dinged and she turned to mix the food again. She hadn't told me, but then she wouldn't need to. If I'd been there, I would've known. She might've discussed her decision or the struggles she was having.

It wasn't that kind of marriage. But it was the kind where she surprised me at home and I took her against the island. I was hungry, but my appetite for her was growing again. My gaze dropped to her ass.

"My supply wasn't keeping up, and I figured we'd had a good six months of nursing. Instead of stressing about why, I figured I'd wean him." She shimmied her shoulders. "I'm sure I'm not supposed to confess that it's nice to have my body back again, but I don't miss the sore boobs."

When she started the microwave again and turned back around, I dropped my gaze to her chest. "What I'm hearing is...I can play with your tits."

Pink dusted across her cheeks. "You played with them before."

"Not with my mouth."

The flush deepened. I loved that damn color.

I could easily love the whole woman.

I turned back to the counter and pushed the cooler to the side. I was falling for Lily.

"Whatever you do, Eliot, don't put your own wants and needs before a woman's." Mom's tsk and sigh rang in my head like she'd told me only yesterday, *"Don't be another Knight to hold a girl back from the life she deserves."*

If I wasn't careful, I'd end up exactly the guy Mama thought I'd turn into.

Lily

I sat at the island and watched a show on my phone. Eliot and I had eaten all the leftovers. On Friday, when he'd gone back outside, I had run to town and bought groceries, including more protection, and endured the small-town stares all the way through the store.

Did they know I was Eliot's wife?

Did they know it was a ruse?

As long as Aunt Linda didn't, did it matter?

On Saturday, I had prepped some quick reheat meals for Eliot for the week. He said most of his employees were returning today, Jasper included.

I checked the time. He'd be back soon. I'd gotten a message that he was taking off three hours ago, but depending on how many potty breaks Cali surprised him with, he could have an hour or two left.

The door opened from the garage. I clicked out of the show and turned with a smile. The guy coming toward me wasn't Eliot. He was a wiry man with shock-white hair and a bushy mustache. He carried a covered round tin in one hand.

"Oh, you must be the missus. Lily, right? All your siblings have plant names."

Pleased I was the first to come to mind, I nodded. I might have a few trust issues left over from Carter, but Eliot was a completely different person and didn't give off those vibes. Yet, I'd be looking for confirmation everywhere for a while.

"Hi, yes. Chambers?"

He shuffled toward me with his free hand out. "At your service."

I got a hearty handshake before he sidled around me.

He set the tin on the counter and withdrew a couple of forks. Then he dug out two plates. "I didn't know you were coming, but I'm sure glad you could make it."

"Jasper helped me figure out a plan."

"I like that kid." He uncovered some sort of pie and sliced right into it. "He gets right to work, and the things he can do with spreadsheets can make an old man feel like he was born in the Neanderthal era."

He scooped a slice of what appeared to be strawberry rhubarb pie onto each plate. He set a fork next to a slice and slid it toward me.

I wasn't hungry, but I wasn't about to turn down pie. That was one of the things I'd never really made after I left home. "Thank you."

"No, thank you. I was worried about that boy."

"Jasper?"

He chuckled. "No, but also yes. It's the parent in me. I didn't like Eliot skipping the holidays. Didn't sit right with me." He shoved a forkful in his mouth.

Then I was glad I surprised him. "It was important to him that his employees get time off."

He chewed while considering me. "We have a rotation," he said around the food, then swallowed. "The guys know when they work holidays, and when one quits or gets fired, the new hire takes over the schedule. It's how it's been run since before Barns passed."

I left my pie untouched. "I know he didn't want to be a bother to his siblings."

"Austen invited him. He was cooking because he and Vienne knew life would get hectic with a new baby under the roof."

"He was invited?"

Chambers nodded.

I chewed on the inside of my cheek. "My parents invited him to their place too."

"That was nice of them. I'm not surprised he turned them down." He put his fork down and bustled around the kitchen, starting the coffee machine, the older type that made an entire pot.

I was bursting with curiosity, needing to know everything about Eliot. What made him think he had to give everything up and didn't deserve the same from others? "Why aren't you surprised?"

"Oh, uh..." He returned to his pie. Mine was still untouched. "What do you know about Barns and Birdie?"

"Birdie was his mom's name?"

He nodded. "I only knew her from around town. She was gone by the time Cody got to high school. But Roxie, my wife, would chat with her occasionally. And she was always complaining. Barns did this; Barns did that. And I heard talk from other teachers. When the boys would get in trouble, she wasn't upset with them like you'd think. She was more like insulting."

"Oh no."

He bobbed his head. "A gal Roxie's friends with had Eliot in first grade." He screwed his face up. "That was shortly before Birdie left. Eliot got into a snowball fight on the playground. What boy doesn't?" He got quiet. "Roxie's friend was so upset after she talked to Birdie. 'Just another disappointment, like the rest of them.' That's what his mom said."

Horror passed through me, curdling in my gut. I would never say that about my kids. "That's awful."

"It wasn't the first or last time this teacher heard things from Birdie about the boys. Horrible things. Can you imagine thinking that about your kids, much less speaking it?" He shrugged. "Now, my daughter's husband, maybe."

My laugh broke the heaviness. Eliot was always doing what he thought was the right thing by the people he cared about. He was that little boy trying to please his mom.

Heat prickled the backs of my eyes. Chambers was right. Eliot went out of his way to keep from disappointing his family, even if it meant staying away.

"Birdie always thought she was too good for Buffalo Gully and for the ranch life." He chuffed. "Too good for Montana. Definitely for being a mom. I can't believe how well-adjusted all those kids turned out."

"Eliot's a decent man." I took a bite of pie. Sweetness burst over my tongue, but I couldn't appreciate it. Would Eliot continue to plan for a divorce because he thought it was best for me?

Hadn't I thought the same? Or was I just another person leaving him to do what he thought was the right thing at the cost of his happiness?

"He's had a pep in his step since you came into his life."

I smiled and dug into my dessert, suddenly self-conscious. "I like him."

"A lot of wives can't make the same claim."

We laughed and ate our pie. I heard a vehicle pull up. "That must be Jasper."

He went to the kitchen window and peered outside. "Looks like he's taking the kids down to the barns."

"I'll never get Cali home."

I was tempted to run out and greet my kids, but I also wanted them to have the freedom to explore. I'd done that a lot yesterday. Wandering around the ranch brought back memories from Grandma's place.

The weather was cool, bordering on cold. Jasper and the kids wouldn't be long. Then it'd be time to go. And I'd be back to wondering when I would see Eliot again.

Eliot

After Lily and the kids left, I ran inside for a bite to eat. A meal would take my mind off how I loved seeing Cali's awe over the ranch and how much Kellan had grown. Chambers hadn't left, and while I always appreciated his presence, I was even more grateful for the noise he was making in the kitchen. Then the place wasn't so quiet.

Chambers was having the last piece of pie. He'd set one out for me by my normal spot at the island. A pile of pie-smeared dishes was next to the sink. Everyone else must've gotten a slice.

I slid into my chair. "Tell Roxie thanks." I cut off a big hunk and stuffed a forkful into my mouth. My bleak long weekend of sandwiches had turned into some damn good food. Instead of me making pancakes, Lily had gotten up and made me breakfast burritos I could take with me to eat.

"You'll never believe it. I made this one."

I stopped chewing. Damn. It was good, but I didn't know Chambers knew how to do anything more than make coffee and eat pie.

He chuckled and licked off his fork. "I have to use a store-bought crust. Can never be patient enough to roll out dough. I'm irate as soon as I get a tear. I want to eat, not patchwork my dough."

Grinning, I finished my slice.

He put his dishes in the sink but didn't leave. "When you going to Crocus Valley next?"

"I told Lily I'd see how the weather is. Cali wants me there for Christmas, but Jasper mentioned his parents might visit the kids so she doesn't have to haul them again."

He watched me with a look from the days I'd been his student, one that said *wrong answer*.

I pushed my plate to the side. "I don't know what else to tell ya."

"I dunno. Maybe 'I'm going down Christmas Eve so I can see the kids open presents Christmas morning.' Or how about 'I'm going to for sure ring in the New Year with my wife'?"

My chest ached to do all that, but I was considering the future. How quiet would next Christmas be? Would I sit on the fringes while my relatives celebrated? "Christmas is my holiday to work."

"Too bad you messed up the holiday rotation, but maybe someone will switch with you." His tone was challenging.

I scowled at him and pushed away from the island. I took my plate to the dishwasher and loaded all the other dirty plates and forks inside. "Holidays are important for family."

"They used to be important to you."

"Why are you here?" I straightened and used my heel to shut the dishwasher door. "It's Sunday and you were supposed to be with your family."

His gaze was measured. "The kids left this morning, and I didn't like the thought of you being alone. And I wanted to show off my pie."

Didn't I feel like shit now? "You don't have to worry about me."

"Lily spent the whole weekend, huh?"

The subject change made my mind spin and cranked up my irritation. "Yes. It was nice."

"More than nice, I imagine."

That it was. Goddamn perfect, except for worrying how bored and abandoned she'd felt inside the house. I'd run back as often as possible.

I'm a prisoner here. Mom's breathy, dramatic voice had echoed in my head all weekend. I'd tried to make up for it when I could with Lily. Usually, with orgasms. And a generous use of condoms because I was better than my father.

"You could have it every day, Eliot," Chambers said.

"Stay out of it, Chambers." I marched out of the kitchen. "Have a good night."

A tiny thread of guilt still clung to me. I joked around

with Chambers, but I wasn't usually a prick. "Good pie," I called behind me.

Lily would have her family around on Christmas. I had missed the kids since I was in Crocus Valley last. The little visit I got today wasn't enough, but maybe I should keep my distance. I should find a random weekend so they didn't associate me with holidays. I didn't want our eventual parting to be hard on them. Kellan might not remember me, but Cali would. I'd have to have a good talk with her.

I had seven months yet.

The pie turned into an iron anvil in my stomach.

In the garage, my phone started vibrating. I answered without checking. "Knight."

"Knight."

I rolled my eyes. "Austen."

"You're a new uncle. Fifth time this year."

My previous dark mood immediately lifted. "Hey, man. Congrats. Vienne and baby doing okay?"

"They're both perfect. Catherine can barely be contained. I think we're going to have to fight her to hold Francine."

"Francine?"

"Yeah." He couldn't sound prouder. "Catherine insisted she needed a fancy name, and she had several options for us to choose from."

"I can't wait to meet her."

"Coming out for Christmas?"

He would be with his wife and new baby. Sutton and Wilder had the twins. Both Cody and Aggie respectively, had newborns. What could I do for them? Lily would have her family. It was better that I keep my own routine.

If her aunt was around for Christmas, I had a legitimate reason. "I gotta work."

"Didn't you work all Thanksgiving? I assumed you switched with someone."

I had let them all assume that. Otherwise, they'd be butting into my business. "We'll have to see what the weather has in store."

"That's a cop-out. You have two other nephews to meet."

I did. Another helping of guilt was heaped on my conscience. I was struggling to be a decent real-but-pretend husband and stepfather, but I was slipping as an uncle. "I'm waiting for newborn life to settle down."

Austen snorted. "That's the quiet time. Life with Catherine is crazy busy, and she's almost legally an adult now."

I was happy for him. I was. But I had work to do. "I can let you know—"

"Christmas."

"What?"

"We're all home for Christmas. All the babies are birthed. Aggie said she can't wait for Cutter to meet all of his uncles. I do believe Tova said something similar about Teddy."

And guilt was roaring back. I was being a shitty uncle. "Fine. I'll see what I can do around Christmas. But I have to make sure it's okay with Lily first. I can't just show up and play husband when I want to."

A high-pitched cry came over the line. "Oh—gotta run. Christmas, bro. We're going to plan something for the day."

"It might not be on Christmas—"

He hung up. Dammit.

Christmas. I'd need to get to Miles City and find some toys. Though from the way Cali fangirled over the horses, she'd love all the little plastic ponies from the hardware store.

What'd I get a six-month-old baby?

What'd I get a wife I was divorcing at the beginning of July?

All I'd gotten her was a cheap silicone ring.

I scratched the back of my neck. I'd figure it out. Then I'd go be a proper uncle and husband for a few days.

Twenty-One

LILY

The Christmas tree was tucked into the corner of my living room. I'd gotten a six-foot fake tree with ornaments and lights already built in. Cali had chosen it. I had some gifts underneath for Cali and Kellan, and then Cali had insisted on getting Bug, Flakes, Pebbles, each barn cat, and her new hamster, Yellow, each a gift.

It was Christmas Eve. Mom and Dad had taken off this morning and would arrive soon. Eliot said he hoped to make it in time for dinner. Dad had asked about inviting Aunt Linda and Uncle Darren. Other than Dad getting to catch up with his sister and mend any rift that might have developed between them about the trust, it'd also be good for her to see Eliot at the house again.

I was excited to see Linda and to have my parents over, but I also dreaded it. It was Christmas, and the visit should be less awkward and more jubilant. I also wanted them to see that Eliot and I were, indeed, close. We at least had a sexual relationship. Yet the motivation behind the visit for me and Eliot would be to dupe her and my dad.

Cali sprinted to the front door at the first flash of headlights. "It's Grandma and Grandpa!"

Bug barked from the basement. I'd bring him out after all the guests arrived so we could work on proper introductions. Otherwise, everyone would get a bear hug from a Dalmatian.

I was excited to see my parents again, but I was anticipating Eliot walking through the door. After Thanksgiving, I wasn't sure whether Eliot would make it or not for the holiday. But he'd called shortly after I'd gotten home and asked if he could come on Christmas Eve and he'd have to leave later on Christmas Day. Maybe he was more invested in this relationship than he thought. He was making Christmas work, and that wasn't nothing.

Maybe I was more invested in our relationship than I should be. Either way, I'd been counting down the days until I could see him.

I peered out the picture window. They'd parked at the end of the driveway, closest to the front door. "Can you see if they need help bringing anything in?"

Eliot would park by the garage like he normally did. He had a spot, and something about that made this whole thing seem less pretend.

Cali ran out to greet her grandparents. They came in on a rush of cold air, large tote bags, and a big cooler.

Dad smiled at me. His jacket was crinkled from the cold, and he had a black stocking hat on his head. "Heya, kiddo. I have a few trips to make with the presents."

I took all the bags hanging off Mom.

She toed off her thick boots and handed Cali her coat.

"The prime rib is ready to throw into the oven, and I have heating instructions on the potatoes and carrots. The dessert can go right in the fridge." She beamed at Cali. "Can you help me with that?"

Cali's nod was enthusiastic. "I'm the boss lady."

Kellan crawled right up to Mom. She stooped to pick him up. "You're going to be faster than me soon."

Cali tugged on Mom's hand. "Want to see our tree?"

"Absolutely." Mom kept Kellan hugged to her and let Cali lead her to the tree. "Oh my. Did you pick out all the decorations?"

I waited, the back of my shoulders growing tight. I had decorated the house each year I was married to Carter and each year his parents found fault with my style and efforts. They never said it outright, but there would be small comments. *My friend's daughter color coordinates her bulbs. She even put them in a nice spiral going around the tree.* Or the *Oh, I expected more...since you're just a tech now.*

"They came with the tree," Cali said proudly. She'd picked out the tree, and the decorations she'd made in school hung on the limbs.

"Oh my." Mom smiled at me. "That's a good idea. Some years, I thought I'd lose it if I found one more tangled set of lights."

I immediately relaxed. Mom always supported me. She might question me, and she'd always treat me like the youngest, but she had my back. "It was probably Poppy or Clover that just threw them in the storage bin."

Mom chuckled. "It was most definitely Alder. Now, the boy will roll them up with military precision." She switched sides she held Kellan on. "I'm going to tackle dinner. You hang out and relax."

"Mom, I can help." It was my turn to host her. There was no Carter to undermine her visit. There was no overwhelm for me. I was in a good place and I wanted her to see it. My wish had nothing to do with the damn trust.

"It's my treat. I'm sure you'll be watching out the door for a certain cowboy to arrive?"

I might've been doing that for the last hour. There was no talking Mom out of her mission. "I'll help Dad and then I'll be back."

By the time I got my shoes on, I heard footsteps crunching on the other side of the door. I swung it open.

"Perfect timing," Dad said as he stepped in, his arms full of red-, green-, and white-wrapped gifts. "Keep the door open. There are more."

I was about to peek out when another person strode in. Eliot grinned from behind two big boxes.

"Eliot!" The butterflies in my belly woke up. I rose on my toes to give him a kiss. He turned to the side as much as possible and met my kiss with an equal energy of his own.

I cupped his face and stole a few more seconds before pulling away. "I'm glad you could make it."

"Me too. Your aunt and uncle just pulled in. Wanna give me another kiss for them?" He spoke loud enough for me to hear.

My thrill from earlier died just a little bit. Was the first kiss for my parents' sake? I wanted to keep my mouth on him for completely different reasons. He pressed his lips to mine, then footsteps sounded outside the screen door.

"Knock knock," Linda's voice rang out.

Eliot straightened. The heat in his eyes brought some of the earlier excitement back. I wouldn't quit hoping he'd come for Christmas because he'd wanted to.

I let my aunt and uncle in. "Welcome."

Linda stepped in and looked around. Darren piled in behind her. Dismay filled her eyes, but she shook it off. "It's looking less like Mom's place." Her smile was hesitant. "Always a little shock, but it looks good. The tree full of presents brings back memories from when you kids were little."

Dad glanced up from where he was squatting, arranging presents. "Maybe with that trust, we'll get another generation of little ones to keep Cali and Kellan company."

Aunt Linda smiled, looking at Eliot and then me.

Oh. She was thinking we were going to add to the kid crew. Laughter bubbled up from my chest. Things were so new. I was falling hard for my husband, but we'd spent only a smattering of days together. Babies? I still had a baby.

The laughter died when I caught a glimpse of Eliot's shuttered expression. He was staring at the floor, but he snapped out of whatever hidden thoughts he was thinking.

"Let me get those for you," he said as he took the bags and presents from Linda and Darren.

Eliot hadn't even taken off his coat and boots. He was rushing to get away from the baby conversation.

Eliot

Lily sat next to me on the couch as Cali ripped open her presents from her grandparents and squealed with each one. Magnolia and Weston were helping Kellan with his. I had my arm around Lily's shoulders. Being away from work was a blessing and a curse. There was supposed to be a storm rolling in the day after Christmas, and I worried about getting back before it hit. I stressed over Jasper being on his own for the first time. He was a quick learner, and he had a strong base thanks to helping Weston's parents ranch in the summers, but he was in charge of everything, and Chambers and his wife were out of town for the holiday.

Yet being in Crocus Valley, getting to kiss Lily and watch her laugh and enjoy her parents' company, was my own Christmas gift. She was relaxed around them in a way she hadn't been with her family when they'd been here in the fall. I loved seeing her happy, and I'd get to be with her tonight and wake up to her. But the pull of my obligations would always be there.

I shouldn't have come. Lily wasn't an obligation, but my absence would've been heavily noted by her aunt and uncle and her parents. It was a good thing I came.

The gift Cali was opening was from Linda and Darren. Cali cheered when she broke through the red Santa wrapping paper to reveal a box with brightly colored plastic bowls and just as brilliantly colored pots and pans. "A cooking set. Thanks!"

Linda spread her hands. "I didn't know what little girls liked these days."

"She'll love it," Lily assured her.

Magnolia helped Kellan finish opening his gift. He tried to put a fistful of wrapping paper in his mouth, but his grandma intervened. "Perfect timing. You can chew on this giant phone."

She wrestled a white plastic phone with multicolored

buttons out of its box. Kellan kicked his legs and reached for it.

Magnolia grinned at Linda. "Another winner."

Darren patted his wife's leg. "We should get going. I think it's going to be a while before the kids are done opening the gifts from their grandparents."

Lily stood with her aunt and uncle. Weston gave his sister a hug and shook Darren's hand. Magnolia encompassed both Linda and Darren in a hug before going back to her grandkids.

Lily walked her aunt and uncle to the door, and I followed to see them out like this was my place too.

"Thank you for coming," she said, giving Linda a quick hug.

Darren handed his wife her coat. "I'll get the car warmed up." He ducked out the door with a general wave at the room.

I slipped my arm around Lily's shoulder. "Nice to see you again."

Linda smiled and shrugged into her jacket. "Yes. Having family in town again is nice." Her expression warmed. "I feel like I've already seen your kids more than I got to see you when you were growing up. And I have to admit, it's comforting to see you both." Her gaze bounced between us and landed on me. "Have you been able to commute like you wanted?"

"We're making it work," I said.

Lily nodded. "The kids got to see the Knight ranch. It's so much more spread out than Grandma and Grandpa's."

"Yes," Linda said fondly. "I've been wondering if they didn't piecemeal their property just for something to leave behind for each grandkid." She peeked out the screen door. "Well, Darren's waiting." She hesitated and glanced at where Weston and Magnolia were with the kids. "You two remind me of them, you know. You thrive on a busy life like your mom, and there was a time when she was home with the kids and Weston was already in Billings for his new job. He spent some time commuting while they sold their old house and built their new one."

Lily stiffened only enough that I could feel it. "I barely remember that," she murmured.

I could hear what was going through my wife's head. Eventually, Magnolia and the kids had moved. They lived together as a family again. Lily and I had never lived together, and we weren't planning on it. Weston and Magnolia hadn't lived separately, knowing they'd be ending in a divorce.

Twenty-Two

LILY

I woke up in the cocoon of Eliot's arms. It was Christmas morning. Uncle Darren had been correct. It'd taken the kids forever to unwrap all the gifts from my parents. By the time they were done, Cali's eyes were drooping, and Kellan was trying to crawl into anyone's lap he could to go to sleep. Eliot said they could save his gifts for today. My parents were at the motel in Coal Haven. They'd be at the Christmas party Aggie and Ansen were throwing.

There was a frantic knock on the bedroom door. "Mom!" Cali whisper-shouted. "Santa came!"

The strong arm around me twitched. "I guess that means no time for frisky business before Santa's presents," Eliot grumbled into the back of my neck.

"You already unwrapped me last night."

He slid his hand down to my thigh where my shorts had ridden up. "You're halfway there. I wouldn't have taken long."

Another knock. "Mom!"

"We'll be right out," I called back. Just how quick could he be? No. It was Christmas. I wasn't making my daughter wait so I could get an orgasm.

"What if we don't have time before I leave?" He pressed a kiss into my hair.

Warmth was kindling in my belly. There would be no fanning of those flames today. I wasn't having a quickie at his sister's place, and he was driving separately to Aggie's and leaving from there. With the impending storm and his staffing already short for the holiday, he didn't want to risk getting stranded.

I reached behind me and stroked my hand down the front of his shorts, loving the way his erection twitched as soon as I touched him. "Then you'll have to call me later tonight."

Eliot groaned and rolled up. "You're a menace. I'll drive too fast knowing your moans are waiting for me."

Grinning, I got out of bed and dressed. I couldn't finish without looking over my shoulder to catch a glimpse of his muscled back. He shrugged into an olive-green, long-sleeved shirt.

Kellan was making noises by the time we exited the bedroom. Cali sprinted to the living room. I cleaned up in the bathroom and Eliot made a bottle, then I got Kellan and dropped onto the couch. Eliot took his turn cleaning up.

Cali pushed a little pile of presents by my feet. One was a hand-decorated gift bag with her gift for me from school. She claimed it was for both me and Eliot.

She grinned as he appeared from the hallway. "Open mine first."

He sat next to me. I had a wiggly baby who was

almost as interested in his bottle as everything else, but I couldn't take my eyes off Eliot's finger-combed hair and the way his dark whiskers dusted his jaw. I'd gotten to feel those between my thighs last night.

I tucked my feet under his butt and enjoyed the little smile he sent my way.

Cali dropped the gift bag on his lap.

Eliot held it and studied her drawings on the outside. "You sure you want me to be the one to open this masterpiece?"

She nodded.

He glanced at me, a question in his eyes, more like he was searching for approval. I nodded at him. "She's been so excited for you to see it."

I didn't know what it was, but her giddiness about it had amplified my curiosity.

He dug through the tissue paper and withdrew a mass of brown paper towels. "Just what I needed to dry my hands," he said.

She giggled. "No, it's inside." She was standing right in front of him, practically jumping from foot to foot.

He peeled off a taped-together wad of towels to reveal a red Christmas tree ornament. On the shiny surface were names. Mine. Cali's. Kellan's. And the one that Eliot kept staring at—his.

"That's gorgeous," I gushed, keeping an eye on his reaction. I loved the handmade craft just as much as I loved seeing all our names written together like a real family. As much as the ornament satisfied me, a spark of worry started that maybe this whole plan was wrong. Cali was going to get attached. Eliot and I had something real, but what if he never acknowledged it? What if he rejected the possibility?

It was Christmas. I couldn't handle those heavy thoughts today. It was the season of hope, right?

His expression was passive, but several emotions played through his eyes: genuine affection and pride, then a hint of fear that morphed into dismay. Maybe some panic?

"Thank you, Cali," he said stiffly. "It's really nice."

No "boss lady"? A low simmer of hurt started in my chest. He wasn't used to kids bringing home presents like this. Was that why he was so wooden, or did he have the same concern over Cali's attachment as I had?

"Mrs. Beeker said to write our whole family's name on it." Cali's grin was huge.

Eliot's brows lifted. "Yeah? It's really nice." Again, his voice was aloof, a little detached.

If only I could know what he was thinking. Would I want to?

He gave me a tight smile. "Want to see it?" He gingerly handed it over, like he was afraid to damage it.

"It's so cute, Cali." I looked over her meticulous letters before handing it to her. "Can you put it on the tree for us?"

She picked a special spot in the middle of the tree. Eliot's gaze was on the floor, but when she turned, he shot her a bright smile. "Ready to open mine?"

The optimism of the morning had dimmed. I'd gone into Christmas morning like Cali, thinking we were a family. Eliot had drawn his line. Would he ever cross it? Did he want to but was scared? Chambers's insight ran through my head. Did Eliot think he didn't deserve this?

He was here. It was Christmas morning. He'd decided to come and celebrate with us. We were going to Aggie's later with his family. Eliot would meet his two nephews and niece. Could my concerns from Thanksgiving be unfounded?

A small pool of uncertainty filled my stomach. Just because I wanted us to be together, and I thought Eliot deserved all the happiness in the world, didn't mean he agreed. I couldn't make that decision for him.

Cali tore off the candy cane wrapping on her gift. "Horses!" The box had a horse family inside—a mare, a stallion, and two ponies, along with a stable that could be snapped together and some picket fence segments for her to make pastures with.

A knot inside my chest loosened. A family-themed gift. I was overthinking. I nudged Eliot with my foot. "You chose well."

"Thanks." His eyes warmed when he looked at me, and he held his hands out for Kellan. "Time for the champ's gift."

Cali pushed another candy-cane-wrapped box toward the couch. I helped Kellan to the floor and he immediately started scratching at the paper like he'd seen his sister do.

"Go ahead and give him a hand," I said to Cali.

Kellan's horse set was more robust, made for babies who put everything in their mouths.

"You got a horse family too!" Cali said.

If I didn't have my toes tucked under Eliot's ass, I wouldn't have felt him stiffen. Yet, when he looked at me and said, "Your turn," he acted normal.

My anxiety rose, but I squashed it. It was Christmas and I wouldn't tear myself apart with questions when I didn't have answers.

His present to me was a small box, but it wasn't jewelry small. I wasn't a jewelry girl. I peeled off the paper.

"Either you're really good at wrapping, or you found someone who was."

His smile was the first natural one I'd seen since we started opening gifts. "I paid to have them look pretty."

Inside was a petite carved horse. Not just any horse, but a gorgeous chestnut Arabian.

I held it up, inspecting the intricate features. "Is this one of Jasper's carvings?"

He nodded. "I saw him doing one and asked if I could commission him."

On the side was a laser inscription of the day we married.

All my insecurities vanished. He'd put our wedding date permanently on the gift he gave me. Unlike the ornament Cali made, this horse wasn't breakable. I was touched and so damn relieved. I ran my fingers over the cool, smooth surface. "Eliot, it's gorgeous."

"You like it?"

"I love it." I turned the date toward him and smiled.

He lifted a shoulder. "Figured you'd have something to remember me by."

My world skidded to a stop. Just as I was thinking the carved date signified the beginnings of a legitimate commitment instead of a responsibility, Eliot produced a shiny pin to burst that bubble.

He was right. I'd never forget him.

<h1 style="text-align:center">Twenty-Three</h1>

ELIOT

My family milled around Aggie's shop. Ansen had cleaned the floor and pushed all his equipment to the side. In one corner, he'd fashioned a small fenced area, not unlike the picket segments in Cali's pasture kit, and had laid a large piece of carpet. The area was scattered with toys. Grayson was reading to Cali and his youngest sister while Kellan scooted around with Ansen's daughter and oldest boy.

Lily's parents had been chatting with me but then Weston had found an opening with Cody. The two weren't just talking oil wells, judging from their laughter.

I was at a table, facing the kids so Lily could catch up with Sutton. Sutton and Wilder each wore a baby in a sling. Austen did the same, Cody too. I was going to feel left out if Ansen showed up with his new son strapped to his chest.

Lily was next to me, pushing mashed potatoes and gravy around on her plate.

"Don't you like the potatoes?" I asked.

When she glanced at me, her gaze was guarded. "No. It's great. I think my appetite is just... I'm not hungry." She pushed her plate away. "There was so much good food."

There was, but she hadn't eaten a lot. We hadn't had time for a large breakfast after opening presents, cleaning up the mess, getting Bug outside for some running before he was put into his enclosure, then preparing everything we might need for today.

This gathering was a present-free zone. I had never been more relieved after Cali's delight over the ornament. A family ornament.

Where would it hang next year? How would she take it when her mom and I came to the inevitable conclusion that this wouldn't work out? Once the stipulations of the marriage were met, there would be no denying that seeing me for a weekend every month or so wasn't enough.

The damn thing had all our names on it, and I'd seen how happy she was about it.

Mrs. Beeker said to write our whole family's name on it.

When Cali had thought of her family, she hadn't put her piece-of-shit bio dad's name on it in her tiny, unwieldy handwriting. She'd written *my* name.

Knight men let down the women in their lives. It's inevitable.

The only way I couldn't fail Lily and the kids would be to step back. I'd known it before I'd seen the gift, and now I was shown why. I was nothing but a heartbreak waiting to happen for Lily and Cali.

So why had I asked Jasper if he could carve a date on the horse?

Something to remember me by.

Wouldn't I want her to forget me and all the ways she had hoped for more? I'd seen the thrill in her eyes die when I told her why I'd had the date etched into the wood.

Something to remember me by.

I was just a guy trying to do the right thing, and I couldn't stop messing it up somehow.

Knight men let down women in their lives. It's inevitable.

Austen sat across from us with a plate of food. Dark circles rimmed under his eyes, but he was filled with a vibrancy I couldn't identify. He was tired but elated.

"Where's Francine?" I asked.

"Feeding time." He sawed off a hunk of ham. "Then Vienne said she'd keep her, and they'd snooze on Aggie's couch. Thought I'd grab a bite where I don't have to worry about dropping food on Francine's head."

Lily smiled. "Mom and baby look well. How are you all feeling?"

He was chewing, but he rubbed a hand down his face. "I thought I was getting too old for early morning formations, but I'd almost trade the middle-of-the-night wake-ups for those." He grinned, looking every inch the smitten new dad. "Almost."

"I like seeing you run ragged."

He'd taken another bite, so all he could do was shoot me a glare. He switched his gaze to Lily. "Do me a favor and send me a picture when he has to drag his ass out of bed sometime between midnight and four a.m.?"

She smiled, and this one lacked the woodenness from

her earlier grins. "I really hope Kellan's past the worst of that."

Austen bobbed his head and shifted his attention back to me. "Glad you decided to make it down for this."

Grateful he didn't know how close I'd come to skipping out, I dipped my head. "Have to keep my favorite uncle status."

"I was worried you'd try to work for martyr boss status instead."

"It's not like you gave me a choice. 'See you at Christmas,' then you hung up."

Lily tipped her head to the side like she didn't hear what I said.

Austen's grin was unrepentant. "I know when pulling rank isn't enough."

Those were the moments when his laid-back style was dangerous. "Well, it worked. I'm here, and I even opened presents with everyone this morning."

"Oh yeah? What gifts did you come bearing?" When his gaze jumped to Lily, his expression flickered. Then he swiveled his attention back to me, and there was a hint of disappointment in his eyes.

I explained the gifts, but I was attuned to Lily. She was quiet and picking at a Christmas cookie that had been part of the catering package.

"Sounds like it was a fun morning." His words were stilted. He grabbed his plate and pushed back his chair. "I'm going to check on Vienne. Merry Christmas to you and yours in case I fall asleep with them."

"Merry Christmas," I murmured at the same time Lily did.

A few moments after he left, she twisted in her chair. "You weren't planning on coming for Christmas?"

Her words vibrated with a sense of betrayal that rocked me back. "I was scheduled to cover Christmas."

"Because you would've gotten Thanksgiving off." At my hesitation, she shook her head. "Chambers said you've had a nice rotation for years but that you went off and did something unusual for Thanksgiving. Was it to avoid us?"

The hurt in her eyes was like claws around my chest. "No. You had plans with your family."

"That you were invited to."

"And then what, Lily? I get all chummy with them and we stay close after the divorce?" I kept my voice hushed. The two of us were an oasis at our table, but from the way we were facing each other, both of us tense, we probably radiated *stay back* vibes.

"Did it ever occur to you that there didn't have to be a divorce?"

"We've been over this."

"No, you have." She grabbed her plate and shoved her chair back in a way that we still faced each other. "You've been over and over the same scenario and nothing ever changes because you don't want it to."

"Lily." I didn't know what else to say. Couldn't she understand I was trying to do what was right by her? By the kids? "I care about you."

"But you could never love me?" She spoke quietly, but the words hit and ricocheted through my head loud and clear. "You know, when I first met you, I thought you were exactly what I wanted. You were everything my ex was supposed to be. And you've only proven that notion correct. But in the end, my ex didn't want to be in love with me, and neither do you."

Indignation blazed a path across the back of my neck. How dare she compare me to the guy who pawned off two kids and stepped all over her heart? "I'm nothing like him."

She stared at me for a moment. "No," she said flatly. "In a lot of ways, you're not." Then she stood and gathered her empty cup and her plate. "I need to talk to my parents. Make sure you tell the kids goodbye before you leave."

And she was gone. Stunned, I stared at the tabletop. I never set out to hurt her feelings. If anything, I was guilty of not realizing that she might be hurt by the way I tried to protect her. I could live with that. She'd realize I was right, eventually. I was ready for it.

What I wasn't ready for was the way my chest was going to crack open and dump my heart on the floor. I rubbed my sternum. Fuck me, this sucked. I could barely take a full breath. As long as I was the one in pain and not her. Never her.

Happy New Year.

I stared at my message to Lily. She hadn't yet responded. It'd been a week since I left Crocus Valley, a week since Christmas. I'd talked to Lily once, and she'd been busy with a hamster on the loose in the bedroom and Bug vomiting. He'd apparently eaten Cali's pretend lunch—plastic bowl and all.

I couldn't bug Sutton about her because my sister-in-law wouldn't return to her regular work for another few weeks. Jasper hadn't been to Crocus Valley since that first family picnic, and if I asked if everything was okay with Lily, he'd ask me why it wouldn't be. He'd wonder what I'd done, and my explanation would sound weak. *I can't fall in love with her, and she's finally realized it and she's upset. But you see, Knight men let down women, and I had to pick which way to let her down the best.*

Would my brothers or I have bought any of that when it came to our little sister?

When Ansen had made some lame excuse about taking money from our father to marry Aggie when he actually seemed to enjoy being with her, we'd still run him off the property.

Only, the ranch was mine, and I wouldn't be running Jasper out. So I didn't ask him.

Instead, I was sitting on one of the little-used chairs in the living room while the wind howled outside.

Chambers shuffled out from the hallway where his office was. "I'd better get going. The wind is picking up, and it's going to kick up all that fresh snow. Roxie won't like it if I get stuck here."

"She knows you might try so you can watch your shows."

He chuckled. "She got me a— What do you call those? A smart TV. Yeah, she got me one of those for Christmas. I can have my shows and my wife during the blizzard. As long as the power holds up. You good?"

I wiggled my phone. "Just worried about Lily. I doubt she's going anywhere for New Year's, but the same weather will go through there tomorrow. I'd like to know she's prepared and ready." Did she have enough food and water if the wind knocked out any power?

"You don't know already? Don't you two talk every day?"

We used to. I looked at my phone every five minutes to make sure I hadn't missed a message. "She's been busy this week."

He blinked, then a long sigh eked out of him and he leaned against the island counter. "What'd you do?"

"Why do you think it's anything I did?" I asked, irritated. It was something I had done. Or didn't do.

A bushy gray brow lifted. "Lily's a levelheaded woman, and she's crazy about you. I don't see her ghosting—is that the right word? It's what my grandson says when a girl quits talking to him. Anyhow, I don't see her ghosting you. She's crazy about you."

She had been. An invisible punch hit my gut. "She might be upset that I went there for Christmas because Austen pressured me."

"That's not how you make a woman feel special."

"It's because she is special that I don't want to lead her on," I said tightly. I glanced out the window. The sun was going down, and with the cloud cover and the wind gusts, it'd be hard to see the road soon. "Don't you have to go?"

His expression turned obstinate, but he looked out the window. "I have some time."

His wife wouldn't agree. She'd have my ass if he got stranded, only I'd punish myself first. "No, you don't. Get home before you go into a ditch."

"I know these roads like the back of my hand."

"But you don't know them blindfolded."

He didn't move. "If I thought you were actually worried for my safety, then I'd go. But you want to get out of talking about your feelings and how you keep hiding from them."

I ground my teeth together. "I am not hiding from them."

"Do you love her?"

"It doesn't matter."

"That's not a no."

The sound of footsteps made us both look over. Jasper emerged from the hallway, pushing up the sleeves of his blue flannel shirt. He stopped and glanced back and forth between us. Chambers was giving me a hard stare, and I was militantly gazing back at him.

Jasper held his hands up. "Shit. What'd I walk into?"

"Nothing," I answered. "Chambers was just taking off so his wife doesn't worry about him."

Chambers's mustache twitched. "Yes. I sure was. Happy New Year, boys."

"Have fun for the both of us," Jasper told him.

I glowered out the window.

"I'd ask if everything's okay," Jasper drawled, "but you look like you'd tell me to fuck off."

"I'm fine."

"Sure, boss."

I winced at his nickname. I should be used to being called boss, but right now, the word only made me think of my little boss lady before I left on Christmas Day and how she'd asked when she'd see me again. As always, I never gave her a definite answer.

She thought I was her family. The stupid ring on my finger said I should be, but I wasn't. I shouldn't have married Lily. I should've known I would be in a position to make a woman feel like she didn't mean enough and to make a kid wonder why she wasn't good enough. Would Kellan remember me at all?

I continued to stare out the window. Chambers claimed I was hiding, but I wasn't. I knew exactly how I felt and I'd face it. Alone.

Lily

I pushed my fingertips to my forehead. Tears streamed down my face, my shame mixed with their saltiness. I should've known better.

I care about you.

After Thanksgiving, I hadn't been ready to admit that I was in love with Eliot. We'd said the words to each other once, over the phone, and we'd never said them again. We'd never mentioned saying them. But his reaction two weeks ago on Christmas morning had shown me exactly where my emotions were. I wouldn't have been so devastated otherwise.

Mom softly knocked on my bedroom door. She'd been staying with me since Christmas. Fuck Carter and the way he nagged on me about my family. I needed them. I needed my mom.

"Have you called him yet?"

I shook my head.

"Okay. I'll make sure to keep Cali and Kellan entertained."

"Thank you, Mom."

I was closed in my room once again. Last week, I'd eventually returned Eliot's message with my own, wishing him a happy New Year. We'd only talked on the phone twice, and there hadn't been endearments. Definitely no more phone sex.

It was time to rip the bandage off.

My heart twisted, but I dialed his number.

He answered with one ring. "Lily pad."

I squeezed my eyes shut. Why'd he have to do that now? "Hey, Eliot. Do you have time to talk?"

"Of course. What's going on?"

The words almost choked me. "I have divorce papers drafted."

I was met with silence. Would he talk me out of it? Tell me no, that he'd changed his mind? Would he tell me that he really was in love with me and he'd figure something out?

"I see. I mean, it's after the first of the year and July will be here before we know it."

My heart sank. He didn't understand what I meant. Spelling it out would be painful, but then Christmas had hurt more than I could've imagined. "No, Eliot. These are for sooner. The lawyer can send them certified mail since I told him we wouldn't be contesting it—"

"What do you mean sooner?"

"You don't want this," I said sadly.

"I want to help you."

"And I want more." Tears continued to gather. "I can't deny it anymore. I fell for you, Eliot. I fell for you really hard. But each time you make an appearance, it's out of obligation. Not once have you spent time with us because you wanted to."

"What was Thanksgiving about?"

Wasn't that what I had been asking myself for two weeks? They'd been blissful days, but he hadn't asked for them. He'd done everything he could to make me feel welcome, and I'd seen the strain on him, running back and forth between me and his chores. "Be honest, Eliot. How badly did my sudden appearance stress you out?"

"It wasn't like that." He made a frustrated noise. "What about the house?"

That was where my parents came in. My dad wasn't a lawyer, but he'd been steeped in legalities for years in the oil industry. Contracts weren't new to him, nor were workarounds or loopholes.

"My parents and I talked with Aunt Linda. Technically, I have six years before I need to get married." Again. For the third time. "It's the middle of winter, and she and my uncle would like someone to keep an eye on the place through the winter. It's old and frozen pipes and all that." If the pipes hadn't frozen over the last several decades, they weren't going to. "Technically, I can't rent, but Dad got it set up that he's going to rent. Nothing in the trust forbids him from renting Grandma's properties."

If I had gone to Dad first, I could've avoided all this. Eliot would've been saved from the mess that was me. But then Linda might not have gone for it. She thought I was just another scorned woman, leaving a man who didn't treasure her like he should.

"As it is, she only agreed to six months. She doesn't want Dad trying to rent every open living space Grandma had owned. It gives me plenty of time to find a suitable place to rent in Crocus Valley."

"Jesus, Lily—"

"I haven't talked to anyone yet about this," I continued, my voice getting stronger. Hearing him distraught would not help me. I had to remember each and every time he mentioned divorce. I could cry—again—when I got off the phone. "I can send your clothing back with Mom, and Jasper can meet her to grab it."

"What the hell, Lily?"

He sounded hurt and frustrated. My heart was cracking deeper. No matter how he felt about me, all this was my fault. "Remember how you said that initially?" I laughed, a hollow sound. "You rose to a challenge that was never yours to face."

"I thought we had an agreement. This summer, so you could get the house."

"Yes. You were clear about the agreement." I let out a long, heavy breath. "I want more, Eliot. I've already had a guy tell me all the ways I don't fit into his life. You might not have asked me to flip my world to make yours easier, but you've made it clear I don't fit in your life. I don't want that. I want a guy who makes room for me. I want a true partner, not someone who finds ways to be absent. I want to get married to a man who really wants to spend his life with me for once. I hope I deserve at least that." I was breathing hard by the end of my confession. My voice had been rising, and I couldn't draw Cali to the bedroom. "I think you need to really think about what you want too. Because I don't think it's sitting out on that ranch alone. You've convinced yourself there's no other way, but you're wrong. If there's one thing I've learned about your family, it's that they're there for you. They're just waiting for you to ask."

I was met with silence again. A hot tear rolled down my cheek.

He cleared his throat. "You'll make sure Cali knows this has nothing to do with her?"

"Of course." Another tear. He wasn't going to fight me on this. Our divorce might be even easier than the one from Carter. My heart was going to crack right in half.

"I really cared about you, Lily."

"That's the difference between us. I fell in love with you, Eliot. You made it easy to fall in love with you, but you made it hurt to stay in love with you." I licked my lips and tasted tears. They were rolling free now. "Goodbye, Eliot."

I hung up before I caved in to what I really wanted to do and begged him to love me.

The complete silence finished wrecking my heart. It was done. Once he signed those papers, I would be single again, and I might just stay that way. One thing the relationship with Eliot did for me was get me comfortable with living alone.

<h1 style="text-align:center">Twenty-Four</h1>

LILY

After a week, I hoped I'd be all cried out. My eyes were bloodshot this morning. I put some toast on a plate and set it on the table.

"We need to eat," I called down the hall. "We've gotta go soon."

I had woken up early and cleared the driveway. I had clipped the monitor to my jacket, and Bug frolicked in the snow while I worked. Now I was showered and running late. I worked the later shift, but there was no more running to daycare after I was done. Doc Julio had started scheduling my shift a half hour early, so I would be done a half hour before daycare closed. Same for the early mornings.

I was humbled I worked for such a supportive clinic. When I had approached Doc Julio with the request, I had been prepared to apologize profusely for even asking. He'd changed my schedule with no issues. Carter wouldn't have even done that for me when I was his wife and the kids were his.

Now, it was just me.

Cali ran into the kitchen, her backpack on her back.

Kellan called out to her from his high chair. He was babbling, but I wouldn't be surprised if some version of her name was his first word.

Cali slid into her seat and devoured the toast. "I wish I could have Eliot's pancakes," she said with her mouth full.

I wished I could have Eliot again. Heat rushed behind my eyes. Nope, I wasn't cried out.

I hadn't talked to Cali yet about the earlier-than-planned divorce. "Yeah, it'd be nice." I sighed and brought my toast to the table. Weight mounted on my shoulders, and my breathing turned shallow. "Cali, we have to talk."

She nodded and kept eating. She was bebopping her head to some music only she could hear. Her backpack had horses on it and underneath one arm was the mare Eliot had given her in the pasture set. She'd named the horse Eli. After Eliot.

I coughed on what I'd been about to say. I swallowed the words. "It's nothing that can't wait. Finish up while I get Kellan loaded."

The pressure eased off my chest. Yes. Telling her about Eliot wasn't a conversation to be rushed before school. Once we were all loaded into the car, I dropped her off at school, then Kellan at daycare. At the clinic, clients were already filling the waiting room, and I happily lost myself in work.

When lunch rolled around, I swept into the break

room. Sutton was at the counter, scrolling through her phone.

"Hey," she said and tucked her phone in her pocket. She wore sweats and a loose top. Instead of a braid, she'd bunched her hair into a loose bun. The fatigue from the last couple of times I'd seen her was gone. Hopefully, she and Wilder were getting more rest.

"Hi. You're back early." I dug my homemade chicken alfredo leftovers out of the fridge.

"I figured I'd start with half days for a couple of weeks and ease into it, but I was hoping to meet with everyone and get a gauge on how everything's been going. I don't want to walk in and pretend it's exactly like it was six months ago."

Those months had gone by in the blink of an eye, but also so much had changed it was like an eternity had come and gone. I was different. Stable. The kids and I had a routine. I didn't worry about the roof over my head, and if I had trouble finding a new house to rent, I had generous, doting parents to help me bridge the gap. I wasn't too immature to rely on them, and I'd never be afraid to again. I'd like to think that when my kids grew up, I'd be there for them in the same way if needed.

She had asked about work, but I needed to clear the air about her brother-in-law. My personal and professional life technically didn't overlap, but they did, and I'd rather have the truth out there. "Have you talked to Eliot?" My pulse picked up. I could delay this conversation with Cali, but I shouldn't with my boss.

She frowned. "No, but Cody mentioned Chambers asked him if everything was okay between you two."

"I asked for a divorce." A tremor traveled through my body. The tears were ready to fall if I let them.

Shock filled her features. "Oh no. I'm sorry, Lily. May I ask what happened?" She held her hands up. "Sorry. You do not have to tell me."

"No, it's fine. He committed to helping me, but he's not committed to me and…" Each time I spoke my feelings, they felt more valid. My parents had listened to me, my siblings, even my aunt and uncle. "I got to a place where I wanted the real thing and not just a handout. My parents helped me buy some time in the house, and my aunt and uncle were willing to work with us."

"I'm sure making you move after you're established and after Cali's started school and during the middle of winter feels a lot harsher."

"I think my aunt felt bad. The pressure to marry and that I fell for him. She had a bad experience when she was younger and probably felt like the trust put me in a similar position." Eliot would never use me though. Our problem was the exact opposite.

Sutton squeezed my arm. "Don't be afraid to ask any one of us if you need anything, okay?"

I nodded, my throat growing thick. They would've been a wonderful family to belong to. I already had one though, and that was why I could move on.

Someday.

Eliot

It was twenty below, and shit was constantly breaking. The hydraulics went out in the Bobcat, spraying everywhere when we tried to use the bucket. Jasper and

Alexander got it towed into the shop. I was elbow deep in hydraulic fluid while they went to repair the bale unroller. The damn thing busted up on them this morning and it was too damn cold to be on the back of a truck tossing hay ourselves.

I had just replaced the line I figured out was leaking in the Bobcat. I tested the lift. The bucket rose. Good. One problem was— A goddamn leak started bubbling from the new connections.

"Fucking motherfucker." I lowered the bucket and whipped the 15/16 wrench at the shop bench. It clattered against the top, the wall, then bounced to the floor, its bangs ringing through the shop. "Fuck you and your hoses too."

"I didn't bring any hoses, but thanks for the offer."

I spun around at Wilder's voice. He wore a heavy black coat, and his breath puffed in front of him. The shop wasn't usually this cold, but it had a hard time keeping up with the wind, and there was likely something wrong with the goddamn heater too.

"What are you doing here?" I wanted to be happy to see him, but for the last two weeks, I'd been steering clear of everyone and everything.

When Chambers had asked who pissed in my Wheaties, I'd tossed the divorce papers at him and walked away. Those damn documents still sat on the island.

Jasper hadn't said anything, but he'd left my box of clothing and toiletries right inside my bedroom door. I'd almost tripped on the damn thing.

I ignored the papers and the fucking box too.

He shrugged out of his coat. "I came to work my magic on that hose."

"I just replaced both lines brand new." I grabbed a rag

from off the bench and wiped the grease and hydraulic fluid off my hands. Barely any of it budged.

Wilder searched the floor until he found where the wrench landed. He squatted. He was wearing the same work clothes he usually used when he was doing shit for Sutton at the clinic. "Did Ken at the hardware store make them for you?"

I chewed on the inside of my cheek. I knew what he was getting at. "He doesn't mess up every DIY job."

"But when he does, it's for this."

My anger notched higher, and the back of my neck heated. I knew to check over Ken's work. He had a habit of not making the fastenings tight enough. The tractor was old, and he had to make some adjustments since we couldn't buy the right fittings.

Wilder grabbed another rag, went to the rear of the Bobcat and started mopping up the fresh hydraulic spray. Then he loosened the hoses while I leaned against the workbench and sulked.

He crossed to where I was and found the plastic bag I'd brought the hoses home in. "Come on. Let's go exchange these."

"You go ahead."

"I didn't come here to do your work for you."

I knew why he'd come. Everyone had to know about the divorce by now. His wife was my wife's boss.

Lily wouldn't be my wife if I signed the papers.

"Don't start, Wilder," I said, weary. I hadn't slept well for almost a month.

"I haven't." He put on his coat and started for the door. "I'll drive."

"Who's with Sutton and the boys?"

"I believe her exact words were, 'I'm not breakable. I

can handle a day or two. Go check on Eliot; you know what a stubborn bastard he can be.'" When I stared at him, he shrugged. "Maybe she just said you can be stubborn."

He walked outside. I glared at his back. Finally, I grabbed my dirty work coat off the hook by the bench and followed him.

Outside, the wind stole my breath, and I tucked my chin into my collar.

He'd parked right outside the shop. Someone must've told him where I was, and he'd kept his pickup running. Did he think I was going to run him back out of the shop? I might've, but I wasn't the only stubborn Knight.

I got into the warm cab and sank into the seat. He put the truck into gear and pulled away.

"Just answer one question," Wilder said after a few minutes.

"I'm not buying that you're only going to ask one." He didn't respond, and for some reason, the silence bothered me. "Fine. One question."

"Do you want to stay married?"

"We've talked about—"

"It's a yes or no question." He used his law enforcement tone on me.

I bristled. "It's not a yes or no answer."

He lifted a shoulder. "A question like that should be an immediate yes because if it's not, the answer is no. But at the same time, if you can't give a resounding no, that also says a lot."

"What kind of response is that?"

"What kind of reaction is yours? You go out of your way to keep from seeing Lily unless you're expected to or she really needs help. Now she's telling you she doesn't need you, that she's no longer your responsibility, and you're dragging your feet."

"It's…" What? A big decision? A hard decision? A decision she already made that I can't agree to? I'd decided to marry her in less time than it took her to explain why she was divorcing me. "It's complicated."

"It's not."

I slid a glare toward him, and he glanced at me, challenging me to argue.

I had no rebuttal. The divorce wasn't complicated. Lily and her family had figured out a workaround, and she'd decided to take the extra time to find something real. I should let her go. But I couldn't. Not yet.

What we'd had was real. I missed the phone calls. I missed the messages. I missed looking forward to seeing her again. I missed walking into a house that felt like a home.

So why had I been avoiding her?

"You ever think about Mama?" I didn't know what made me speak, but there was a pressure valve inside of me that needed a little release before I ended up like the Bobcat's hydraulics.

He grunted. "Maybe not as much as I should, but then she never gave me much thought either."

"But you remember what she used to say?"

"A lot of bullshit came out of her and Barns's mouths."

"Yeah."

Houses on the edge of town were coming into view. Our talk would be paused once we reached the hardware shop. I needed to get this out. There were some things my brothers and I had never talked about.

"She didn't like having boys, that's for sure," Wilder said.

"She said it's inevitable that Knight men let down women in their lives."

He blew out a breath. "Damn, I forgot about those tirades. She wasn't right though. I mean, yeah, for many years, I wasn't what Sutton needed, but I got there. I let her go because I didn't want to be like Barns and coerce her into staying when she was unhappy." He slowed as we got farther into town. "Maybe that's why Austen stayed single so long. And you. But Cody didn't let down Meg, and he sure as fuck isn't failing Tova."

"Yeah." Was I the anomaly? The one to prove Mama right?

He took a few turns and then parked in front of the hardware store. Exhaust billowed around us from vehicles left running in the frigid cold.

"Is Mama why you think Lily's better off without you?" he asked.

I scrunched my face up. "No." That was a lie. "Maybe. Being married had me thinking of Mama a lot."

Wilder barked out a dry laugh. "Our parents are not ones to take advice from. They weren't role models, and they were two of the most selfish people I've ever met in my life." He shook his head. "We've all had to get over shit from them. All of us. Even Aggie, and we know how Mama thought girls were better."

I didn't realize I was nodding at first. I'd been in on some of those talks with my siblings as they found the loves of their lives. I'd found mine, and I'd been too afraid of fucking it up.

"What if I don't know how to love?" Did that question sound as stupid as it felt?

He snorted. "You could've fooled me. You came down when you heard she was sick."

"She had no one to help her."

"You drove in a storm so you could be with her on Halloween."

I had to look out the passenger window. "Because it was supposed to be our first time together."

"No shit?" Surprise rang in his question.

I nodded.

"You've gone longer than that without getting laid. You sure it had nothing to do with missing out on trick-or-treating with kids you adore? That you hated not being there for Lily? Maybe you hoped she'd wear a sexy vet tech costume."

"She doesn't need a costume. She's already a sexy vet tech."

"Eliot, you've got it bad."

I did. Would admitting the fact help me get over her? "She said she deserves better, and she's right."

"Yep. You've gotta be her best, and if you're not willing to do that, then you need to let her go." He turned in his seat until I looked at him. "You need to decide what you want. *You*, Eliot. Not everyone around you. Yes, our parents were selfish, but you're not. You deserve better too. You deserve a life you look forward to, not one you've settled for. Letting yourself love her and spend your life with her isn't selfish. That's real commitment, and that's one of the many things our parents were missing. So if you're not willing to commit, then you gotta let her go."

Lily

The kids were dropped off at school and daycare, and I was heading to work. It was Valentine's Day. At some point, I would have to confess to Cali about my breakup with Eliot, but I also would like the legal papers to be filed before I broke her heart. When she asked about him, I gave her generic answers. He's busy. The roads are bad. Maybe soon.

I hadn't been brave enough to call Eliot about the papers, but I'd messaged him. **Have you signed yet?**

He'd replied an hour later with **No.**

No other explanation. That was two weeks ago, and I hadn't dared message him again. Did I need to call him? I had no assets. I'd talked to the lawyer about a clean split. We'd each leave with what we came with. Was that no longer the case? I should call to make sure.

No. If I heard his voice again, I'd regress. I wasn't crying every night anymore. I got to skip at least every other second without fantasizing about him turning up and ripping those damn papers up.

Once Valentine's Day wasn't looming over my head, I'd give it a shot. The day of love was not it. The day when couples celebrated each other would not be when I pestered my pretend husband about divorce.

Cali had wanted to do handmade cards she could pass out and write a special message for each classmate. It'd taken hours, but her excitement made it worth it. A nice task to take my mind off being alone for the day.

To make things even better, the day landed on a workday. Monday. I could see all the flowers that my coworkers got from their partners. I was happy for them. But I was still sad for me.

I pulled into a parking spot and went inside. I dropped my coat and purse off in the office and took my lunch bag to the break room.

Sutton came out of an exam room, and her eyes widened when she saw me. "Oh, hey. You're here. Hi."

She wasn't usually flustered. She was back to working full days, but she also split her time between clients and office work.

"Yes, I'm here. Did I get my shift wrong?"

"No." Her pitch went up. "I actually need help in Exam One. Right now."

Was she feeling guilty that she was handing off a tough animal? I relished the challenge. When all of my brainpower was required for a wild patient, then I couldn't think about my impending divorce. "Whatcha got?"

"Uh..." She stepped closer and put her hands on each side of her head. "Just know—whatever happens in there, it has no effect on your job."

"That bad?"

"I don't know. You'll have to let me know." She rushed down the hall.

That was weird.

I opened the door and stepped in, checking the exam table and then the floor when I saw the table was empty. "Hi, how's it going today?"

My gaze landed on a pair of cowboy boots. The scent of leather and sandalwood hit me, and I let the door fall shut behind me. My heart hammered hard as my attention wandered up a very familiar long-legged stance.

Oh god. It was him. He was here.

I brushed my gaze over his wide chest, covered in a loose red-plaid shirt over a black T-shirt. When I landed on his face, taking in his serious expression, I swallowed hard. "Eliot?"

I looked around the room. No cat? No dog?

Why was he here?

"Lily." He crossed toward me.

My back hit the wall. I stared up at him. He was here. For me?

Was he dropping off the divorce papers in person? Oh god, I could not face a regular workday after seeing his signature saying we were officially done.

He touched two fingers under my chin. "How are you?"

He would be sweet while severing ties between us, wouldn't he?

"Not well," I answered honestly. Who was I kidding? I'd been emotionally white-knuckling through each day.

"Me neither." He searched my eyes.

I was either going to melt into the floor because he was touching me again, or I would combust from anticipation. I could not get my hopes up. "Why are you here?"

"For you." He dug out folded-up papers that had been stuffed in his back pocket. He unfolded them, and I recognized my lawyer's letterhead. "I came to find out what you want me to do with these."

This was it. The pressure to sob pumped behind my eyes. He didn't need me to tell him what to do. Was he shoving them in my face? Was that why Sutton was almost apologetic? "You can probably just run them over to his office."

"No, Lily pad."

I had to close my eyes at his use of the nickname. "What do you mean?"

"Do you want me to sign them?"

A tremble whispered through me, leaving a tiny thread of hope winding through every cell of my body. "You haven't signed them?"

"I had something to run past you first. Like, what if I move a few horses to your property after the mares drop their foals and they're all healthy enough to relocate? What if I hired Jasper as the ranch manager, and when he moves on, I'll hire another? Then I could live in Crocus Valley. The ranch would still be going, but the Arabian breeding operation would downsize even more and be right in your backyard. And what if I had a special pony already picked out for Cali? And what if I trained one of the new arrivals this spring to be a good horse for Kellan?"

Those hopes of mine rose up from the depths of my soul, shaky but there. "What are you saying?" I whispered.

"What if we didn't divorce? What if, on our first anniversary, we renewed our vows in front of our friends and family in a big-ass Knight-and-Duke picnic at our place, which will officially be your place? Because there's no way your aunt and uncle won't know that I'm committed to you and those kids forever."

It sounded absolutely perfect. A dream. But how did I know he wasn't doing this because he felt bad? "Eliot, it's okay if I don't get the house. I'm going to be okay. I have a big family, and I'm not afraid to use them anymore. You don't have to do this for me."

Bewilderment flared in his eyes. "It's for me." He winced. "That makes me sound selfish, but dammit, I am around you. I want to do this for us. I want to do this for those kids. I want you. And them. I want this family. I want to live under the same roof as you so I can tell you I love you every damn day. I'll do it in text too. I'll wake you saying it. I'll go to bed with you every damn night and whisper those words in your ear. I love you, Lily. I love those kids. I might be selfish, but it'd be an honor to spend my life with you."

His words stole every molecule of air. He loved me? He wanted to be with me? Eliot wasn't a liar, but he was finally being honest with himself. It must not have been easy. And he was here, telling me everything I wanted to hear because it was exactly what he wanted too.

"Eliot." My voice shook. "Are you serious?" *Please say yes. Please don't make me go through all the heartbreak again.*

He brushed his fingers down my cheek. He was so close. "You're not the only one who fell hard. Honestly, as soon as you brushed me off with those indigo eyes, I was yours."

That would've been the cookie incident. "I really liked when you asked if I wanted cheese on my burger." I was serious, but gosh, that sounded insane.

He blinked, then his lips twitched. "Lily, that was not our first meeting."

"Before that, you were just a really hot apparition I embarrassed myself in front of."

"I'm not sure what you're talking about. I remember a really nice set of tits."

I laughed and rested my cheek on his chest. He pulled me closer to him. This was real. He was real. His words were real.

My dream was coming true.

"Are you sure?" I was scared to ask.

"I've never been more sure of anything. I've been so damn miserable without you. Chambers complained about how cranky I was, and my brothers and Aggie wouldn't leave me alone." He pulled back and met my gaze. "Being married to you is the happiest I've been all my life, and that was with me being a half-assing idiot. I'm all in, Lily. I want to spend my life with you. If you want me."

My breathing turned shallow. All in. If I wanted him. I was on the edge of a precipice. I just had to leap.

He'd been there to catch me so many times. And when he hadn't? I had the support system a shitty ex tried to take away from me.

"I love you, Eliot. I want to spend my life with you too."

A slow grin spread across his face. "Remember when we said that over the phone? I never thought I'd be lucky enough to hear it for real. I love you, Lily pad. I always will. I love those kids, and I can't wait to raise them with you." Alarm filled his expression. "Will this be a mind-fuck for Cali? I took so long to plan everything and get ready to move, but I was also worried that I'd do more damage—"

"I didn't tell her."

Surprise lifted his brows and hope filled his eyes. "No?"

"I never got a call from the lawyer that you returned the documents."

The smile returned. "And you never pressured me."

"I guess my hope never officially died."

"Lily Knight, I'm gonna make you my wife every

damn day of our lives." He dug in his pocket and withdrew something I couldn't make out.

Then he stepped back and dropped to a knee. He was holding a small black velvet box.

I covered my mouth with my hands. I was getting proposed to. Properly. Romantically. I didn't care if we were in a veterinary clinic exam room with the smell of cleaner surrounding us.

"Will you stay married to me?" he asked and opened the little box. A square diamond ring in a platinum setting sparkled inside.

"Yes. Ohmigod, yes." I had my arms around his neck before he fully stood up.

He planted his mouth on mine and pressed me against the door. I savored his taste, the hardness of his body, and the fact that he was here.

He pulled back like he needed supreme strength to break contact. "If I don't stop, I'm going to walk out there with an erection that won't go away. But everyone's going to know you're my girl." Juggling the box, he took the ring out and slid it onto my finger. A perfect fit. Just like us.

Eliot

Lily pulled into the garage. I wanted to go out and help her, but she thought Cali would love the surprise.

Cali breezed through the door from the garage and stopped in the laundry area. She dumped her backpack on the floor and flung her coat off. She stepped out of her snow boots and danced into the kitchen. She stopped when she saw a little carved horse at her spot at the table. There was another in front of Kellan's high chair.

"Is Uncle Jasper here?" she yelled toward the garage door where Lily was coming inside with Kellan.

"No," I said, entering the kitchen. "Happy Valentine's Day, boss lady."

"Eliot!" She launched herself at me.

I crouched and caught her. She'd grown again, and I'd missed it—for the last time.

"It's been forever!"

I laughed. "You sound like Ivy." My niece loved the drama, and Cali loved her new cousins.

I stood and led her to the table. "I asked Jasper to carve this for you." He'd captured the traits that made an Arabian stand apart—the arched neck, high tail, and dished facial features. "You know why?"

She shook her head, dancing from foot to foot.

"Because that carving looks exactly like the horse that'll be coming to live here this summer. Your horse."

Her mouth dropped open, and she gasped. "My horse?"

"Your horse."

"What's her name?"

I chuckled again and ran a finger along the carving. "You're getting a gelding. A nice, mellow boy who loves to listen and learn. I saved him for you." I had known he was something special. A good horse for kids. I couldn't send him to be a show horse whose only purpose was to win money. "His name is Starry Night."

"Star? His name is Star?" She squealed and whirled around. Lily came to stand by me.

I held my arms out for Kellan. He grinned and reached for me. I lifted him. "Kellan's horse isn't stained yet because it's not born yet. Once we know the color, Jasper said he'll finish it."

"The mommy is still pregnant?" Cali's voice was full of awe.

"Yup. Uncle Ansen is going to help me train both of them for you two."

"Can I help?"

"We'll have to ask." Ansen would probably love to pass on his knowledge to young horse owners. It made his job easier when he knew a client would continue supporting the training long after he was done with the animal.

I put an arm around Lily. She felt good pressed against my side. Just like it felt right to be in this house without a deadline hanging over my head.

"I'm going to be living here now too." I was almost afraid to say it, as if Lily would wake me up and tell me I'd been dreaming. "Is that okay with you?"

Lily squeezed her arm around me. Her reassurance was appreciated.

Cali jumped up and down. "Yay! Can you take me to school tomorrow?"

"Absolutely. I'll take you to school every day this week." And the next. And the one after that.

Cali snatched her horse off the table and then threw her arms around me. She clutched me and the figurine tight. "I love you, Daddy."

Hell. My throat grew tight. I never thought I'd be called Daddy. I had been afraid I wouldn't be worthy of it. But right now, I knew I'd spend the rest of my life proving that I was the right man for Lily and a good dad to these kids.

"I love you too, boss lady. I love your brother, and I'm so in love with your mom."

Epilogue

LILY

At my first wedding, there hadn't been that many people. All my siblings had shown. I'd chosen a simple white dress that could double as a summer party dress. My in-laws had been dour-faced and disapproving. Carter had been a smooth talker, and I'd been excited to jump right into a family. Yet I hadn't been able to escape the feeling that the mood of the day had been a warning sign for the marriage.

My second wedding had a desperate cloud over it. Eliot had been quiet but kind and maybe a little confused. I had been timid and upset at myself and the world for putting me in such a position. Yet I hadn't felt like a dark cloud hung over us. Just a resigned one.

This was still my second marriage, but my third wedding. Eliot was in crisp black jeans and a white dress shirt. His dark hair was ruffled from the light wind, and he'd left the scruff on his face because I'd asked him to. I wore a flowing, off-the-shoulder wedding dress. I had on a new pair of cowboy boots underneath.

Bug had behaved very well for the vow renewal ceremony on our property. There were a lot of kids who were wrangling him, and now he wandered freely, completely played out but unwilling to nap through the excitement.

The old red barn had been our ceremony backdrop and the whole day was perfect. Laughter rang across the lawn. The sounds of kids' delighted screams and yells while they played were the perfect music.

Aunt Linda had happily signed off on our marriage as legit, and then she and Uncle Darren took off on a trip to Alaska.

All of Eliot's family was here. I couldn't have asked for better in-laws. I had a large group of friends who were now family. Sutton, Aggie, Tova, and Vienne had incorporated me into their dart nights. I couldn't aim, but they didn't care.

A few months ago, Violet had been in town, and she'd come along for darts. She and Willis had broken up, and she'd needed to get away. I was flattered she'd chosen to spend her time with me, but then I saw her with Cali and Kellan. She'd needed sister time, yes, but she'd needed to be the fun aunt more than anything.

Still, I was worried about her.

Eliot held my hand. We didn't have to mingle. Everyone came to us. Catherine was following Kellan around now that he could walk and tried to keep up with his much older cousins.

Sutton took a drink of her fruit punch. "Do you think anyone else is going to meet the terms of the inheritance?"

I shrugged. My oldest brother was chatting with Dad and Cody. Alder worked at King Oil with Dad and loved his job. I doubted he'd give it up for a year just for a house and some land. Jasper was chatting with Eliot and Chambers on the other side of me. He loved what he was doing, but maybe he'd decide to form his own business. At the cost of being married? I wasn't sure I could envision Jasper settling down. Poppy and Clover were chatting with each other. Neither one had brought a date or mentioned that they were seeing anyone.

"I don't know," I said. "I can't even guess who'll be first."

"What about last?" She took a drink from her punch cup. "I would've said Austen and Eliot were going to stay single forever." She smiled. "I'm so glad I was wrong."

I was too. "When the snow melted, I stopped by the cemetery and thanked Grandma for meddling in my life. I can only hope it turns out just as well for the rest."

Her gaze caught on Wilder coming out of the house with Drew and her expression turned dreamy. Alex was in my mom's arms.

Tova and Vienne approached.

"Your sisters are a riot," Tova said.

"You mean Poppy and Clover?"

She nodded. "Violet too. I was just hanging out with her, Ivy, and Cali."

"Violet's a riot?" Shock filled my voice. I loved my sister, but a riot? That was not Violet.

"She's one of those serious ones with biting sarcasm that's hilarious if you're not on the receiving end," Vienne said.

Violet did have a dry sense of humor. "I hope her ex was on the receiving end for once."

Aggie joined us and gave me another hug. "I can't believe I grew up the only sister and now I have four."

"I more than doubled the number of sisters I have." And it was amazing. "Brothers too."

Ansen slipped an arm around Aggie's waist. "Welcome to the family, Lily." The corner of his mouth lifted. "Again."

"We like to have two weddings around here," Aggie joked.

Tova's eyes went wide. "Oh my god, you're right."

"Wait." Vienne's brow furrowed and she toyed with one of her four necklaces. "Aggie and Ansen didn't go through with the first wedding."

"But we were minutes away," Aggie said. "Everything was set up and ready for me to walk down the aisle."

"I've only been through one wedding," Tova added. "But Cody's been married twice."

"Same with me and Austen," Vienne said. "Austen's been married once, but I've been married twice. Wilder and Sutton. Now, Lily and Eliot."

"We'll do anything for a reason to party." Aggie grinned and leaned her head on Ansen's shoulder.

Violet approached Poppy and Clover. I gave Eliot's hand a squeeze and released him. "I think Violet might be taking off. I'll be right back."

"Take your time," Sutton said. "And like Ansen said —welcome to the family." She grinned. "Again."

I was still smiling when I reached my sisters.

Violet's gaze lifted to mine. Her eyes were tired, but she still had an energy around her that Willis had sucked away. "Will you be upset if I take off early?"

"Are you feeling okay?"

"Of course." She didn't sound convincing. "I've just been tired lately. My appetite's off."

"Oh no." Horror crossed Poppy's face. "Willis didn't implant his arrogant alien seed in you, did he?"

I almost laughed it off, but shock was scrawled over Violet's expression. "No." Her voice pitched up. "Not Willis. He probably got a vasectomy at eighteen and never told anyone."

True. "I'll walk you to your car." The driveway looked like the parking lot of a county fair—a line of dusty pickups.

"No." She squeezed my hand. "This is your day, and I don't want to take you away from anyone. It's just been a long few months, but I'm going to be back. Visiting my family is so much nicer when I don't have to drag a man-child along." She rolled her eyes. "Or argue with him about going in the first place. Enough about him. I love what you and Eliot have done with the place."

To keep himself busy until he could get the horses moved, Eliot had started renovating the house. He'd opened up the living room and kitchen, removed the wallpaper, and painted. The work helped distract him from a calving season he was minimally involved in. Jasper and Chambers kept him updated. "Thanks. I love what he's done."

"Have fun on your honeymoon. Vegas?"

My parents were staying to help watch the kids and animals, and Eliot's siblings would take care of the horses. "He hasn't traveled a lot outside of work, and I suggested it as an adult destination. He might hate it."

"He's going to love it because he's with you." She sighed wistfully. "I'm happy for you. Really."

I hugged her, then she started for her car, one of the few in the row of vehicles.

When I turned, Poppy was scrutinizing me. "You almost—*almost*—make me think that old house is worth hooking up for."

Clover lightly swatted her arm. "It's a *marriage*, not hooking up."

"Whatever. There's some guy renting the house that's supposed to be mine anyway." She held her hands up. "I'm staying far away."

"It's our no-man era," Clover announced.

I smirked. "No man, no land."

"What's this about no man?" Jasper jogged up to us.

"I don't know what the rhyme would be for you," I said. "Are there a lot of marriage options in Buffalo Gully?"

He blanched. "Uh, no. But there's this lady named Carla whose car keeps breaking down on the road between the ranch and town. Only it's always when I've seen her in town and then I'm heading back."

"She's stalking you?" Poppy asked.

"Wilder and Sutton warned me about her. She's looking for her third husband. Or is it the fourth?"

Alder wandered up to us. "You're becoming the fourth husband. I can see it."

Jasper scowled at him. "No, we're taking bets on when you're getting married to get your land."

Alder's jaw hardened. "It's not right." His gaze softened. "But I'm glad it's worked out for you. I'd say Eliot's a nice addition to the family, but I feel like we've all been added to his."

I glanced at the way Mom danced and laughed with all the kids. "It goes both ways. Mom considers everyone hers. I heard her tell Cody he's a good kid and should be proud of himself."

Alder snorted, but his fond gaze was on Mom.

A wall of heat came up behind me. Eliot wrapped his arms around my waist. "The DJ wants to know if he can start the music."

The DJ was Cody's oldest son. "Yes, absolutely. There's a cowboy I need to dance with."

Country tunes started to play out of the speakers. Eliot twirled me into his arms. "You realize that I'm going to sneak off with you after a few songs?"

"You don't think anyone will notice?" Did I care?

"My side of the family will expect it since I know for a fact they all snuck off at their weddings."

"Well, then we have to complete the cycle."

The corners of his eyes crinkled with his smile. "I love you, Lily pad."

"I love you too, Romeo."

"I love our family."

"Good. Because it's growing."

He blinked once. Then again. "Seriously?"

"As serious as the will and trust. It's early yet, but—"

He whooped and picked me up. His mouth was on mine as he whirled us around. When he set me down, neither of us looked around to see if we made a spectacle. It was a wedding. We'd announce the new baby later.

"When should we tell the kids?" Eliot asked. "Kellan might say 'no,' but that's the only word he can say. And I'd like for us to talk to them about the official adoption first."

"Cali's already calling herself Cali Knight. I don't think she's going to protest."

A proud smile stretched his lips wide. "I can't wait. We're going from a family of four to five."

We started dancing again, and I laid my head on his chest. Horses grazed in the pasture closest to the house. "At least all the new animals aren't my fault."

"They're my job. I'm justified." He tipped my chin up. "I'm also so damn grateful I'm one of the critters you took in."

"You cuddled better than Flakes."

He laughed, and we danced until the song changed to another. Then he found Cali and danced with her. My mom was in line for the next dance.

I chatted with my sisters until Mom walked Eliot over.

"He's such a good guy," she gushed and turned to him. "I'm proud to call you my son." She crushed him in a giant hug. When she let him go, a stunned expression was on his face. He blinked like it was the first time he'd been told someone was proud of him.

I loved my family more today than I ever had.

Mom glanced at my sisters. "I'm not going to be one of those mothers who pressures you. I want all my kids to be choosy about their partners. But...I'd love to meet them before I die."

Poppy choked on her punch as Mom wandered away.

"No pressure," Clover said around her laugh. She shot me a fake glare. "She didn't talk that way when Carter and Willis were getting brought around, but you had to open a can of worms with *that* guy." She jerked her head toward Eliot.

"I'm not guilty at all." I took Eliot's hand again.

"Ladies, I need to steal the bride." He slowly towed me away.

"Get 'em, gurrrrl," Poppy called after us.

Eliot led me to the house, but we ducked into the garage where people would be less likely to look for us. His pickup was inside and would offer us some shelter if someone walked in.

He opened the back door and lifted me onto the seat, then he kissed me. A slow, sweet kiss. When he pulled back, his eyes were full of love. He was my future. "One year ago today, I knew you were everything I wanted. But at the time, I thought I couldn't have you."

"I'm yours."

"You're all mine. Forever. Together, we're going to make endless memories."

———

Thanks for reading!

All the Knights have settled down, but Lily has five siblings who need to find love or they'll lose their inheritance. What happens when Violet lets loose for one night with a guy she meets at a bar in Coal Haven? She has only a first name, and no way to find him to tell him he's going to be a dad. Until one day when she confronts the renter currently in the property left to her.

Evander Barron returns home after more than a couple of decades in the army to find his one night stand throwing up on his porch. Then she tells him the news. He should be elated, but his past hasn't made it easy to trust, and he doesn't trust Violet. So it's best to keep her close. It'll be his worst decision, or the best thing he ever did, in Violet Promises.

Want to keep reading more of Lily and Eliot? Join them at the ten year reunion of the camping trip with all the Knights. Sign up for my newsletter on mariejohnston writer.com and you'll get access to all my bonus material.

Marie Johnston writes paranormal and contemporary romance and has collected several awards in both genres. Before she was a writer, she was a microbiologist. Depending on the situation, she can be oddly unconcerned about germs or weirdly phobic. She's also a licensed medical technician and has worked as a public health microbiologist and as a lab tech in hospital and clinic labs. Marie's been a volunteer EMT, a college instructor, a security guard, a phlebotomist, a hotel clerk, and a coffee pourer in a bingo hall. All fodder for a writer!! She has four kids, cats, lots of cats, and a corgie.

mariejohnstonwriter.com

Follow me:

Also by Marie Johnston

<u>Return to Coal Haven</u>

Violet Promises

Daisy Whispers

Poppy Kisses

<u>Crocus Valley</u>

A Reckless Memory

A Temporary Memory

An Unfinished Memory

A Fearless Memory

An Endless Memory

<u>Coal Haven</u>

Make Me Whole

Make Me Shiver

Make Me Blush

Make Me Dream

Make Me Exhale

<u>King's Creek</u>

King's Crown

King's Ransom

King's Treasure

King's Country

King's Queen

www.ingramcontent.com/pod-product-compliance
Lightning Source LLC
Chambersburg PA
CBHW021244190726
48289CB00005B/1475